ISBN: 979-87-15437-93-8

BLOOD

AND

JUSTICE

Also by J.J. Miller

Brad Madison series:

FORCE OF JUSTICE

DIVINE JUSTICE

GAME OF JUSTICE

Cadence Elliott series:

I SWEAR TO TELL

THE LAWYER'S TRUTH

Email: jj@jjmillerbooks.com

Facebook: @jjmillerbooks

Blog|Website: jjmillerbooks.com

BLOOD

AND

JUSTICE

(Brad Madison Legal Thriller, Book 4)

J.J. MILLER

PART I

1

"Brad Madison!" the voice barked into my ear, making the greeting sound more like a command.

I'd answered an unknown number, but I recognized the caller immediately. Even after twenty-plus years, the gravelly tone was unmistakable. A deeply ingrained Pavlovian response had me in two minds: should I drop and give him twenty, or snap to attention?

"It's Henry Tuck here," he said, but the reminder wasn't needed. For thirteen long weeks, I ate, slept, breathed, and crossed five realms of hell to the tune of that voice. As my drill instructor, or DI, at Marine Corps boot camp, Sergeant Henry "TNT" Tuck was my ceaseless tormentor. In the perverse way of the military, that made him my mentor.

What does he want with me now?

And how did he get this number?

Tuck had not been put through by my secretary, Megan Schaffer. He hadn't looked me up online. Someone had given him my private number.

In the brief conversation that followed, Tuck offered no reason for the call. He just said he wanted to come and talk to me face to face. Then, once the arrangements were made, the call was over. Whatever it was that Tuck wanted, I felt I owed him. Big time. I was indebted to that man for life.

Tuck had taken a shine to me at boot camp. At least, he'd taken a shine to seeing me with my face buried in the ground, shouting, "Yes, sir!" "No, sir!" "Aye, aye, sir!" through a mouthful of Parris Island dirt.

No recruit wants special attention from their DI, but that's what Tuck gave me. In the process, he instilled in me the life-and-death virtue of obeying orders. To civilians, this may sound like little more than power and pedantry. But in the heat of battle, when you have the lives of a dozen or more men riding on your decision, you need to get shit right. Not by doing it your way. Not by weighing up pros and cons while precious half-seconds slide by. Not by wondering whether you want to or not. *A Few Good Men*'s Colonel Jessop may have lost the plot like Colonel Kurtz, but no one said it clearer or saner: "We follow orders or people die. It's that simple."

When the civilian version of Henry Tuck walked into my office three days after he called, it took a little adjusting to see him without his wide-brimmed smokey. That hat had a rancor all its own. When his eyes drilled into you, it stared you down too, as though you'd also roused its wrath. His hair was thinner and silver all over but still cropped short. He was in his mid-sixties now with all the facial lines to show for it, but he looked fit and sharp. As he stepped toward me and offered his hand, he showed me something I'd rarely witnessed all those year ago: his smile.

Addressing him as Henry, as he insisted, took some adjusting too.

He ran his alert blue eyes over my office and the shelves of books I'd surrounded myself with, and nodded his head with satisfaction.

"Glad to see you're doing well for yourself, Madison."

"You look fighting fit, Henry," I said as I invited him to sit. "I bet you could still put recruits to shame in the gym."

I wasn't humoring him. He was a lean two-hundred pounds, about my height—six, two—and he moved as lightly as a man half his age.

"What can I say?" he said as he took his seat. "I watch what I eat, I stretch, and I can still bench two-sixty. How about you?"

"Two-eighty-five. But I'd be more than happy with two-sixty at your age."

"Listen," Tuck said as he tapped a hand on his chair, "I didn't mean to be all top secret on our call the other day. I just hate talking on the phone—never liked it—and so I always keep it super brief. But the reason I'm here is that I have two problems I'd like your help with. Kevin Allman recommended you. Said you were a good operator."

Allman was a former DI of Tuck's generation who now worked for a non-profit called Second Life that helped vets with PTSD. He'd sought my input on a fundraiser five years ago and I've helped out occasionally ever since. That Allman saw fit to give Tuck my private number was okay with me.

"What kind of problems are we talking about, Henry?"

"Two divorces, you might say."

Henry then paused, disinclined by nature to be expansive. I didn't want to have to prod him to go into more detail, so I waited for him to fill the silence.

Henry breathed in deeply then exhaled.

"I've been married to Laura for twenty-seven years," he said. "And, for longer than I can remember, if it hasn't been me threatening to leave, it's been her. But we stuck at it. Recently, though, I decided I couldn't do it any more. So I moved out, and now I want to proceed with a divorce."

I felt deflated all of a sudden. That's what family law does to me. I hate it. Give me criminal law any day with its cast of lowlifes and liars and its smattering of innocent souls. It's not every day that I fight to save a client from a travesty of justice, but when I do there's no better job in the world. Family law is a downright ugly, sordid mess that I was happy to steer well clear of.

Problem was I'd just recently defied my own conventional wisdom and take on a divorce case. A bitter one—surprise, surprise. But I only did so as a favor for a friend of a friend. Well, a friend of my ex-wife Claire, who practically begged me to help.

Henry must have guessed I was considering looking for an out.

"I know divorce is not your bag, Madison. If you want me to go somewhere else, I will."

I waved my hand. That was never going to happen. Like I said, I owed Henry.

"Don't be silly, Henry. Of course, I'll help you. But tell me this: who is she?"

"What are you talking about?"

"You know exactly what I'm talking about."

The skin on Henry's face was still taut and, as I guess he had done every day since his late teens, he'd shaved that morning, so there was no hiding the fact that he was clenching his jaw.

"Her name's Fernanda. Fern for short."

His manner was ever so slightly defiant.

"And she's how old?" I persisted.

"Thirty-four," he said. He tilted his head to adjust the aim that his eyes kept on me, alert for the slightest hint of ridicule, I suspect. "And don't try that all-your-Christmases-coming-at-once line on me. We had the DI reunion last weekend in San Diego and the boys never let up. But they're nothing but jealous. They even admitted it. And as it happens, it was talking about Fernanda that led me to you. Kevin practically insisted I come to you."

I could just imagine those DIs standing around, ribbing Henry for all it was worth before getting back to hanging crap on their former recruits.

"So, your relationship with Fernanda is out in the open?"

Henry shrugged. "There's nothing to hide. We're in love."

I was leaning back in my chair now, relaxed and impartial.

"How'd Laura take it?" I asked.

Henry's lips pressed into a flat frown. "As well as can be expected. She thinks I'm a fool."

I paused for a moment to consider what I was going to tell Henry. Yes, my instinct was to think that Laura was right but he didn't come to me to be judged. "You want my best advice, Henry? Get your settlement with Laura agreed on with little or no input from lawyers."

"Too late for that," he said, shaking his head. "When I told her that I was coming to see you she said the next call she was making was to her own lawyer."

"Any idea who that might be?"

"Don't know for sure but I could take a pretty good guess. A couple of years ago, her sister Martha took her husband to the cleaners after he cheated on her. And I'll never forget the name of those lawyers after Laura told me. Paxton and Punch. Man, did they give that fella the old one-two."

I had heard of Paxton and Punch. My reservations about dealing in family law only deepened.

"Henry, that firm may as well be called Paxton, Punch and Pitbull, because that's what they are. They're ferocious. And if Laura has engaged them, you're in for the fight of your life."

"Come on, Madison. There's plenty of money to go round. I'm not looking to screw Laura over. I just want to get on with my life."

"You say there's plenty of money, Henry. But sometimes plenty ain't enough. Just how financially sound are you?"

"Well, that's the other thing I wanted your help on."

"The second problem?"

"Yeah, the second problem. You could say it's another divorce."

"God Almighty, Henry. You better not be telling me you've got two wives you want to leave."

"No. It's a business. Something that I poured a lot of money into."

"And?"

"Well, when I told my business partner that I want to get my money out, he wasn't real happy. He said it wasn't a good time. He wants me to wait a year, at least."

"How much money are we talking?"

"About two million. It's a security company that's gone from strength to strength. It's been growing fast for five years."

I raised my eyebrows. Some business smarts must be nestled in that love-addled brain of his.

"And you don't want to wait, obviously?"

"Madison, I don't want anyone telling me to put my life on hold. I want to cash in my chips, and I want to cash them in now."

"Okay," I said, tapping away at my computer keyboard to bring up my calendar. "We're going to have to make another appointment. Thursday or Friday next week looks free if that suits you. Meantime, I'd like you to send me the partnership agreement."

"Okay."

"Is there a dissolution strategy in the contract?"

"A what?"

"A dissolution strategy. It's kind of a prenup for partnership agreements."

"I have no idea."

"Okay, I'll check that out. Have you got all the financial statements?"

"Yes."

"Send me those too, will you?"

"Will do," said Henry. He was looking relaxed now. Having someone to help was clearly a weight off his mind. "I think I came to the right place. Thank you, Madison."

I stood up and put my hand out. "I want that paperwork ASAP, okay? I wouldn't mind betting Paxton and Punch have already gotten a head start on us."

I walked Henry to the door. As I returned to my desk, I heard Megan book him in for the following Thursday at three o'clock.

A couple of days later, I got an email with a rudimentary list of Henry's assets. The email was sent from his girlfriend's account.

But he never showed for his three o'clock.

A few days after leaving my office, Henry Tuck took hold of his Beretta M9 service pistol and fired a bullet into his right temple.

2

I fell in with a line of men entering the small chapel and took a seat in a pew midway up the aisle. The place was three-quarters full and more mourners were still coming in. Men, mostly. Some wore suits while others looked like they'd had to rummage deep through their drawers to find a suitable tie—heck, any tie. And then there were the bikers. They may never have met Henry, but when word gets around that a soldier has fallen, a lot of vets make a point of attending the funeral. They'll be damned if they'll let someone who'd had the balls to serve leave this world alone.

Like me, they'd always carry survivor's guilt. Funerals bring death near again, to coldly graze the soul. They give rise to sobriety—there by the grace of God go I, and all that—and gratitude for having the fortune to be alive.

"Always go to the funeral." I don't know who came up with that as a guiding principle to death, but I agree with it wholeheartedly. Do it if not for yourself but the deceased's family. They'll take heart from those who show at the service, the strangers in particular. It's something I will instill in my daughter, Bella.

But I wasn't here for the family, I was here for the dead. For the life of me, I could not work out why Henry would choose to kill himself so soon after our meeting. He'd displayed the verve of a man who relished the future. I did want to pay my respects, but I also wanted answers.

Henry and I had unfinished business. He walked out of my office with a spring in his step and a glint in his eye. He did not look like a man fixing to kill himself.

Not long after I'd taken my seat, a man crossed in front of two people to claim the place beside me.

"Madison," he said, still on his feet. He held his smile and an outstretched hand while I took a couple of seconds to recognize him.

"Pete Chang," I said, standing up and taking his hand enthusiastically. "Good to see you. My God, you haven't aged a day."

"What can I say? It's the Asian genes. My grandfather could pass as my older brother."

"What are you doing here, anyway?"

"Same as you, I guess. When I heard old TNT had kicked it, I got down and gave him fifty."

When I got the news of Henry's death, the first thing I did was call Doug Ward, an LAPD detective whose nephew I'd helped beat a first-time DUI. Ward told me Henry's death was a boilerplate suicide. Besides the fact that there was no note, Henry had done a meticulous job of it. He had gotten dressed in his good clothes, laid himself down on his bed, and fired. Ward said no one reported hearing a shot. What they did report was a godawful smell coming from his apartment. Forensics estimated Henry was dead for three days before they found him.

It may have made sense to the cops, but to me it just didn't add up. I came to the service hoping either Henry's wife or his girlfriend could help me make sense of it all.

Sitting across the aisle from me in the front pew was a woman I assumed to be Laura Tuck. In a yellow floral dress, she sat staring ahead, waiting for the minister to begin speaking. Now and then she dabbed her eyes with her handkerchief.

I then scanned the crowd and, to my surprise, there was no one who could be Fernanda.

"You know she left him," Peter said in a hushed tone, leaning sideways into me.

"He told me he left her. After twenty-seven years of not quite marital bliss."

"No, not his wife. The girl he ran off with."

"Fernanda?"

"You know her?"

"No. He told me a little bit about her. Well, a little bit about his situation. He came to see me about handling his divorce."

"Well, it looks like he jumped the gun." Pete shook his head. "Shit, I didn't mean that pun."

"Who told you she dumped him?"

"One of Henry's DI buddies. You remember Sergeant Longley? I was speaking to him before I came in."

As the service got under way, we fell silent, but I ruminated on what Pete had told me all the way through. I may not have known Henry too well, but from our brief contact I knew that if Fern had dumped him it would have been a crushing blow.

After the service, the crowd began to shuffle out from the pews and into the aisle. Pete and I were standing together when he grabbed my shoulder firmly.

"Listen, Madison. I've got to go now, but what are you up to tonight?"

I had absolutely no plans other than a few hours at home watching SportsCenter.

"Not much," I said.

"Why don't we grab a meal together, have few beers and do a proper catch up?"

I'd been keeping to myself in recent months. So much so, turning down social invitations had become a reflex. But not this time. Pete was a good man, and the thought of us hanging out and shooting the breeze appealed to me. Besides, I wanted to know what else he knew about Henry's situation.

"That'd be great, Pete," I said. "Let's do it."

"My family's got a restaurant. China Doll. It's on Sunset. How's seven?"

"Seven's fine."

"Don't you dare pull out on me, Madison."

"I won't."

We shook hands quickly and Pete shifted into the aisle and made for the door. After a moment, I followed him then waited outside to see if I could get an opportunity to speak with Laura Tuck.

A string of mourners consoled her before she began making her way to the parking lot.

"Mrs. Tuck," I said as I approached, and she turned to face me.

"Yes?" she said and waited for me to introduce myself.

"I'm so sorry for your loss, ma'am. Please accept my sympathies."

"Thank you," she said flatly. Her tone surprised me. It was like I'd earned her disapproval without ever meeting her.

"Mrs. Tuck. My name's Brad Madison. I'm a friend of Henry's. Well, I was one of his recruits."

As I spoke, her expression hardened into a glare.

"So you're Brad Madison."

"Yes, ma'am."

"Well, you have some nerve approaching me."

"I'm sorry. I don't understand."

"Don't play me for a fool, son. You were helping Henry to divorce me."

I guess he must have told her.

"Well, Mrs. Tuck, the truth is we never got that far. And to be honest—"

"Don't play the nice guy with me. And don't introduce yourself as a friend when you're just his lawyer. You were going to leave me destitute."

"We had one conversation during which Henry made it clear he wanted to do right by you."

"If you were any kind of friend, you would have advised him to come to his senses and save his marriage."

"I didn't get the chance to advise him on anything, ma'am."

"Sure, you didn't. If you had done the right thing instead of trying to make a buck out of that fool, he'd still be alive today."

"I'm sorry you feel that way. I won't bother you anymore." I bowed my head quickly and turned to walk away.

"I bet you feel proud of yourself," she called out to me as I walked. "I suspect you'll be chasing some kind of payment to come out of his estate. You leech."

I kept silent. I kept walking.

Family law. Like I said, it's the pits.

3

When Pete Chang said China Doll, the name rang a bell. I'd never eaten there but I'd heard good things about it. A quick scan online revealed it was one of LA's best Chinese restaurants. Standing in the foyer, I got an immediate sense of why.

Ahead of me was a vast dimly lit room filled with round, white-clothed tables—enough to feed an army. Exposed beams and columns of dark teak framed the space, a white wooden framed lantern hung over each table, and golden dragon statues were stationed in every corner. Beside me a water feature bubbled away soothingly while the combined smell of incense and roasted duck filled the air. Across the room to my left was the exposed kitchen, and behind a glass panel hung about two dozen glistening birds. All of a sudden, I was ravenous.

As I resolved to claim one of those ducks as my own, a woman in a red cheongsam approached me. Her straight black hair arced down from a fringe to frame a face of striking beauty.

"Mr. Madison?"

"Yes," I said, both surprised and delighted she knew my name.

"I'm Pete's sister, Marcia," she said, extending her hand. "He told me to keep an eye out for a handsome man who looks a little lost."

"He said that?" I quickly wondered what sad tale Pete had spun about me. A divorced, chronically single workaholic with (very) occasional bouts of PTSD. What's not to like?

"The first bit. The second was my little joke. I can see you haven't been here before."

"Guilty as charged. Thanks for coming to my rescue. I can't believe you're Pete's sister."

"We're fifteen years apart, and we've got five siblings in between. Come with me. I'll show you to your table."

I fell in behind Marcia as she walked gracefully between tables, leading me to a secluded area at the back of the restaurant.

"Where's Pete? Doing his nails?" If there was one thing I remembered about Pete Chang from the old days, besides his exceptional fitness, it was that he was an obsessive groomer. I hadn't thought about him for years but the memory of him always holding us up before we went out to a bar came back to me.

Marcia laughed. "Probably. Once he's done with the mud mask treatment he borrowed off me."

There was a flirtatious warmth about Marcia that enlivened me. Twenty minutes earlier, I was half tempted to turn the car around and head home, calling Pete to say I wouldn't be coming. To some extent, I was inclined to hide from the world, which may sound odd given my often high-profile cases. But since my divorce from Claire, I hadn't held onto any relationship long enough for it to get serious. And on the two occasions I tried, I was cut loose. I was conscious that a grim acceptance of singledom was setting in, and I wasn't sure if I wanted to embrace or reject it.

"He won't be long, Mr. Madison."

"Please, call me Brad."

"Okay, Brad. Pete's just helping Mom out with a business matter that's just come up."

"No worries."

"I'll get you a drink. What would you like?"

I asked for a Tsingtao and Marcia swung away to oblige. No doubt about it, Mr. and Mrs. Chang had something special in their DNA, producing such fine-looking offspring.

I'd barely had the chance to check my emails when Marcia returned with my beer. As I took the ice-cold green bottle in my hand, Pete appeared.

"Madison," he said. I released the beer and stood to shake his hand. "I'm glad you made it, bro."

"What makes you think I wouldn't?" I asked, like pulling a no-show had never crossed my mind.

"Are you kidding me? I bet your yearbook superlative was 'most likely to get a better offer.' Something tells me you haven't lost that Madison magic." Pete put his arm behind the small of Marcia's back. "Don't get any thoughts about Marcia. She's taken."

Pete lifted her left hand to show off an impressive engagement ring. Marcia beamed, clearly enthralled with the ring and what it signified. I suddenly felt way too old for allowing myself to think she was flirting with me.

"He's a lucky man. Congratulations, Marcia. When's the big day?"

"That's partly why Pete was late. We are trying to settle on the best date so we can have the reception here. And if you know anything about Chinese weddings, you know it's going to be bigger than Ben-Hur."

"Getting our guest list down to three hundred is going to be tough, given the size of our extended family," said Pete.

"Good thing your brother has a fine brain in that pretty head of his. I'm not surprised your mom is leaning on his management skills."

Marcia took her brother's arm. "And I'll be leaning on him to walk me down the aisle." The two of them looked at each other so sweetly, I couldn't help myself.

"Pete and Marcia. Are you sure your surname's not Brady?"

They laughed briefly before their smiles both faded as one.

"Well, with Dad no longer being with us, I wouldn't want anyone else but Pete beside me."

"I'm sorry, I didn't know."

Pete patted my shoulder. "How could you? Dad passed away six months ago but he left a big hole. Come on. You hungry? Let's eat."

Once Pete sat down, he looked up to Marcia knowingly. "Okay, Sis. Like I told you, bring it on."

"I hope you came with an empty stomach, Brad," she said with a smile before leaving us.

After a few rounds of dumplings, a waiter wheeled a whole duck to the table and began slicing off pieces and laying them onto a platter. That done, he took the rest of the carcass away to be transformed into sang choi bow.

"Pete, I wanted to ask about Henry," I said, placing a slice of crispy-skinned duck into a pancake and drizzling hoisin sauce over it. "Are you saying his girlfriend dumped him, so he went and killed himself?"

"That's what Longley told me. When they found him he was holding a photo of her, and there was a Dear John text on his phone, apparently."

Detective Ward didn't tell me that. Maybe they hadn't processed Henry's phone data by then.

"Did you know Henry at all? I mean since boot camp, obviously."

Pete finished his mouthful and took a swig of beer. "Wouldn't say I knew him. I just knew we were in the same industry. Well, that's my understanding at least. I heard he'd pumped some money into the rival of the company I used to work for."

"Which company?" Henry never told me the company he wanted to extract himself from.

"HardShell Security."

"Never heard of it."

"I'm not surprised. It's only been around a few years and it operates in a pretty niche field."

"What kind of field?"

"The cannabis kind. When Prop 64 passed to legalize recreational cannabis use, the industry blew up. And this guy called Quinn Rollins saw there was a gap in the market and he stepped in to fill it."

Pete told me HardShell was a private security company that specifically catered to businesses thriving in the burgeoning cannabis economy. The growers, dispensaries, and labs that were making a lot of money in the new "green rush" found themselves with a major problem. Cannabis was now legal in California, but as far as federal law was concerned it was still illegal, classed as a Schedule 1 drug under the Controlled Substances Act.

"That means if a traditional bank accepted cannabis money they could be prosecuted for money laundering," I said. "Or aiding and abetting a federal crime. I'm starting to see the problem."

"Exactly. So now you've got a lot of cash—and we're talking a mountain of cash—that can't just be wheeled down to the local Wells Fargo branch for safe keeping. You have to find something like a sympathetic credit union, of which there aren't that many."

"So just to get your money banked and to be able to access it when you want is a major issue?"

"Yeah. Then there's the other big issue."

"Which is?"

"Think about it. You've got literally a truck-load of cash that you have to transport to a credit union a few hundred miles away. You've just become the biggest target for road agents since the Prohibition Era."

"And that's where HardShell stepped in?"

"Yeah. They collect your weed and/or your money and get it to where it needs to go. Guys with guns riding in unmarked armored trucks, ferrying millions of dollars' worth of cash and weed across the state."

"Sounds like the private contractors running amok in Kabul," I said. And I could see where the company name came from: in conflict zones, a hard-shell vehicle meant armor-plated vehicle.

"It's not too different. Most of Quinn's men are vets who went on to work for private military contractors overseas."

"How do you know all this?"

"I used to work for Rollins' competition, Bravo Security."

"And Henry Tuck had invested in HardShell, is that right?"

"That was the word on the street. It wasn't out in the open. As far as I understood it, he was a silent partner."

"Did Bravo pay well?"

"They paid very well."

"So why aren't you still working for them?"

Pete shook his head and reached for his beer. "It was getting too crazy."

"How so?"

"It was like the Wild West, Madison. What I said about road agents wasn't hypothetical. Our vans were like stage coaches, and we drew the bad guys out of the woodwork."

Now that Pete mentioned it, I'd read about a couple of incidents where cannabis dispensaries had been ram raided with the crooks making off with a cash-laden ATM.

"They hit your vans?"

Pete nodded. "First time I got stung, we were making a run from Eureka up in Humboldt County down to one of our compounds in San Diego. We pulled over for a piss break, middle of nowhere, and a bunch of guys with masks and guns appeared, tied us up, and stole one and a half mill."

"Inside job?"

"Had to be."

"And that wasn't the only time. We were about to do a pick-up at a grower's farm, but fifteen minutes before we got there, it was raided. This time they left no witnesses alive. Three people dead and eight-hundred grand's worth of weed gone."

"Same guys?"

"Who knows? But my guess is yes."

"And that's when you got out?"

"No. I stuck it out for a while longer. Then I made the decision to leave a couple of weeks ago."

"How come?"

"I saw the writing on the wall. Another company got hit. Three dead and one in hospital. It's out of control, Madison, and the cops and governments won't do anything about it. Until the feds change the classification of cannabis, nothing's going to change. It was only a matter of time before I got hit again. I've got a wife and kids. To hell with that. From now on, the only business I'm interested in is feeding people."

"I had no idea it was so hectic. Sounds like you made a wise move."

"I now realize how much of a lifesaver the cashless economy is. If someone comes in to rob my restaurant, there's no till to empty. All they'll get is a couple of PIN pads. They're never going to bother. That's peace of mind for me, right there."

A waiter came with more food and more beer. Pete took a swig and leaned back in his chair. "Enough about that, Madison. What's going on with you? When I saw you today, I just got a sense everything's not A-OK with you. How are you doing?"

Through dinner, I sensed this was coming and was ready to wave Pete off. But with a few drinks under my belt, and the genuine care Pete displayed, I decided to let my guard down a little.

"I don't know, nothing's majorly wrong. Work keeps me busy but outside that I'm just going through the motions right now. My life's fine. It really is. I mean, I'd like to have more time to spend with my daughter, but that's not something I can change."

"You got a good woman in your life?"

I laughed and leaned back. I looked at Pete like this topic was territory that I didn't want us to wade into. Any higher than ankle deep, anyway.

"I guess the straight-out answer is no."

"As far as I can tell, that would have to be on your account. I can't imagine you'd have too many issues finding yourself a girlfriend. Hell, the way Marcia was looking at you I thought her wedding might have to be put on hold."

I laughed. "Yeah, right. But thanks for the flattery. I've been divorced over five years now. And I can tell you there have been some fine women in my life since. But just when things seem to be going right, they go all wrong."

I went on to tell him a little about Abby Hatfield, the Hollywood actress I fell for right when Claire and I decided to get divorced. Then there was Jessica Pope, the prosecutor who I battled in the courtroom and enjoyed a friends-with-benefits relationship with. Then, right when we both realized we wanted something more, she up and moved to Washington D.C. Six months later, Jessica told me she was engaged to a senator.

"Who'd have thought it. The great Brad Madison, getting dumped. Not once but twice."

"I don't need sympathy, Pete."

"It's not sympathy. It's funny."

"Prick."

We laughed and proceeded to demolish our banquet. It felt good to get that off my chest. I don't know whether I felt more or less like a loser.

4

I got the Uber to pull over at a 7-11 a block or so from my apartment building. I was pretty drunk but not so much that I forgot I was out of coffee and that I'd need a heart-starter in the morning courtesy of my espresso machine.

I liked living in Santa Monica. I was close to Bella, who lived with her mom Claire in a fine house on the Venice Beach canals. How I came to be a Santa Monica resident was a long story. The apartment used to belong to my younger brother Mitch. About two years ago, he told me he wanted to sell. He never gave me a convincing reason why, and pressing him risked pushing our relationship back to where it was for most of our adult years—that is, almost non-existent. All he said was that he needed a change, had to get out of LA, and was thinking about moving up to San Francisco to join a real estate firm. The apartment was actually a gift from me—which is a long story in itself—but I saw this as my cue to get out of my rental and into a near-new apartment complex in the heart of Santa Monica. I offered Mitch market price and he accepted.

I hadn't heard from my brother since, but that was not unusual. With his history of gambling, I figured he'd sold out in order to settle some kind of debt. When I offered to help him out if he was in a financial bind, he denied it and reassured me it was nothing more than a mid-life crisis.

I shifted my supplies to my left arm as I dug into my jeans pocket for my keys. Looking ahead, something I saw at the entrance to my building made me slow my pace.

Two men were standing there, both wearing sleeveless leather jackets, jeans, and boots. One of them was huge. Six-six at least, with a torso that had the girth of a tree trunk. They made it clear they were watching me approach.

Adrenalin pumped fast through my body, sobering me up just a little. Not that I was kidding myself that I could fight my way out of trouble here.

As I got near, I nodded a greeting and reached for the door. The big biker stepped across to block my way. A waft of his acrid armpit musk hit my nose and his frame practically filled my vision. Greasy long hair was parted at the side, revealing a broad brow that was furrowed with scorn.

"You the lawyer Madison?" he said in a soft rumble.

I cast a quick glance at his sidekick, a wiry, wary-looking specimen who wore his beard in a long plat beneath an almost glowing white, shaved scalp.

I could tell by their colors that they belonged to the Iron Raiders. My mind flicked through my most recent cases in an effort to unearth anything I'd had to do with outlaw motorcycle gangs. I came up with nothing. Over the years, I'd defended a few bikers and to some extent I was familiar with the way they did business. They hardly ever relied on phones to send a message. They favored having a couple of brothers deliver the memo in person. It was never a cheerful encounter. Even to pay my fees, they could pull a stunt like this, showing up at two in the morning to hand over a few grand for services rendered. But I had the feeling that these guys had not come to line my pockets. I'd never represented an Iron Raider, so the best I could hope for was that they were here to ask for my help.

Turns out I was right. In a sense.

"Yes, I am. What can I do for you guys?"

The stinking bear had yet to blink, and he looked through me with an implacable expression devoid of mercy. It was as though I'd somehow insulted his mother and he was just taking a moment to decide just how he was going to dismember me. Then, quicker than lighting, he shot his right fist into my solar plexus. It was like a battering ram. My feet just about left the ground with the force of the impact. I staggered back a little before crumpling down to the pavement, somehow managing to clutch my bag of groceries as I went.

For a few seconds I struggled to breathe. But the blow didn't just wind me, it created a terrible force in my stomach. Within seconds I was ejecting a full belly of Chinese food and booze onto the concrete.

"What the fuck!" I said after I was done wiping my mouth. "What the fuck do you want?"

The Bear dropped to one knee. He then dropped the other onto my neck. My attempts to regain my breath were now blocked.

He put some weight into his knee. The blood pressure in my face reached the point of searing pain.

"Now you listen to me, lawyer man. And you listen good. You stay clear of Chip Bowman, you hear?"

"I don't know a Chip Bowman, you fuck," I squeezed out.

He jabbed his knee harder into my neck.

"You better watch your mouth, cocksucker. Just tell me you understand. You are not going to defend Chip Bowman under any circumstances. You stay the fuck away from him. Got it?"

With a two-hundred-pound biker leaning his whole bodyweight into my neck, I lost the wherewithal to reply at all. The Bear sensed that and backed off to give me some air.

I sucked a few quick breaths into my lungs before replying with haste. "I got it. I don't defend Chip Bowman."

"Good."

With that, the biker released his knee, and he and his sidekick walked slowly over to their Harleys. The Bear straddled his bike and watched me get to my feet. He kicked his machine to life.

"You do anything for that prick, lawyer man," he shouted over the engine noise, "and I'm going to break every fucking bone in your body."

With that, they roared off.

All I could think was, *Who the fuck is this Chip Bowman?*

5

I was woken at God knows what time by the ringing of my phone. I picked it up and saw it was Claire, my ex-wife. Although it's been years since we split, seeing her name on the screen at odd hours still stirred up a stock response: I've screwed up somehow.

"Hello," I said.

"Hi Brad. I woke you. I'm sorry," she sounded genuinely apologetic. "I take it you didn't get my message."

"What message?"

"Damn. I'm so sorry. I tried to reach you last night." The slightly beseeching tone in her voice told me I hadn't screwed up, even by missing her call. "Listen, this is so last-minute. Something's come up and I have to head out to Palm Springs for work. I was wondering if Bella could spend a few days with you."

I sat myself up in bed. A pain in my stomach made me grimace and I was reminded of the lovely reception I'd gotten from my Iron Raider friends.

"What's the matter?"

"Nothing. My head hurts a little. That's all."

"You had a big night?"

"Kind of."

"How big?" Claire asked warily. She couldn't help but imagine the worst. She'd seen me leave a trail of destruction several times during our marriage. Mostly it was down to a PTSD episode, which would occasionally spiral into an alcoholic binge.

"I just caught up with an old buddy of mine, but it wasn't over the top. If you called, I just didn't notice."

"That's okay. But here's the thing. I'm downstairs with Bella. Can she stay with you?"

"What? You're downstairs?"

"Please, Brad."

"Yeah, of course she can stay," I said, getting off the bed and biting down on the pain in my gut. "Come up. I'll buzz you in."

I reached the kitchen and pressed the button to open the security door. Through her phone, I heard the door unlock and Claire open it. "See you in a bit."

As I spoke, I smelled vomit on my breath. I went to the bathroom, brushed my teeth, splashed cold water on my face, and ran wet hands through my hair. Back in the bedroom, I pulled on some jeans and a t-shirt. I was feeling awake now and surprisingly sober. That fat biker did me a small favor emptying my gut of booze. The place where his fist landed burned when I stood tall, but it was nothing debilitating. My neck, though, felt stiff and sore. I quickly massaged some of the pain out as I moved to the kitchen and made some coffee.

It was only then that I looked at my watch, realizing I had no idea what time it was. It was just after seven.

The buzzer sounded and I went to the door.

There was a time when Bella would launch herself at me at first sight. She was a little older now, a little cooler, but her smile upon seeing me was something to treasure.

Looking relieved, Claire gave me a quick kiss on the cheek as I drew Bella in for a hug and stepped into my apartment. She couldn't help but cast an eye over the place but cut it short to explain herself.

"Thanks for this, Brad. We're shooting a multi—platform campaign in Palm Springs, and it's starting to go sideways. I need to get there ASAP."

Just before we got divorced, Claire founded a jewelry enterprise that proved to be incredibly successful. "Claire Hall" (her maiden name) was now one of the biggest jewelry brands in the US.

"I got it," I said. "But I want it on the record that I'm doing this under duress," I said, giving Bella a squeeze that triggered a giggle. "I don't know who this young woman is or what she thinks she's doing here, but I'll just have to go along with it. But any nonsense and I'll be taking her straight to the authorities."

I bent over and kissed the top of Bella's head.

"Have you had breakfast? You hungry?" I asked her.

Bella nodded.

"Go grab some juice while I talk to Mom. Then we'll make pancakes."

Bella skipped off to the kitchen.

"What's going on?" I asked Claire.

"One of the models has gone postal. Seems the photographer was screwing her and she just found out he's also screwing her best friend. The hotel had to call security on her, and now we're rushing to get a replacement and... do you really want to know all this?"

I shook my head with a smile. "No."

"I'm going to have to stay there for three days, and Bella's got school tomorrow. You okay with that?"

"Of course. Where's Marty?"

Marty was Claire's husband, and Bella's step-dad. He seemed an okay guy. He was good with Bella and never seemed inclined to over-step his role. He and Bella got along but were not tight, and Marty left all the parenting decisions in their house to Claire. He was aloof toward me, and I felt he was a bit of a try-hard. But he did well for himself working for a big finance company that seemed to have a hand in everything from Hollywood movies to renewable energy. Call me cynical, but he seemed a bit dull for Claire, as though she'd opted for a safe harbor after her tumultuous experience with me.

"He's away."

"Let me guess. Golf?"

Marty appeared to do a lot of business on the golf course. During one brief conversation I had with him, he let it slip he played off a handicap of two and had considered going pro when he was younger.

"Pebble Beach. It's his annual trip. Left yesterday and won't be back for a week."

"Okay. No worries."

On paper, our custody arrangement was clear. I got Bella every second weekend. Claire was flexible, though, so I also got to take Bella on ski trips or up to Boise to visit my folks.

"Thanks, Brad. She's excited."

"Can't see why."

"Ha," Claire smiled. "She loves every minute she spends with you," she said and looked at her watch. "I gotta go." Claire then turned back to me with a caring look and touched my arm. "You okay?"

She didn't have to say that I looked rough.

"I'm fine. Just a bit hungover."

"A few drinks with a Marine buddy, you say? Are you sure it wasn't a big date with someone special?"

Claire couldn't resist the temptation to tease me, and to pry a little at the same time. Everyone was on my case about "finding someone." Even my ex-wife.

"Yes. His name's Pete Chang and we're very much in love."

Claire laughed. "Whatever happened to Jessica?"

"She's in DC. And she's counsel for the President."

"The President?"

"Yep, she's spending a lot of time in the White House. And she's now married to Senator Ryan Fielding."

"The Republican from Florida?"

"That's the one."

"That's a shame. I thought you really liked her."

"I did. That's why she left," I joked.

Claire looked like she felt sorry for me. "You'll meet someone. If you'll only let them in. Hell, you're one of the hottest forty-something men in LA. Don't tell Marty I said that. Take care, Brad."

Claire walked to the kitchen to kiss Bella goodbye before returning to the door.

"Good luck with the shoot," I said.

I saw Claire out then went back to join Bella. "Okay," I called out as I approached the kitchen. "Pancakes it is. Right, let's get the ingredients."

"I'm way ahead of you," said Bella, stepping aside and waving her hand over the flour, sugar, baking powder, egg, milk, mixing bowl, utensils, and measuring cup that she'd set out on the bench.

"You go sit down, Dad. I can manage," said Bella as she began scooping flour into the bowl. I watched her for a moment, marveling at my beautiful daughter.

"What do you want to do today?" I asked.

Bella didn't look up from what she was doing. "Don't know. I'm easy."

We hung out down at Santa Monica. Went ice skating. Saw a movie. Walked down to the pier. Then had an early dinner.

It was a perfect date with the perfect girl.

6

I was surprised to find Megan Schaffer busy at her desk when Bella and I arrived at the office on Monday. It was just after seven-thirty. Normally, she would not have appeared for another hour.

When I raised a "what are you doing here?" eyebrow, she folded her arms and returned my expression with playful exaggeration. "The Lindstrom case?" she posed in an effort to jog my memory. "You said I could leave early Friday so long as I got the brief ready first thing Monday. So here I am. And here it is. And my goodness, good morning gorgeous Bella. What a lovely surprise."

Megan got to her feet, pushed the file into my stomach, and embraced Bella warmly. Megan and Bella were very fond of each other. I'd given Bella the option of us staying at my place or hanging at the office before school, and she chose the latter on account of Megan.

"Thank you," I said to Megan. "You didn't have to get here this early. How'd the move go?"

"Great," Megan said. "I mean, a lot of packing and unpacking but I got it all done, and now it feels like home. My home." She bounced a little and addressed Bella. "I just bought a condo. A very small condo. But it's mine."

This was a huge step for Megan. I valued her for many reasons, such as her intelligence, humor, and charm, but I was particularly grateful for the loyalty she'd shown me. When I decided to relocate from Downtown to the Third Street Promenade in Santa Monica, the move added forty minutes to Megan's commute. Now, as the proud owner of a one-bedder on Stanforth Street, she could get from door to door in less than twenty minutes.

"Glad to hear it, Megan. You should be proud of yourself."

"Let's not pretend I could have bought a condo without those bonuses you gave me."

"Bonuses you earned," I said. "And then saved, and then spent wisely."

"How long are you staying with Dad?" Megan asked Bella.

"A few nights," Bella beamed.

"Have you had breakfast?"

"No, Dad said we could get breakfast burritos."

Megan turned to me. "Why don't I take the lovely Bella with me to get us some food?"

"Great idea. I'll have coffee and one of those burritos too." I raised the Lindstrom file. "And thanks for this."

As Megan and Bella left, I walked into my office with my nose buried in the file. Nina Lindstrom was a friend of Claire's who was going through a bitter divorce. Claire recommended me not just for my abilities as a lawyer, she knew I'd be silly to turn down the potential money on offer. Nina and her soon-to-be-ex-husband Eric were at war with each other. I'd been trying to get the most basic terms of a settlement down but it was proving damn near impossible.

I walked into my office and sat at my desk. I liked my new office. It was close to home, close to Bella, and close to the beach. In summer, I could get in an early surf and maybe one at lunch during winter, if the waves were inviting enough. Calling my own hours was one perk of practicing solo that I made full use of. I'd once entertained the idea of returning to a big law firm but that was never going to happen now.

My office was on the fifth floor of a ten-story building that housed a variety of small businesses and interests. I say interests because directly above me was the office of none other than Wesley Brenner, a Republican vying for election to the Californian State Senate. Brenner, a former pro wrestler, was used to drawing all sorts of attention to himself, and on several occasions I'd had to work my way through a media scrum to get into my building because he was holding court in the mall.

I wouldn't say I was repulsed by Brenner's politics. It was his boisterous, bullying persona that rubbed me the wrong way. He was a big, tall man with a bald head, silver goatee, and a diehard propensity to behave as if the cameras were always rolling. To avoid being caught with him in the elevator was the main reason I often took the stairs. In recent weeks he'd launched his own podcast, which he recorded in his office that sat directly above mine. I knew this not because I listened to his show but because I'd hear him sharing the subject of each episode with anyone he managed to corner.

After I'd digested the Lindstrom file, I found myself wondering how the hell two people who had once walked down the aisle and professed undying love for each other could become such bitter enemies. It made me thankful that Claire and I were on good terms.

I heard my door open and saw Megan enter holding my coffee in one hand and my burrito in the other. She quickly closed the door with her foot and stared at me with a puzzled look.

"What is it, Megan?"

"You've got a walk in."

"What?" I looked at my watch. "It's five past eight. I don't have time. I have to get Bella to school, and I told Nina Lindstrom I'd be at her house by ten."

"He looks desperate."

"Where's Bella?"

"She's fine. She's in the conference room."

"Good," I said. I pulled up the front desk security camera on my computer. I'd had my fair share of crazies barge into my office, or at least try to. The man was sitting on one of the waiting room chairs, switching his gaze from my door to the elevator. I didn't recognize him at all.

"He's not scary desperate, Mr. Madison. Just anxious, as far as I can tell. He practically begged me to let him see you immediately."

I really didn't have the time. "Megan, can you please just get this guy to make an appointment?"

"He said it was a matter of life and death."

"Oh, for God's sake. Of course, it is. Did he give you a name?"

"Yes, he did. Chip Bowman."

7

I sprang to my feet and, after Megan had stepped aside, whipped the door open and walked out.

Upon seeing me, the visitor got to his feet, albeit with some difficulty. He placed his hands on his right thigh and winced as he rose. He was a mild, inoffensive looking man in his mid-thirties. Beneath a black Orioles cap was a thin face that bore a worn-out expression. There were bags under his eyes, and his pallid skin had sprung a few days of light brown stubble. He looked like he kept himself very fit. The short-sleeved checked shirt he wore was tucked into beige chinos, and nothing hung over his woven leather belt.

He bowed slightly, hunched his shoulders, and made a quick adjustment of his cap. He then held out his hand and walked toward me with a limp.

"Mr. Madison," he said, "I'm sorry to—"

I kept my hands by my side. "What are you doing here?"

"What? I need a lawyer."

"LA's got a million lawyers. Why me?"

The guy was taken aback by my tone. His mouth hung open as he tried to find his words.

"I need help."

"If I don't get a straight answer from you right now, I'm throwing you out, got it? I'll ask you again: why did you choose me?"

"Henry Tuck."

"What about him?"

"I knew Henry. When he needed a lawyer, someone gave him your name and he asked me to check you out."

"What do you mean, check me out?"

"He wanted some due diligence done before he came to see you. He wasn't great with computers and he asked me to see if you were the right fit for him."

I couldn't help thinking of the huge biker with his knee crushing my neck, telling me I was dead if I went anywhere near Chip Bowman.

"Did you take any precautions to make sure you weren't followed here? Or did you just wander in?"

Bowman stood a little straighter and hit me with a trusting look. "Mr. Madison, my life is in danger. I can't afford to let my guard down for a second, and I assure you, as a fellow Marine, that no one followed me here. I swear."

"A fellow Marine?" I looked at him soberly and nodded.

"Henry was my DI too. He told me you were one of his best ever recruits."

That was news to me, not that I'd ever expect to hear such flattery from Henry's mouth.

I walked to my office door and extended my left arm out. "Come in and take a seat. I'll be with you in a minute."

Bowman flattened his mouth in a humble display of gratitude and stepped past me. I closed the door behind him.

"Megan," I said, digging into my pocket. "Do me a favor, would you? Take my car and get Bella to school. And then if I'm still busy with this guy when you get back, call Mrs. Lindstrom and tell her I'm going to be late. Any time after twelve that suits her."

"Got it, Mr. Madison," said Megan, taking my keys and handing me my coffee and breakfast. "Get some of this into you."

As Megan set off, I sipped at the coffee. It was barely warm, so I threw it down in about four gulps. I tore open the paper and took a bite out of the burrito and walked into my office.

"You got me at breakfast, so I apologize," I said to Bowman through a half-full mouth.

"I'm sorry. Please, go ahead and eat."

I sat down. "Let's keep this moving. Are you and Henry friends?"

"Not really. Our paths hadn't crossed since basic training. But he somehow knew I was employed at HardShell Security and contacted me."

"What do you do at HardShell?"

"Basically, I work as an armed courier. That's what most of the guys are hired to do. You know, carry a gun and chauffeur piles of weed and cash around."

"I know a little about HardShell, as it happens. Did Henry work there?"

"No. He kept his involvement in the company real low key. He never spoke to anyone there, but one day he approached me. We spoke a few times after that, and then one day he told me he was concerned about what was going on in the company. He asked me to check on a couple of things."

"Such as?"

Bowman shifted in his seat. "Mr. Madison, with all due respect, that's not why I'm here."

"Well, right now that's what I'm interested in. What did Henry want you to look into?"

"He thought Mr. Rollins was getting into some illegal activity."

Right, I thought. *Maybe sharing poolside pina coladas with Fernanda wasn't the only reason Henry wanted to pull his money out.*

"And was he?"

"I wasn't sure."

I leaned back in my chair and studied Bowman. He was for all the world one of the most unassuming individuals you could ever behold. He looked like the excitement of his week was tending to his stamp collection.

"I want to thank you so much for seeing me, Mr. Madison," Bowman said politely. I held up my hand to stop him.

"Tell me why you're here."

With that, Bowman took a deep breath. "The truth is I'm scared, Mr. Madison. My team was robbed. They made off with a million dollars and a lot of weed. They killed both my partners and shot me in the leg. I think the cops think I did it."

"Did the cops tell you that you're a suspect?"

"No, not in so many words. I just started to feel like one."

"Is that what you're scared of?"

"Well, yes. Them. And Quinn Rollins. I'm sure he thinks I was involved somehow."

"What about the Iron Raiders?"

Chip Bowman's face slackened with mild surprise. His mouth opened again but offered nothing.

"You know, the motorcycle gang, the Iron Raiders," I prodded. "Why the hell would they threaten to turn me into ground beef if I helped you?"

I was leaning forward now. Bowman looked puzzled. His jaw moved from side to side. He then tilted his head quickly in preparation to talk.

"I think I can explain."

I looked at my watch.

"You've got two minutes. Convince me fast or I'm kicking you out of my office."

8

"The bikers," said Bowman quickly, like he was thinking on his feet. "I have no idea why they'd do that to you."

"Really? No idea at all?"

"Look, like I told you. Henry thought there was some dodgy stuff going on at HardShell. And so did I. But I never found anything. But I think there was something sketchy going on. And I think that the bikers may have lost more than just money in the robbery."

"And they think you're in on it?"

"I guess so."

"And so does your boss."

"Yes."

"And so do the cops."

"Yes."

I looked at my watch again. "Time's getting on, Mr. Bowman. From what you've told me I'm not inclined to touch this case."

"I didn't do it, Mr. Madison. You've got to believe me. I've got two young daughters and a wife I love very much. All I wanted to do was do my job well, build a good life for my family, and save enough to put my girls through college. I've got no reason to do something like this. How they think that I'm part of this crime is beyond me. But, like I said, I checked you out for Henry's sake. You're one of the best defense attorneys in Los Angeles. You've proven that time and again. And from what I read you're prepared to fight for justice. And Marine to Marine, sir, I'm begging you to fight for me."

I was leaning back in my chair now, weighing up Bowman's words. I was also weighing up the wisdom of provoking a return visit from my biker friends. Why would I risk that? Why should I? I didn't know this Chip Bowman guy from Adam and, what, I'm supposed to put my life on the line for him? But his last line echoed in my mind: *Marine to Marine, I'm begging you to fight for me*. This was an appeal that was almost impossible for me to ignore.

Almost.

Bowman began fiddling with his phone. I was about to suggest that he get his focus back on our conversation when he stood up and presented the screen to me.

"This is Carrie," a pretty woman smiled at me from the phone. Bowman flicked to another photo. "And this is Tracy and Hannah. Tracy's four. Hannah's two." In the photo, the two blonde-haired girls were seated beaming on their father's lap. "I live for my three girls, Mr. Madison. I've done some stupid things in my life but here are three things I got right. They are my world and I would never do anything to put that world at risk."

Bowman stepped back and resumed his seat. "I swear to God, Mr. Madison. I had nothing to do with that robbery."

I looked at my watch again. The gesture wasn't to put any pressure on Bowman. Rather, it was a reminder that I'd given him a commitment to decide, and now *my* time was up.

"Okay, Mr. Bowman. I'm going to need to know a lot more about your situation. I want you to start by telling me what happened that night, and then tell me everything you've told the cops."

Bowman relaxed somewhat and took a few moments to gather his thoughts. Then he began, telling me that he and two other employees, Bo Hendricks and Nathan Reed, were tasked with a collection run that went from Los Angeles up to Humboldt County and back. It was a four-day job. It was a twelve-hour drive up to Humboldt where they collected cannabis and cash from various growers and then returned to Los Angeles.

"How much were you carrying?"

"It was only a small load by usual standards. We had a hundred pounds of cannabis and a million dollars in cash."

"Small, you say," I said with raised eyebrows. "Go on."

"When we got back to LA, we headed to a warehouse on Mission Street that HardShell leases."

"Is that where everything was supposed to be stored?"

"No. There are no vaults there. It's a new property, and it hasn't been fitted out with all the usual security equipment yet. It was a place where we'd store the vans and we'd leave our cars there while we do the runs."

"Were you scheduled to stop there on this run?"

"No. But then Bo got a call from his girlfriend. He was pretty upset and didn't tell us too much but he said he had to go see her as soon as possible. That was okay with us because, you know, there was still Nate and I to secure the delivery."

"So you pulled into this warehouse lot. Then what happened?"

"Well, I was driving, and I remember getting out of the van, but that's about it. Next thing, I wake up. I'm lying on my back, there's these paramedics leaning over me, and lights flashing all around. I've got a bullet in my leg, a big lump on the back of my head, and a powerful headache."

"That's it?"

"That's it."

"Is this what you told the cops?"

"Pretty much. They wanted to know where the money and cannabis was meant to go."

"And where was that?"

"The HardShell head office. There's a couple of big vaults there. We'd lock everything up in there overnight, then the next day, we'd take them out to where they were supposed to go."

"Where to?"

"The weed was destined for dispensaries and labs. About two-hundred grand was going to the California Credit Union over on Rosenell Terrace. But most of it had to go to City Hall."

"City Hall?"

"Yeah."

"I don't understand."

"Taxes. Most of the money was the monthly installment of five of our clients. Because of the banking situation, they can't cut City Hall a check or wire their money from a cellphone. They have to physically hand their tax money over to the Finance Department."

"Hell, that kind of cash must make those government workers jumpy."

"It sure does," said Bowman. "And all they have to do is count it. There are growers, dispensary owners, and other businesses out there that take the risk of driving their cash and weed around themselves. No security. It's a crazy situation. Everyone in the chain is watching their back, scared of getting jumped."

"And that's what happened to you?"

"Yeah. Like I said, I pulled into the lot, got out, and after that I don't remember much."

"You blacked out."

"I think I was knocked out, sir. I mean, Mr. Madison."

"Call me Brad."

"I asked the paramedic what was going on but he didn't tell me anything. I turned my head and saw my buddies lying on the ground nearby. They had paramedics on them too. Then the paramedics stood up and that's when I saw that Nate and Bo were dead."

"They weren't knocked out like you?"

"No, I could see the paramedics being mindful of where they stepped and when I looked I saw they were stepping over pools of blood. And there were some bikers there."

"What? At the crime scene?"

"Yes."

"What were they doing there?"

"I don't know. But I heard them shouting. They were pissed about something."

"You didn't hear what they were saying?"

"No. I was in a kind of haze."

"Okay. What else do you remember?"

"I started screaming, asking what the hell happened to Nate and Bo but no one explained anything to me. They just told me to calm down. They told me that I'd been shot and that they were going to take me to the hospital. Then they loaded me into an ambulance and took me away."

"Where were you shot?"

"Here." Bowman tapped his right thigh. "I was lucky the bullet didn't hit the bone. Just muscle. I got the stitches out a week ago. It's healing fast but it's still sore."

"Whereabouts were your co-workers shot?"

"Twice in the head. Both of them." Bowman looked guilty as he said this. "I have no idea why I wasn't killed, if that's what you're going to ask."

"No, but I bet the cops asked you that."

"Yes, they did."

"How many times have they questioned you?"

"Three. Twice in the hospital and then once at my house."

"Did you get their names?"

"Yes. Detective Ed Frierson and Detective Lou Morello."

I wrote the names down. "What about security footage? Surely, there were cameras monitoring the place?"

"No," said Chip shaking his head. "As I said before, this was a new lease for HardShell. Nothing had been set up yet. It was little more than a parking lot and an empty warehouse."

"Okay. So why are you here? You haven't been arrested for anything?"

Bowman moved forward to perch himself on the edge of his seat.

"Sir, I mean Brad. I don't know what to do."

I drummed my fingers on my desk.

"Did you have anything to do with this crime, Mr. Bowman?" I asked, studying his face. Bowman began shaking his head, slowly and deliberately. If he wasn't being honest, he was damned good at pretending to be.

"Brad, I swear on my children's lives: I did not do this. Nate and Bo were my friends. I was just doing my job, earning good money, and trying to build a good life for my family. Now I could lose everything. There's no way I'd ever take such a gamble. There's no way I could shoot Nate and Bo like dogs."

"I've seen men abandon their families for far less than a million in cash, Mr. Bowman."

"Brad, you've got to believe me. I'm innocent."

I don't know why but I was inclined to believe him.

"But you're telling me the cops don't believe you, your boss doesn't believe you, and that a criminal gang doesn't believe you either."

"I think they're going to try and pin it on me. They all are. I'm a scapegoat."

"Or else someone's trying to frame you."

Bowman nodded. "That could be true, also."

"Hypothetically, why would your boss want you to take the fall for this?"

Bowman sat back in his chair. He looked down at his hands as he flipped his phone around with his fingers. "I've given that a lot of thought, Mr. Madison. I always thought Mr. Rollins liked me. But you know how Henry asked me to see if anything shady was going on? Well, there were a couple of times when I thought the other guys loaded black market weed and cash into the van."

"Did you check the van?"

"Yes, but I found nothing. Then I went to Mr. Rollins and asked if he had ever given other members of my team permission to take on any goods that were not listed on the manifest. And he said no. And he told me to tell him if I saw anything untoward going on."

"That's good, isn't it? That means he trusts and values you."

Bowman lifted the corner of his mouth and tilted his head. "That's what I thought too. But then after all this went down, I started to look at things differently. Like, maybe he thought I was out of line with raising my suspicions with him. Maybe he thought I should just turn a blind eye and shut up."

"You think Mr. Rollins was doing business with illegal growers?"

Bowman shrugged his shoulders. "Maybe."

"So this whole robbery double murder might have been a plot to get rid of you?"

"Maybe."

"Why wouldn't he just fire you?"

Bowman bent forward and put his head in his hands. "I know. It's ridiculous. I mean, he might have thought I might squeal if he fired me. But I didn't know anything for sure. I had nothing to go to the cops with. And he knew that."

"Maybe he just thinks you did it."

Bowman straightened. "Yes. You're probably right."

"Still, I am interested in the Iron Raiders. They sure as hell don't like you. What have you done to earn their wrath?"

"Could be that they just think I'm guilty too."

"Could be."

"Or it could be... No, I'm just getting desperate."

"Could be what?"

"Well, what if the aim of the robbery was not just to steal all that money and weed? What if there was something else in the van that was not on the books? Something the cops don't know about because Mr. Rollins could never report it to them? Something that the bikers knew was there and that they knew was stolen? Something small, very valuable, and easy to hide?"

"Like what?"

"There are no diamonds up in Humboldt County. There's only one thing I can think of that fits, if I was to guess. Meth."

9

Nina Lindstrom lived a comfortable life in a Hollywood Hills mansion, and she intended to keep it that way. When her husband Eric finally admitted he'd been cheating on her, she kicked him out. The confession confirmed, or at least justified, all the suspicions she'd put to him over the years that he'd flatly denied. She told him she'd found incriminating photos and emails on his phone. He promptly deleted them and smugly told her she had nothing. That's when she revealed she'd sent all the material to herself and that she'd secured a lawyer. And because Nina was Claire's friend, that lawyer was me.

Chip Bowman's drop-in meant I was running ninety minutes late. Before Bowman left, I told him to think about a safe house for his family. He said he'd already made plans along those lines. He had a sister in Napa Valley that Carrie and the girls could stay with, if things got dicey. I told him to get a burner phone and use it to contact me.

The last thing I said was that he had to stay put. If he relocated, it would be suspicious. If the bikers wanted to kill him, he'd be dead already. That they hadn't paid him a visit like they'd done to me was curious. Maybe they simply wanted to ensure Bowman had nothing better than a stock public defender representing him.

On the way to Nina Lindstrom's house, I called my investigator Jack Briggs. He and his wife Chanel had just welcomed a baby boy into the world.

When I say just, I mean three months ago, but Jack's commitment to being a hands-on dad meant he'd made himself unavailable for work. Noah was their second child, so this was the second sabbatical Jack had taken. And while I understood and applauded his decision, it meant I'd had to make do without the brilliant investigator who'd helped me no end to win cases and build my name and business. Over the years, we'd built a great friendship, strong enough for him to ask me to be godfather to both his children.

"About time you called," Jack answered. "When are you going to come visit your godson?"

I hadn't seen Noah since the christening. "Some of us have work to do."

"Whoa. Check your lazy patriarchy at the door, buddy. What I'm doing is more valuable than any job I've been paid for."

"I never said it wasn't. But working's always been kind of optional for you, hasn't it?"

Jack was a man of many talents, one of which was being astute enough to invest in certain tech stocks that proceeded to go through the roof. Before that he was a promising quarterback. I'd heard it said many times, and not just from him, that if he hadn't busted his throwing arm in college, he'd have rivalled Tom Brady in ability, not just looks.

But Jack kept a constant sunny demeanor about him, which was to some extent a shield against a family tragedy. His elder sister Nora went missing in Australia years ago. Then it was discovered she'd been murdered, and the killer refused to reveal where her body was, a secret he took to the grave.

The pain of that experience, for Jack himself and his parents, forged in him a desire to aid the cause of justice. He was broad-minded enough to understand that justice wasn't all about putting bad guys behind bars.

At some point, he came to see deep value in saving someone who was innocent from the hell of a wrongful conviction. One day many years ago, after he'd read a story about one of my cases, he knocked on my door to offer his services as a private investigator. Every success I've had ever since has been due in no small part to Jack's input.

"Is there some point to this call? I'm about to give Noah a bath."

"Well, yeah," I said. "I wanted to see if you could pull your head out of baby-bliss-land and do some work for me. You won't even have to leave the house or wear a shirt that doesn't have baby puke on it. I just need you to do some good online research."

"What's the subject?"

"Check your inbox. I've sent some info about a new case. Guy called Chip Bowman. He was injured in a fatal robbery and the cops might be shaping to pin it on him."

As I talked, I could hear Jack was walking. I heard him enter his home office and close the door. I waited while he tapped away at his laptop.

"Okay. HardShell Security, huh?"

"Yeah. You've got the names of the victims, and the founder Quinn Rollins. Most of these guys are vets who went on to work for private security companies. I want you to dig around and see what you can find. You able to do that?"

"For sure. How deep you want me to go?"

"Just see what you can get over the next two days and let me know, would you?"

"No worries."

"Great."

I pulled into the Lindstrom driveway, and by the time I reached the front steps, Nina was standing at the door waiting for me. In her early forties, she was a vivacious brunette who carried herself with a dignity weighed with lament. She was saddened and somewhat ashamed that her marriage had failed, even though it was not her who steered it onto the rocks. She didn't enjoy the thought of being a divorcee.

In the meetings I'd had with Nina Lindstrom to date, I'd admired the way she managed to keep her enmity in check. In a way, she felt sorry for her husband, who, although I hadn't met him, appeared by way of anecdote to be a conceited fool. The luxury car business he had built from scratch afforded him the mansion, a Downtown apartment, and a villa in Los Cabos, to name a few of his prized possessions. Now he was in danger of losing a big chunk of them, if Mrs. Lindstrom and I had anything to do with it. I'd already sensed via his lawyers that Mr. Lindstrom was intent on hanging onto everything as aggressively as he could.

"Hello, Nina. I'm so sorry I had to push our meeting back. Thanks for being so accommodating."

"That's okay, Brad. Please come in."

She led me through a luxurious sitting room where we sat opposite each other on broad floral sofas.

"This won't take long, Nina. Just a few things for you to read over and I'll need your autograph where the yellow tabs are."

I set the documents out on the table between us. She took them up to read. "I take it you got my check?"

"Yes, I did. Thank you. It was hand-delivered to me last Friday by your driver. What's his name? Xavier, wasn't it?"

"That's right."

"Well, we're off to a good start. But you said you had something to show me."

"Yes," said Nina, picking up a file and handing it to me.

"What's this?" I said as I took it.

"It's from Eric. He's filed a counterclaim."

"On what grounds?"

"That I cheated on him first, and that he was the one who initiated the divorce."

"It really doesn't matter who initiated the divorce."

"Well, he claims he can prove I cheated on him."

"Did you?"

"No. He's being ridiculous."

I didn't say anything as I read through the claims made in the file. It went into some detail, alleging multiple indiscretions by Nina. Among them was a claim that he had caught her in bed with Xavier.

"Nina, is there any substance to these allegations?"

She scoffed. "Of course, not. Like I said, the man is desperate and ridiculous. Look at the settlement he wants."

That's exactly what I was looking at. In his proposed terms of settlement, Eric Lindstrom wanted the mansion and the villa, leaving the condo to his wife.

"He wants you out of here," I said.

"Over my dead body," she said.

"It's not going to come to that, Nina. Unless he has actual evidence that you were having an affair, he can't prove anything. It changes nothing. We'll just stick to your original settlement terms: this house plus half his business and personal assets."

"Good."

"I'm sure that will enable you to get on with your life."

"In the manner to which I've become accustomed," she added with a sad weight that such a spent cliché could so profoundly apply to her.

"In the manner to which you deserve," I said with a smile.

We proceeded to run through the status of the case and I explained to her what our next move would be.

"I don't want you to worry about this, Nina. This is just the standard kind of brinkmanship you get in divorce cases. Next, we'll be hearing how poor your soon-to-be ex-husband is, and that his wealth is all on paper. But we know otherwise, don't we?"

"Thank you, Brad. I feel much better about things. I just want it to be over."

"I know but I'm afraid this is only early days. And I expect it will get much uglier before we're done."

The sadness in Nina's eyes returned. She sighed. "I suppose you're right. I'll just have to endure, won't I?"

"Indeed. Now, I need to get back to the office."

Nina saw me to the door. As I walked to my car, I noticed a red Lexus parked fifty yards down the street. It was in a line of cars but it caught my eye because I detected movement inside. The incident with the bikers had put me on edge, a feeling compounded by the fact that I'd done expressly what they'd told me not to do. Small wonder I was a little twitchy about being followed.

I watched the car for a moment. The man behind the wheel of the Lexus was checking his phone. He had short hair and looked like he was wearing a suit. He certainly didn't look like a biker, and I figured it would be a cold day in hell before an Iron Raider would allow themselves to be seen in a red Lexus.

On Santa Monica Boulevard heading west, the Lexus kept at least three cars behind me but changed lanes swiftly whenever I did. At one stage, I got a clearer look in my rearview mirror. The driver had company. Another guy in a suit.

If it wasn't the bikers, who was it? Had Quinn Rollins assigned a couple of staff members to keep an eye on me?

The identity of my pursuers wasn't the issue. I felt threatened again, and it warmed my blood to a simmering rage.

I was not going to lead them back to my office. And I wasn't going to initiate a high-speed chase, as much as I would have loved to pit my Mustang against that Lexus. I had to get to a place where I could get the upper hand.

I cruised for a few miles before pulling into Roxbury Drive. Just before I reached Wiltshire, I swung into a multilevel parking garage. In my peripheral vision, I saw the Lexus entering the street. I climbed up the ramps fast, my tires squealing all the way. I pulled into a space and jumped out of my car. I could hear the Lexus screeching a couple of levels down. Pressing the lock button, I ran for the stairwell door.

Once inside, I turned and put my weight into the self-closing door to hurry it up. The moment it clicked shut the squeal of the Lexus' tires were right outside. As I leapt up the stairs, I heard two doors shut and footsteps approach the door. I had no way of knowing if these guys were armed. But my plan was not to make myself a sitting duck in a dingy parking garage stairwell.

I saw the handle turn, then the door was shoved open hard. One of the men entered and I could see he wasn't armed. I turned and ran upstairs. They heard me and resumed the chase.

Two floors up, I opened the door to the garage, and ducked behind a van. The stairwell door had not yet closed before the first man appeared again. He made the mistake of coming out too far and I swung around and delivered a kick just above his right knee. The loud crack told me I had found my mark—either his knee was broken or ligaments snapped. He screamed and collapsed to the ground.

The next guy burst through the door and for a second I thought he was going to draw a weapon. I rushed him and tackled him high, slamming my shoulder into his chest. He was smaller than me and I quickly knew I could overpower him. I got my hands behind his neck and laced my fingers as I wrenched his head down and delivered my right knee hard into his face. I repeated the dose twice more and felt his body go limp. He fell to the ground.

I bent down and grabbed the first guy by the collar.

"Easy, man! Take it easy!" he said, holding up his hands.

"Who the fuck are you? Why are you following me?"

"We're PIs."

"PIs. Bullshit. Who are you working for?"

"Eric Lindstrom. We're tailing anyone who has contact with his wife."

"You're looking for dirt?"

He nodded, gritting his teeth at the pain in his knee.

"You're trying to make out I'm having an affair with Nina Lindstrom? Is that it?"

He nodded. "Doesn't have to be you. It could be anybody."

In one way I was relieved. These guys had nothing to do with Chip Bowman. In another way I was pissed. I knelt down beside him.

"Now, you listen to me. I've got a message for Mr. Lindstrom. You tell him he's going to agree to giving his wife the house and seventy percent of the rest of his assets. Got it?"

The guy nodded. "The house and seventy percent."

"And he's got to agree to it today. I want confirmation this afternoon. If he refuses then tell him that, so help me God, I'm going to do to him in court what I did to you two clowns. I don't tolerate this kind of shit. You understand me?"

Both of them nodded.

"Good. Now, if I don't hear from his lawyers with anything other than a total agreement before five o'clock today, that's it. I'll assume the answer is no and I'll come at him with every detail of every indiscretion that prick ever made. And I bet he's got plenty. Tell me you understand what I'm telling you."

"I understand."

"You want me to put it in a voicemail for that dipshit boss of yours?"

"No. We're clear."

"Good."

I stepped over them and went back down the stairs and got into my car.

"Family law," I said to myself. "It's the fucking pits."

10

Detective Ed Frierson's desk was located in the corner of an LAPD cube farm, his section marked by a "Homicide" sign hanging beneath off-white ceiling squares and fluorescent panels. I figured the open plan would suit Ed Frierson. From what I knew, he wasn't inclined to hide his feelings or thoughts from anyone—defense lawyers, especially. I'd crossed paths with Frierson a few times over the course of ten years, after he'd moved out of Vice. His attitude toward me had mellowed since our first meeting, but only slightly.

I first met Frierson through a client of mine who'd been charged with murder, Charles Elliott Davis. This was not the noblest of cases, mainly because Davis was a vile beast of a man, a lowlife pimp who'd cut one of his hookers to pieces. It was a judge-appointed case, and I just had to steer this animal through the channels so he got what he deserved but without prejudice. And that's where Frierson took exception to my role in the legal system. He had no question about Davis's right to a defense. What he did have a problem with was the kind of man who took up such a job.

Sitting in on the interrogation of Davis, I interjected. This prompted Frierson to ask me to step outside. He just wanted me to know that by offering even the slightest impediment between Davis and death row, I was no better than a hooker-slashing pimp myself. I thanked him for his insight, spared him a lecture on where a proper defense sits in the scheme of the justice system, and suggested we go back in and complete the interview. He seemed all the better for getting his opinion of me out in the open.

That was water under the bridge now. I wouldn't say Frierson and I had become friends, but we had developed a working relationship. I'd earned enough begrudging respect for him to address me by name—as opposed to "guys like you" or "you fucking lawyers"—and take my calls.

Frierson was actually on a call when I arrived. As he saw me approach, the look on his face told me I was just one more addition to his day's tedium. He got to his feet, held a palm up, and then turned his back on me. Frierson was a large, roundish man in his mid-fifties who wore braces, a crew cut, and a big Seiko dive watch on his left wrist.

"Are you done?" he said loudly into the mouthpiece, throwing his fleshy paw out at the glass window. "Are you done? Because all I'm hearing is the same bullshit you've given me before, Macdonald...

"Now shut up and listen...

"No. Next time I catch you taking a shortcut on crime-scene procedure I'll have your fucking badge...

"No...

"No... It's not...

"You're a lazy piece of shit, Macdonald. You know what? Fuck next time. This is going to be the last time you compromise one of my investigations. I'm done with warnings...

"No, I'm writing you up. Internal affairs can deal with your incompetence. Okay?

"Bye now, asshole...

"Bye bye."

The last two words were delivered in a light "ta-ta" manner but he slammed the phone into its cradle like it was Macdonald's face.

Frierson kept his head bowed as he sucked in a few deep breaths to collect himself. After a few moments, having succeeded in switching his mind into the here and now, he turned to face me.

I smiled. "Glad to know it's not just lawyers who fail to meet your professional standards, Ed."

Frierson's body relaxed as the tension was released. "Madison, you have no idea. Seriously, I don't need lawyers to undermine all my good work. Sometimes I get that kind of help in-house. What you after? Let me guess. The double homicide."

"That's right, Ed. Is Chad Bowman a suspect?"

The big detective breathed in and out swiftly and loudly. He grabbed a chair from the next cubicle and rolled it toward me.

"Take a seat."

I did as he asked. "Ed, I don't know exactly where you're at with the investigation but I wanted to get your take on it, if that's okay. I want to get a sense of what to be ready for."

"Well, that's easy. Get ready to defend Chip Bowman on a multitude of charges, including robbery and two first-degree homicides."

"How? He was a victim. Just like the other two."

"But unlike the other two, he survived."

"He was shot, Ed. And he was lucky to survive. Are you saying you've got evidence he killed his colleagues?"

"I'm not going to brief you on everything we have in terms of evidence. As far as I'm concerned, you will get that after we've filed with the DA. And I'm happy to leave that up to him as to how much he shares with you and when."

"No worries, Ed. But consider what would happen if Chip Bowman decides to run. That would make a fugitive case out of it, at which point the feds could say, 'Thank you, very much, Detective Frierson, we'll take it from here.' And consider that if my client—or would-be client—got some sound advice from his smart lawyer not to succumb to the temptation to flee then, you know, you and I could go about our work from both sides of the fence."

It was clear that Ed saw the logic in my argument.

"Okay, Madison," he said, leaning closer. "Let's just say it's highly likely that your boy is going to wear some serious charges."

"Are you saying you have no other suspects in this case?"

"I'm not saying that. Maybe we do, maybe we don't."

"Are you exploring links to other robberies that have targeted cannabis businesses over the past year?"

"Of course, we've considered that but that's not where this investigation is going. At this point, all roads lead to your boy."

"This was not a crime carried out by an individual. You know that."

"Yes, I do. But maybe things didn't go as planned for Chip Bowman. Maybe he had to take one for the team. And maybe you should encourage him to tell us who else was involved."

"He's a victim, not an accomplice."

"Well, I'm seeing what the evidence tells me. And the picture of what went down is getting clearer."

"What are you talking about?"

"Let's just say we have reason to believe your boy has come into a whole lot of money. Money that he didn't think anyone else would find."

"How much money?"

"I'm not going to specify. Could be that his rich old uncle died and answered all his prayers. Or could be he just got caught red-handed with the proceeds of a fatal robbery."

"Right," I said as I tried to process this information.

"He didn't tell you about the money, did he?"

"He's not actually my client yet, Ed. We're just getting to know each other."

"I can read you like a book, Madison. He hasn't told you. He's lied to you. And that's what he's gonna keep on doing."

"Thanks for your time, Ed," I said as I stood up. "I'll let you get back to work."

Frierson smiled.

"You just made my day, Madison. Thanks for stopping by. I guess you thought you had another innocent client to save from the blind gears of injustice. Sorry to disappoint you, my man. You might want to consider that Chip Bowman is just another deceitful piece of shit who's taking advantage of your bleeding heart. Almost makes me feel sorry for you."

"Good to know you care, Ed."

"Get a job with the DA, Madison. I won't hold any grudges. I'd be happy for us to work the same side of the street. And you'd get the chance to make up for the sins of the past."

"Thanks for your words of wisdom, Reverend Frierson. You going to hand around the collection plate now?"

"Keep your money, Madison. My job's got a peace of mind that no defense attorney's salary can buy."

"Nice seeing you, Ed."

"Thanks for dropping by, Madison. And you keep your word, you hear? Your boy better not run."

"He's not going anywhere."

As I left the office, I fumed as Ed's words rang true in my head. For all his harmless appearance, it just might be that Chip Bowman was a cold-blooded killer. There was every chance he wasn't that rare tonic that every half-jaded defense lawyer craves: an innocent client.

Outside the LAPD building, I called Bowman.

"Hello?"

"Chip. It's Brad. I've just been speaking to Detective Frierson."

"Yes?"

"And you know what he told me?"

"No. What?"

"He said he discovered that you have just come into a small fortune. He implied that this money had been found in an account that you thought no one else would see."

I heard Bowman's exhale sharply.

"Shit. They must have found it. Fucking Scooter."

"Found what? Who's Scooter? Actually, don't answer that." I needed to cut the call immediately. Most likely, the cops had already secured a warrant to bug his phone. "Where are you?"

"I'm at home."

I checked my watch. I had to go and pick Bella up from school.

"Stay there. I'll be around to see you in the morning."

I hung up, thinking that nothing about Chip Bowman or this case was as it seemed.

11

"Sweetheart, I've got a couple more things to do before I can wrap for the day," I said to Bella as we walked from the elevator to my office. "Then we'll go have a meal somewhere. Okay?"

Bella grinned. "In-N-Out?"

"Sure. If that's what you feel like." I opened the conference door for Bella. "Just settle in here. I'll be an hour or so. You good?"

"Yes," said Bella, pulling her iPad out of her bag. "I've got some reading to do."

I walked out the door and looked back through the glass as Bella buried her nose in her device. Having her near me just made everything right in the world, in spite of everything that was horrible and wrong with it.

"This just arrived for you," Megan said as I reached her desk. She was holding up a large envelope.

"Courier?"

"No. A guy in a suit dropped it off. A lawyer type."

"Thanks," I said as I took the package. I read the sender details as I entered my office. It was from Reinhart and Muntz: Eric Lindstrom's lawyers.

I sat at my desk, cut open the envelope and pulled out its contents.

I smiled as I read the front page of the document. I fished my phone out of my pocket and tapped on a contact.

"Nina," I said when she answered. "I've got some very good news. It's over. You won."

"What are you talking about?"

"I've just received some paperwork from Eric's lawyers."

"Not more of his counterclaim nonsense."

"No, actually. It's a surrender. A complete surrender. He's agreed to everything, and more."

"I'm not sure I follow. I thought he wanted to fight nasty."

"Well it seems he had a change of heart."

"My goodness," said Nina, her voice light with surprise and relief. "You said everything and more. What does that mean?"

"It means you get the house plus seventy percent of his assets and business, or the monetary equivalent."

Nina laughed. "I don't believe it."

"You'd better believe it. It's done. You can get on with the rest of your life."

"Thank you, Brad."

"No problem. You should celebrate."

"I think I'll open a bottle of champagne and drink a toast to my future."

"That sounds like a great idea."

"Why don't you come over and join me?"

We both knew where that might lead, and as much as I thought Nina Lindstrom was a beautiful woman, she was also emotionally vulnerable and I didn't want to start anything with her that I wasn't prepared to stick with for a while. In any case, I wasn't available.

"Sorry, Nina. I can't. I have plans."

"Of course you do. I bet she's a knockout."

I laughed.

"She is. I'm putty in her hands."

"Must be a hell of a girl. I always thought Claire was crazy to let you go."

"I don't know about that. She's pretty happy now, so it seems it's worked out for the best."

"I wouldn't be so sure about that."

"What's that supposed to mean?"

"Nothing. Nothing. Just saying relationships are rarely as rosy as they seem. That's all. You and I both know that, don't we?"

"Yes, I guess we do. Anyway, congratulations. I'll speak to you soon."

After I hung up, I felt a flush of pride in stopping Nina from being fleeced by her cheating husband. I guess family law didn't suck all of the time.

I walked out of my office and filled Megan in about the Lindstrom case.

"You off now?" she asked.

"Yes. You should call it a day too."

"Okay. I'll come out with you."

I moved over to the conference room, tapped on the glass to let Bella know it was time to leave. She shoved her iPad away and the three of us made for the elevator.

As Bella and I ate our burgers, I couldn't help thinking about what Nina had said. It left me with the impression all was not well between Marty and Claire. At some point in my life, I'd have taken this as a cue to raise my hopes of Claire and me getting back together again. But that was a long time ago. I cared about Claire in that I didn't wish her to be in an unhappy relationship. And that got me to my main concern: if the relationship wasn't good, how was that impacting Bella?

Before I could figure out how to approach this with some sort of tact, Bella spoke.

"Dad, can I come and live with you?"

Given the train of my own thoughts, the question floored me. Bella had stopped eating and was looking at me with a sad, beseeching expression.

I put my food down. "Honey, what's wrong?"

"I want to live with you. I don't want to live with Mom any more. That's all. I like being with you."

"And I love being with you too, but listen, this has taken me by surprise. It's serious stuff and we're going to have to unpack it, okay?"

Bella nodded. "I thought you'd say something like that."

"Well, let's start with why you're unhappy living with Mom. Did you two have some sort of fight?" I'd never known Claire and Bella to be anything other than tight. They never fought.

They had the odd disagreement but that was it. Bella loved her Mom to the moon and back, and Claire would be devastated to hear Bella saying she wanted to leave.

"No. But she's not around like she used to be. She's always working."

Bella's words made my blood run cold as my mind leapt to the possibility that her step-father might be the problem.

"Is Marty upsetting you in any way, sweetheart?"

Bella shook her head. "No, Dad. He's okay. He's away a lot."

"If you and Mom aren't fighting and you and Marty are getting along just fine, what's the problem?"

Bella was pouting now, deep in thought, and forming her next words carefully.

"I don't know, Dad. Mom's away a lot. Marty's away a lot. And he's not my dad. And sometimes I feel like we're just three people who happen to live in the same house. It's just that sometimes I just don't feel like I'm part of a family anymore. Does that make sense?"

"I think so."

"Are Claire and Marty getting along okay?"

Bella shook her head. "No, not all the time. Mom's on his case about all his golfing trips."

I put my hand over hers. "Listen here. You and I are a little family. That's never going to change. Ever."

Tears began to well in Bella's eyes. "Daddy, can I just come and stay with you?"

I felt my heart ache. "Honey, I'd love you to, but as you know there's your Mom's feelings to consider and then there's the legal custody agreement which, by and large, we have to stick to. What I can promise you is that I'll raise it with Claire. I think the three of us can sit down and talk about it. I hardly ever have PTSD episodes now, but I think you'll remember how scary they could be. And that's a key reason for you living mostly with your Mom. It's about your safety and your welfare. And I promise you, your Mom puts that above everything."

"Really?"

"Of course, she does. When she gets back we'll have that talk, okay?"

"Okay."

"Come on. Eat up and we'll head home and watch a movie on Prime. How does that sound?"

"Great, Dad."

12

After dropping Bella off at school the next morning, I drove into work, parked my car, and made my way to the café across the street from my office for breakfast. My plan was to head out to see Bowman and ascertain whether he was full of shit and should be dropped like a stone. But as I approached the café checking my phone, I saw Jack had emailed me his report on HardShell, and I wanted to digest it before I confronted Bowman.

I grabbed a table near the front window, ordered, and put my headphones on. They were not for music. I'm not the kind of person who can focus while listening to music, no matter if I love it or loathe it. I could no more do that than tap dance while trying to shoot leaves off a distant tree. To concentrate, I needed sounds that my mind won't wander into, sounds that channel my mind into focus mode. And for me, that's the sound of thunderstorms. So, while I sat in the shade of a sunny Southern California day, my mind was treated to distant thunder, wind, and the sizzling patter of falling rain.

Jack's report began with some background on Quinn Rollins. He'd gone to college, joined the 75th Ranger Regiment, and found himself taking part in Operation Desert Storm. He then went into the private security sector that was making billions from a State Department keen to outsource more and more of its overseas military projects. Rollins did stints at both Dyncorp and then Blackwater. In 2005, he set up a security guard franchise called Rampart with a Blackwater colleague named David McClean. This business ended bitterly with

Rollins accusing McClean of embezzlement. They fought in court for three years, an effort that almost bankrupted Rollins. Then five years ago, he founded HardShell to service the cannabis economy. McClean, having observed Rollins' success, set up a rival company named Bravo that had not come close to matching HardShell's success.

Rollins was now in his early fifties. In the recent photo Jack supplied, he looked fit and happy. His sandy hair was cropped short but most of his scalp was bald. His beard was neatly trimmed and graying at the chin. The image, lifted from the HardShell website, projected reassurance to potential clients—here was a man who could solve civilian problems with military-grade acumen.

I scrolled down to Jack's notes on the robbery victims, Bo Hendricks and Nathaniel Reed. As I began to read, a male voice broke through the sound of torrential rain. I ignored it and kept my eyes on my phone. Then a hand waved in front of my face. I looked up to see a man standing at my table.

It was Quinn Rollins.

"Mr. Madison? Brad Madison?"

"Yes," I said, pulling my earphones down to my collar.

"My name is Quinn Rollins."

I pretended that I'd never heard such a name in my life nor ever seen his likeness. But unlike the rather cheerful image I'd just seen, the man standing before me was the image of stress. No optimism shone from his eyes or glowed from his cheeks. His expression was stern and intense.

"Yes? What can I do for you?"

"I wonder if we could talk?"

"Do you know what I do for a living, Mr. Rollins?"

"You're a defense lawyer."

"That's right. How did you find me?"

"I looked you up."

"And you've been waiting outside my office since when?"

Rollins nodded. "Well, I—"

"So, you saw me come in here and you've been watching me for how long?"

Rollins shook his head in denial. "I haven't been spying on you, Mr. Madison. My company is going through a very difficult time, and I'm working round the clock to hold it together. I did see you come in here, but this introduction was delayed by an important call."

I didn't buy it. It was my bet that Rollins had been watching to see if someone joined me. Someone like Chip Bowman.

The waiter brought me my food—a jalapeno cream cheese bagel. I looked down at the plate but didn't touch it.

"What is it you want to speak to me about?"

"I think you know the answer to that question."

Unless Chip had disobeyed my clear instructions and told Rollins he'd visited me, there was only one way he could know: Frierson.

I picked up the bagel and fixed my eyes on Rollins. "How about you state your business now or leave me in peace? You're not the only one with a long to-do list. I came here for a quick breakfast, not to play guessing games with strangers."

With that, I took a bite, caught the eye of the waiter, and signaled for my check.

Rollins bent down to bring his face level with mine. His agitation was bordering on panic. "Look, I know Chip's been to see you," he said. "My company's going to hell because of what's happened, and every hour of every day is vital to me. The sooner this mess is cleared up, the better. I came to see if I could help. That's all. Can I sit?"

I nodded. As far as I was concerned, he could do the talking. I was going to tell him nothing.

Rollins sat himself down and stared at me. I dabbed a finger onto some poppy seeds on my plate and ate them. He kept his back straight and clasped his hands on the table. When a waiter came with my check he asked if Rollins wanted to place an order. Rollins released his right hand to perform a short cut through the air, dismissing the waiter without a word.

"I understand that you won't confirm or deny anything that you and Chip discussed, as your profession demands. But two of my staff members are dead. A small fortune has been stolen off me. My company has taken a massive blow. And the families of those two men deserve answers, and they deserve justice. The money that was stolen has not only hurt my business cash flow, it has damaged the trust I've established with my clients. The credibility of my company is in tatters."

"Have you got insurance?" I asked.

Rollins nodded his head. "I have good coverage, thankfully. The premiums are through the roof, and I'd hate to think how high they'll go if things like this keeps happening. Anyway, as you'd expect, no insurance company is going to just pay me out. They have to investigate."

"Of course. It must be difficult. And I can understand that you want to stay abreast of what's going on in terms of the investigation into this crime. But other than that, I don't know what I can offer you."

"I'm not here to ask anything from you, Mr. Madison. I just want to offer my help, like I said. I was very fond of Chip. Well, I am very fond of him. And I don't like thinking that he played any role in this crime but I'm also a realist. We deal in a lot of money—all of it cash—and it's enough to turn anyone's head."

"I take it you believe the robbery was an inside job."

"Of course, it was."

"And you think that Chip was behind it."

"What can I say? It's certainly not out of the question."

"If that's the case, who else would be involved?"

"What do you mean?"

"I mean, if you assume Chip was in on it then at least one of your other employees was too."

"Well, of course I'm looking at that."

The tone of Rollins' response did not suggest he was out to help me at all. He was most likely just fishing for information.

"Okay. Look, I need to get to the office."

Rollins leaned in closer. "Mr. Madison. This is a cut-throat industry I'm in. My competitors are circling like sharks, and I'm not prepared to just wait around to see what the cops come up with. I need to get to the bottom of what happened ASAP. And I'm offering to share whatever I learn with you. And, like I've told the cops, if there's anything you want to know about my company, I'm happy to tell you."

"Shouldn't you be offering your help to Chip directly?"

Rollins had to think for a few seconds.

"I last spoke to him a week ago."

"After the heist then?"

Rollins nodded. "You must understand. My reserves of trust are at an all-time low. If Chip is innocent, great. And I'd very much like to think that he is. But what's abundantly clear to me right now is that I've got at least two traitors working for me. Probably more."

"This last conversation you had with Chip, did you call him or did he call you?"

"I called him."

"And?"

"It was not the warmest of conversations. But I want answers. I can't wait around for any kind of trial. I need to rebuild the trust in my company pronto."

"Did you ask Chip if he did it?"

"Yes. I asked him straight out."

"And he denied it?"

"Yes. But—"

"You don't believe him."

"I didn't just ask him that. I wanted to know everything he knew. And he was so hazy on the details. If he had nothing to do with this crime, he'd want to shed light on anything that could expose the true perpetrator. But he gave me nothing. He remembered nothing."

"Do you think he's keeping something from you?"

"I'm not sure."

"And what if you were convinced that Chip was guilty?"

"Then between now and the time they lock him up for the rest of his life, he had better start praying that I don't get my hands on him. I think he knows that he's not going to last more than a few weeks inside. He's crossed some ruthless people. The kind of people who will not feel satisfied in him losing his freedom. They will want him to suffer worse than he could ever imagine."

I was right to tell Chip to get his family out. I made a mental note to insist when I go see him that he doesn't waste a moment longer.

"Mr. Rollins, if, in fact, Chip is charged and he calls upon me to defend him, then yes, I would seek your help."

Rollins was grinding his jaw.

"Name it."

"I'd want to speak to every staff member and examine how you go about your business."

Rollins appeared nonchalant. He nodded his head but it was clear that he did not like the idea of giving me so much access.

"Of course. I'd be glad to have you see how I run my business. I have nothing to hide. And in return, I'd ask that you keep me abreast of any developments you find that shed light on this crime."

I raised my eyebrows.

He raised both his palms.

"Anything outside attorney-client privilege."

"I'll keep that in mind, Mr. Rollins. Now, I must get to work."

With that, we both got to our feet and shook hands. As we did, Rollins held my eye with an intense look. It was not hard to tell he was struggling to keep his rage at bay, and something told me that, sooner or later, I was going to end up being the target of his fury. I could not help but wonder if that had already come to pass, that the bikers on my doorstep were sent by him.

But if that was the case, why didn't Rollins double down on the threat? Was he playing good cop to the bikers' bad cop? Did he hope to get something from me that he could confront Chip with?

Many other questions came to mind. And I was all the more eager to put a few straight to Chip Bowman.

13

The address Chip had given me was a modest one-story house on North Orchard Drive, Burbank. The exterior was painted light green and striped awnings hooded the street-facing windows. A driveway ran alongside a neat patch of lawn, through a carport where the entrance was, and into a double garage out back.

After I pressed the doorbell, I heard little feet approach quickly and two young faces appeared at the side glass. The sight of the children, however sweet, struck me with alarm about the danger Chip and his family were in. A man's voice spoke and the girls disappeared. I heard the deadbolt being unlocked before the door was opened and there stood Chip.

"Hi Brad," he said quietly, stretching his head to the left to survey what he could of the street.

"If you're worried about me being followed, I wasn't. Not that you're hard to find. And your kids should not be coming to the door like that."

Chip nodded. "Yes, I know. I've told them several times but I'm afraid it hasn't sunk in yet."

Once inside, I found myself standing in a hall. At the end, the two girls were staring back. A woman appeared from a room behind them and cradled them to her as she looked at me.

"Brad, this is my wife, Carrie," said Chip.

Carrie came up and gave me an uneasy smile. She was about five feet tall, with light brown hair pulled back into a ponytail. Her face was rounded, her features soft and her brown eyes looked slightly haunted. She was wearing a floral blouse over slim, white three-quarter pants, and I could only think how conventional her dreams of married life must have been until her husband got caught up in a double murder. A slight pleading in her eyes and manner suggested she hoped I might be able to return their lives to normal.

"Nice to meet you, Mr. Madison," she said. "Would you like some coffee?"

"No, thank you, Carrie. I've already had enough this morning."

She picked up the younger child and took the other by the hand. "This is Hannah," she said of the younger girl on her hip. "And this is her big sister, Tracy." Turning to Chip, she said, "I'll leave you two to talk. Just call if you need anything."

"Thanks, hon."

The interaction between them was somewhat weary, as though it took all their mental effort to focus on the here and now.

"Come on," Carrie said to the children. "I'll make us some hot chocolate and then we'll finish off that puzzle."

The girls' eyes lit up and they raced to the kitchen.

Chip waved for me to follow him into the living room.

"You've got a nice family," I said as we sat on opposite brown leather sofas that were deep and soft. Both of us sat perched on the edges.

"They're everything to me."

"I'm sure they are. It must not be easy walking out the door to go do a high-risk job."

"That's true. But unlike the Marines, I'm only gone for a day and I'm not fighting in a war." His own words tripped him up. "At least, it never seemed like I was in a war until this shit happened."

"But you faced very real dangers."

"Yes, and especially lately. With all the other hold-ups and robberies going on, it seemed almost like it'd only be a matter of time before it would happen to us, to me."

"Chip, like I told you, I went and spoke to Detective Frierson."

Chip let out a huff. It was only natural to have a dislike for the man who you suspected was hunting you down. "And what did he have to say? That he thinks I'm innocent, and that he's got the real culprits in his sights?"

"No. We both know he's zeroing in on you."

"How could I have done it, Brad? How?"

"Chip, don't kid yourself. They can convince themselves that you did it. You had help—another insider or two—and you made it look like you were the victim."

"Is that what you believe?"

"No, I don't. You've told me you're innocent, and I want you to keep convincing me."

"Then you don't actually believe me."

"Chip, as much as I ask my clients to be honest with me, I rarely get the whole truth. Most times, I have to work off half-truths and gut instinct."

"And what does your gut tell you?"

"That you're very eager to make money."

"Who isn't?"

"That you're willing to take a great deal of risk to make that money."

"The risk I've been taking is nothing compared to war. I thought you of all people would understand that."

"I do. But I also know how much we can miss war, Chip. All the modern comforts society offers can be almost suffocating to vets. The safety of civilian life can be confronting, oppressive even. I remember coming back from Afghanistan and lying in my bed feeling so snug and free from harm, it was like I was in the womb. And it was actually disturbing. Unless you've been to war, you can't fathom how unsettling, how nauseating it can be to feel safe. That's why a lot of vets act out. We lived hypervigilant lives to cope with violence and chaos. Then once the existential threat is gone, we create it for ourselves with substance abuse and violence."

This was partly an attempt to get Chip to level with me. He didn't know what Frierson had told me, but I could see he was reading between the lines of what I was saying to him.

"I know what you're saying, but that's not me. And that's not why I took the job at HardShell. I liked the job, I was suited to it, it paid well, and I wanted the best for my kids."

"You're working for their future?"

"Of course. I've got college funds set up. I want them to have that opportunity if they want it."

"What's this money that the cops have found?"

Chip flinched ever so slightly, like he was surprised by my question. Then he looked annoyed. "No one was supposed to know about that money."

"How much is in there?"

"Five hundred grand."

"What? Was it placed in that account after the robbery?"

Looking deflated, Chip collapsed back in the sofa. I was disappointed. My client was looking guiltier by the minute. He looked around the room as though he was deciding whether to come clean and by how much. It was a look I'd seen a hundred times before and I didn't like it. It was a look that told me I was about to hear some bullshit.

"Yes, but Brad, I can explain," he said with nerves tightening his voice. "That money was not from the heist. I swear. I just moved it around to make it easier to access."

"You mean easier to run."

"No, Brad. That's not what it's for."

"Well, that's what it looks like. And now the cops have a pretty clear read on what went down. You survive an attack, a million dollars in cash goes missing and then exactly half of that appears in the kind of account that crooks use to hide ill-gotten money."

"It wasn't—"

"We're not talking a checking account here, are we?"

"No, it's a crypto-account. You know, Bitcoin."

"But it's an account you clearly thought the authorities wouldn't find."

"How did they find it?"

"They're not stupid, Chip."

Chip looked away. "Scooter must have helped them," he said ruefully.

"Who's Scooter?"

"He's the chief financial officer at HardShell. Because of all the problems with banking the proceeds of legal cannabis, he built a system where that cash can be banked with credit unions and then shuffled into crypto accounts. That way it's safe."

"He does this for clients?"

"Yes. He customizes a money chain for each client, if they want. It's complicated but he makes it simple. He sets it all up, gives them a PIN and they can see where their money is and can access it whenever they want. And depending on the legitimacy of their funds, he provides various channels to back their money."

"And to hide it too, right?"

"I guess."

"Sounds like this is a way to launder money."

"Right."

"Where did that five-hundred grand come from, Chip?"

"Brad, I swear it wasn't from the robbery. I swear I had nothing to do with it."

"But you said yourself you're planning for your kids' future. And you like risk. You've taken a shot at a huge pay day and thought you could get away with it."

"No."

"That's what the cops are going to think. And you'd better start telling me a more convincing story."

"I've told you the truth, Brad. I didn't do it."

My phone started ringing. I dug it out of my pocket and checked the screen. The caller ID was blocked. It could be important. I raised a finger at Chip as my thumb pressed down on the answer button.

"Brad Madison," I said.

"Madison. Ed Frierson here. Where are you?"

"I'm with a client."

"Well, I hope that client is Chip Bowman because we've got a warrant for his arrest. We're on our way over."

"What about the media?" On the rare occasion I get a courtesy call from the cops about a client, it's usually accompanied by a press release.

"No one's been told. We're not looking to make a show. No press. We hit the road just as soon as the DA gave me the warrant. I just wanted to give you a heads up."

"Got it," I said casting a quick glance at Chip who was locked in on my conversation, looking panicked.

I stood up.

"He's where he should be, I take it?" asked Frierson.

"Yes."

"Good."

"Just make sure he doesn't run, okay?"

"We'll be here."

I hung up and gave Chip the news. His anxiety went up a notch. He began pacing down the hall and back. Suddenly, he stopped dead still and wrung his hands over his head.

"I can't," he said breathlessly. "I can't. I didn't do this. They're going to come and cuff me in front of my kids."

"Chip, there's not a lot of time. Go and speak with Carrie and tell her what's going on. She can keep the girls inside when the cops come."

"They're taking me to jail?"

I nodded.

"They'll hold you until you have a bail hearing in a couple of days, and that's when I'll be asking them to release you back home. There'll be some strict rules you'll need to adhere to, but you'll be back home in no time. Seventy-two hours tops."

I didn't quite believe my own words. Given the charges would be felony murder and robbery, and that the judge would be informed of Chip's hidden account, he was a strong flight risk. I was willing to bet I could get him bail, though, so long as he did what I said.

Chip was pacing in front of me, limping slightly on his wounded leg.

"Chip, go and speak to Carrie."

He went down the hall and I watched the two of them talk. Carrie burst into tears and hugged him. After a while she released him and walked up to me with a defiant look in her eye.

"Mr. Madison," she said. "You can't let them do this. They were his friends that were killed. He would never do that."

"Carrie, I'll do my best to get him back here soon. He'll have a bail hearing, and you'll be eating meals as a family right after. Okay?"

"That's bullshit, Madison," hissed Chip. He was looking at me with fire in his eyes. Suddenly, I was not on his side. I was in on the conspiracy to pin this crime on him. "They're not going to grant me bail, and you know it."

With that Chip grabbed Carrie, pulled her in tight, and pressed his lips against hers. "I love you," he said. "Make sure the girls always know that I love them."

Carrie's face contorted with confusion. She tried to hold her grip on Chip's arms but he pushed her away and jogged for the back door, his limp even more pronounced.

"Chip!" I yelled. "Don't be a fool! Come back here!"

At that moment, the doorbell rang.

I heard Chip burst out the back door. I quickly moved to the kitchen to see him hobbling as best he could across the back yard.

Frierson pounded on the door. I made no move to open it. The least I could do was buy Chip a little time, even though it was pointless.

The next knocking rattled the door in its frame.

"Chip Bowman. It's the police. Open up or we'll knock the door in!"

I moved to the door and worked the deadlock open. As soon as there was the slightest gap, Detective Frierson and three other cops charged in.

"Where is he?" Frierson demanded.

"He's on the john," I said. "Can't a guy take a dump in peace?"

As Frierson stared at me in furious disbelief, the sound of yelling erupted from the back of the house. Actually, it was two men yelling the same word. A word the whole neighborhood would just about have heard clear as a bell.

"Freeze!"

Detective Frierson looked at me with disgust. "So you decided to help your piece of shit client to run. You're just like the rest of them."

"I could say I tried to keep him here, but I doubt you'd believe me."

"No, I would not. You think we're so stupid we wouldn't have the back exit covered?"

I shrugged. "No one likes being arrested, Frierson."

"Well, they shouldn't go around killing people and stealing a million bucks."

Frierson marched toward the back door.

"And he's just blown any chance of getting bail," he called over his shoulder.

It sure looked that way. If the judge was in two minds about Chip Bowman posing a flight risk, he'd now have the arrest report to go by. Chip had zero chance of getting bail.

And if I couldn't help him beat whatever charges he got slapped with, he was never going to enjoy another meal with his wife and kids again.

14

Three days later, I was in a Men's Central Jail visitation room. Frierson was right about Chip getting bail. Judge Marcus Cordukes, who presided over the hearing, responded to my arguments with a kind of baffled wonder at how an accused could so effectively self-sabotage his shot at bail. He denied it like the snowflake's chance in hell that it was. And to top it off, I spoke with Deputy District Attorney Dale Winter right after the hearing. He told me that a plea deal would only be offered if Chip was willing to divulge the names of his accomplices. With Chip sticking to his innocence, there was no guilt to admit, no names to divulge, and little else to discuss. Winter couldn't hide his relish.

"The DA's got a jones for this case, Madison," Winter said. "He's fed up with these cannabis cowboys. Your boy thought he was too clever and got himself caught. Either that or he got double-crossed and is too scared to come clean to you and me both. But that's giving him the benefit of the doubt to a ludicrous degree, if you ask me."

"No one's asking you, Winter," I said. I had no particular feelings about Dale Winter. He was a good prosecutor who was all about hard work and dedication to the cause. His physical appearance was a mid-forties stereotype—medium height, soft-bellied, balding, and goateed. He had a broad, youngish, and fleshy face that a retreating hairline made look oversized. There was nothing flash about Winter, neither in dress nor manner. He was a no-nonsense doer, a function over form operator, but one that seemed to really love his job.

"We'll be having ourselves a trial then," he said with a quick grin. "Bring it on."

He then strode off, no doubt entertaining the brownie points he'd earn by convicting Chip. He may have been plainer than budget stationary, but that didn't mean he lacked ambition. And he had reason to feel upbeat. Both of us knew my case, as it stood, was as weak as water.

But every weakness contains within it an element of strength. And I was now on a mission to find it.

I'd been waiting five minutes before the door opened to the sound of shuffling feet. Chip, dressed in LA County blues, had his hands cuffed behind his back. The sheriff's deputy behind him was six-foot tall and athletically lean. He was only in his mid-twenties but he looked as grim as anyone ever did who'd punched the clock in a prison.

"You got an hour," the deputy barked, his voice bouncing off the cement floor and grey brick walls.

"The cuffs," I said as the deputy turned to go. He huffed, spun around and undid the lock of Chip's hand cuffs with speed. He then looked at his watch.

"Eleven thirty-six."

"Eleven thirty-six," I said, checking my watch.

I motioned for Chip to sit as the deputy left. He looked exhausted. No surprises there. Nothing can prepare you for being locked up in prison, and especially one as notoriously volatile as Men's Central Jail. Except, of course, prior experience. Only days ago, Bowman was at home with his family. Now he was occupying a cell with five other inmates and allowed out for just one hour a day.

"How are you doing, Chip?"

He let out a quick, rueful breath. "Just dandy, Brad. How are you?"

I didn't answer.

"I know. I know," he said. "I shouldn't have run. That was stupid of me. And now I'm stuck in this shithole. Did Carrie work out the payment?"

I nodded. "Yes, she did. Thank you."

I was not in a position to work for free, so Carrie had leaned on her parents for a four-grand upfront payment, which was half the flat fee I said I'd charge. Given the expenses of Megan, Jack, and whatever experts I needed, eight thousand was a fraction of what this case was likely to cost me. Megan chided me for letting my heart get the better of my head. As right as she was, she understood that when it came to helping a fellow Marine, profit was never going to be my motive.

"Are you having any issues with your cell mates?" I asked.

Chip shook his head. "Nope. If anything's going to kill me in here it will be the boredom."

I'd warned Chip about everything from K9s, or snitches, who might befriend him to bikers and their associates who might shank him. He was no safer in jail than on the outside, I warned him. And this was a county jail; his cellmates may only be there for a few days before being transferred to state prison. So he was going to have inmates coming and going and any one of them could be a threat. In Quinn Rollins, the Iron Raiders, the veterans who mourned Bo Hendricks and Nate Reed, and any other client who lost money in the robbery, the ordinary-looking man in front of me had managed to make a world of dangerous enemies.

Once I'd reiterated the need for him to keep his mouth shut, I moved on to his case.

"Chip, you need to help me understand a few things."

He nodded. "Like what?"

"What's the connection between Quinn Rollins and the Iron Raiders?"

In the material Jack had dug up was a case file on the notorious bikers. Its members were implicated in various criminal activities: murder, kidnapping, arson, prostitution, extortion, weapons trafficking, and motorcycle theft. Their chief source of income, it was claimed, was the manufacture and distribution of methamphetamine. They had chapters all across America but their biggest was in Ventura, the site of their founding clubhouse.

"I don't know for sure," said Chip, shrugging his shoulders. "I mean, they've got legal cannabis farms up in Humboldt but who knows what else they get up to on the sly."

I tapped one of the documents I'd laid out on the table. "This police report says the bikers that turned up to the crime scene were Iron Raiders. The same gang that threatened me. Why would they be there?"

"Some of the weed we were carrying was theirs."

"How much?"

"Not much. Ten pounds."

"The way they've been acting, I'd swear they've lost a lot more than ten pounds of weed. Did Henry think that Quinn was trafficking illegal drugs for the Raiders?"

"He didn't have a clue. All he knew was that Quinn was obsessive about expanding HardShell, to the point where Henry felt Quinn did not care which way he made a buck."

"Okay," I said. "Let's look at what we know. My investigator tells me that the Raiders are suspected of manufacturing the drug ice. He says they own property up in Humboldt County, which gives them a perfect secluded location in which to operate a clandestine lab. Quinn's company HardShell's stock business is running cash and weed for Humboldt County's legal cannabis producers, right?"

Chip nodded his head. "That's where most are. There are some in other areas now. But like I said, I saw no evidence of illegal activity at HardShell. I don't know how many runs we made up to Humboldt, but every leaf and every note was legal and accounted for."

I leaned in over the table.

"You know what else this forensics report says, Chip?"

Chip shook his head and looked like he didn't want to know the answer.

"It says they found traces of methamphetamine on your hands."

Chip looked mortified. "What? That must be a mistake. I swear, I've never touched meth in my life. I never saw any meth at HardShell. That's the God's honest truth."

"They swabbed you all over Chip, and they found ice on both your hands."

"Well, someone must have put it there!" Chip said, on the verge of tears. He pressed his lips together grimly. "I don't know who, Brad, but they're trying to frame me."

"Who would want to do that to you?"

Chip shook his head. "I've got no idea."

"How did you get on with Nate and Bo?"

"Those guys. Well, they were both loose cannons. They could get real wild, especially when they got on the booze, but as far as I knew everything they did at HardShell was above board."

I tapped another document. "My investigator tells me that these guys were anything but law-abiding citizens. They were in Iraq as private military contractors for the Fortis company. It seems Quinn was their boss there and both of them were sent home when accusations surfaced about unarmed civilians being killed by Fortis personnel."

"Yes, I heard about that. But only vague details."

"Okay. Let me ask you something else. Say I'm a grower up in Humboldt. I've got a million dollars' worth of cannabis that I need to get to retailers in Los Angles and I've got two-hundred grand in cash that I need to give the Finance Department in LA for tax. How does HardShell give me peace of mind that my assets will get to where they need to go?"

"Well, one thing is our team members. All have combat experience. All know what to do under fire. Then our vehicles. They are state of the art when it comes to armor protection. And then there's the tracking service we provide."

"What's that?"

"All the cash and cannabis are placed in sealed bags which are barcoded and microchipped. Using our app, a client can see where his money and weed is at any given time."

That struck me as odd. "Really? Isn't there a danger that the tracking information can get into the wrong hands?"

"There are checks and balances. The destination is not given, neither is the route taken, and the information the client has is not real time. There's a time delay of thirty minutes."

"So that's how the bikers knew where you were?"

"Yeah, they would have been monitoring the run. Maybe they noticed a delay and came to see what was going on."

I picked up the police report.

"The cops are building a strong case against you, and we've got jack shit. Let's go through what they have so far. You've got no alibi, for starters. They've got traces of meth on you, so they'll be convinced that HardShell was trafficking illegal drugs and that you were in on it. They've discovered that a lot of money suddenly appeared in a secret account of yours, and what's your explanation for that?"

Chip had already told me before the bail hearing, but I wanted to hear his stupid story again.

"I'd made some extra money helping out Scooter and, along with my bonuses, it was all adding up and I didn't want the IRS—"

"That's right. My client, who's charged with committing double murder in a robbery that saw a million dollars disappear, is a tax cheat."

I folded my arms and looked at Chip. "Let me ask you something. Given everything we now know, who would you say was behind this?"

"Brad, I just don't know."

"Well, if you didn't do it, it still looks like an inside job."

I was watching Chip as I said this. I saw his eyes light up.

"Maybe it's not quite an inside job." he said.

"What are you talking about?"

"Bravo."

"You mean Bravo Security? Owned and run by David McClean—Rollins' rival?"

"Yeah. But's it more than a rivalry. Those two are like mortal enemies."

15

You won't find HardShell Security's street address listed anywhere online. The only contact options offered by the company website is an email.

I'd called Rollins to tell him I wanted to speak with his money man, Scooter Slovak. Rollins said no problem and gave me the address. He wouldn't be on site when I visited because he had some work to do on a property up in Santa Barbara.

The HardShell compound, a single-level, cinder-block building painted olive green, was unmarked aside from its street number. I parked next to a large roller door. I walked round the corner to find a large window with thick glass and blinds that blocked the view inside. My bet was that if an RPG ever hit any part of this building, it would bounce off it like a stray bug.

I came to an unmarked door with an intercom. When I pressed the button, a voice came crackling through the speaker a split-second later.

"State your purpose, please."

"I'm Brad Madison. I've got a meeting with Scooter Slovak."

"Present your ID to the camera, please, sir."

I hadn't noticed at first but lodged in the corner of the alcove was a camera encased in a dome of glass.

"Driver's license?"

"Driver's license works just fine, sir,"

I pulled the card out of my wallet and held it up to the camera. The lens inside the glass dome shifted forward as the operator zoomed in on my ID.

"Come through, sir."

A loud click indicated the door was unlocked. I turned the metal handle downward and pushed. Instantly, I sensed the immense weight of the door and I had to put my shoulder against it to get through. As I passed, I saw the door was half a foot thick.

As the door retracted slowly behind me, a guard holding an M4 assault rifle greeted me in the entrance hall. He was mid-fifties, medium height, and thick set. His tactical vest was fully loaded with everything from ammo to a secondary weapon, a pistol.

"Step this way, please, sir," the guard said, motioning for me to pass through the metal detector beside him, all the while keeping his index finger laid across his trigger guard. Any threat from me and he could sweep his gun onto me and empty half his clip before I got a foot closer.

Once through the scanner, the guard asked me to follow. We turned a corner and continued down a hallway. At the second door on the right, he stopped and held it open for me.

"In here, sir."

I did as he asked and walked into a dimly lit office. A man in his early thirties sprang up from behind a bank of computer screens and came toward me. He was about six-feet tall, a few inches shorter than me, his face was freckled and tanned, and the blonde hair that sprang out from his weathered black cap looked bleached by the sun or surf. The guy had an outdoorsy vitality about him that belied the sedentary, dark confines of his office.

"Mr. Madison," he said, offering his hand. "Scott Slovak. But everyone calls me Scooter." He then looked at my escort. "Thanks Cliff. I'll take it from here."

With that, Cliff moved behind Slovak, placed his weapon in a gun rack, and sat himself down at a desk beneath a bank of security camera screens.

"Please, have a seat," said Slovak.

"Thank you for seeing me."

"No problem. Quinn said you were defending Chip and that I should tell you whatever you want to know."

"Chip tells me you got him a job here."

"That's right. I was here from the get-go, and when we needed more staff, I sounded him out. And he wasn't happy where he was so we wasted no time getting him on board."

"Where was he working?" Chip had not mentioned this to me.

"Security for a high-end jeweler. Standing around making sure some little old lady doesn't make off with a diamond-encrusted broach."

"I understand why he'd switch."

"Who can resist a job with a bit of kinetics? You know what I mean. Quinn told me you served."

"Seems like a long time ago now."

"Well, as I'm sure you can appreciate, vets like jobs that add a little risk to the daily grind. A little spice. We were expanding and needed to up capacity in both men and vehicles. Quinn's thing was that HardShell was always going to be staffed fully by seasoned vets. He didn't want anyone who hadn't been shot at and shot back. So, I recommended Chip."

"You served together?"

"Not quite. We both did a stint with Fortis in Afghanistan, doing poppy eradication."

"Right. And you recommended him because he was your friend?"

"Not just that. I owed him."

"How so?"

"Chip saved my life. We were overseeing an eradication effort in Nad-e Ali when we came under fire. We had to retreat and my ATV got stuck in a river. Chip ran back for me and maintained suppression fire while two Afghan police and I wrestled to free my vehicle. Chip's a crack shot and within half a minute their guns fell silent and we all got out alive. Thanks to him."

Slovak took a moment to dwell on the memory.

"Can I ask you something?" I asked.

"Quinn said to tell you whatever you need to know. Shoot."

"Do you think Chip killed your colleagues and stole that money?"

Slovak took a breath and adjusted the brim of his cap. "It's not what I want to believe."

"That's not what I asked."

"I know. Let me put it this way: I don't know. But what I do know is that a big pile of money is enough to turn anyone's head."

"Was he unhappy with what he was getting paid?"

"I couldn't say. But he was taking home twice as much than he was at that jewelry job. And with bonuses he was doing pretty well for himself. Still, he's got a family and always seemed to be saying you can never have enough money. He wanted to set his girls up for life. Nothing unusual about that."

There was something Slovak wasn't saying.

"But?"

"What can I say? Like I said, these guys are driving around with lottery money under their feet. Who knows what goes through their heads."

"Sounds like to me you think he did it."

Slovak shrugged. "All I'm saying is we're all human."

"If Chip did do it, he didn't do it alone."

"True."

"How do you and Rollins know each other?"

"Fortis, again. After that incident with Chip, I went to Iraq to join Quinn's team in training, arming, and housing the local police. That's where I met Nate and Bo too."

"I see. And now you're the finance brains of HardShell, I take it. Can you tell me about how the system works?"

Slovak gave me the rundown on what HardShell offered their clients. They had vaults on this premises as well as other compounds in LA. All their bases, Scooter said, were safer than banks. Slovak said he took an early interest in Bitcoin and had suggested to Rollins that they could sell finance systems to clients as an add-on to the couriering service. He made crypto accounts easy for HardShell clients. A safe, discreet way for them to store money. And the fact that Bitcoin and others had shot up in value brought a smile to all involved.

"So how's business?"

"Booming. It's going off the charts. At least it was until Chip screwed it up."

"So you do think he did it?"

As I said this, I noticed that, over Scooter's shoulder, Cliff was paying close attention to our conversation, his eyes fixed on the back of Scooter's head.

Scooter, realizing he'd spoken too readily, sought to modify his position. "All I know is that we're struggling to keep our clients now. They're a nervous bunch of people anyway, and this bullshit has scared the shit out of them. We handle millions of dollars. That's our stock trade. If we can't be trusted to handle millions of dollars safely, then we have no business. It's not rocket science. Our reputation has taken a blow, and Rollins is out there trying to stop clients from pulling out."

"For argument's sake, let's say Chip was in on it. He had to have inside help, right?"

"Not necessarily. He could have gotten anyone to help him if he planned it. And I don't know anyone at HardShell who'd be willing to kill Nate and Bo in cold blood."

Slovak's face had hardened with anger.

"Is that why you put the cops onto Chip's money?"

"What do you mean?"

"I mean you look pissed. Did you know half a mill had just dropped into Chip's account after the robbery?"

"No, I didn't. How could I? I can't access Chip's account. I just gave the cops the block chain, or account data. They did the rest."

"You had no problem helping the cops investigate Chip, the guy you say saved your life?"

"Look, of course I was torn. But they'd subpoenaed our own financial statements. They were going to find it one way or another."

"I see."

I switched my eyeline to Cliff, who was not looking happy and shaking his head. Then, as soon as he realized I was watching, his head went still immediately.

Slovak surmised that I was skeptical. "Mr. Madison," he said, leaning forward in his chair. "Just come out and say it. You think that because I'm the money guy here I helped Chip steal from my own company? You think I'd do that? For a million dollars?"

He shook his head and scoffed. "Look, I'm not on the Forbes rich list or anything but I'm doing okay. And the idea that I'd risk not only destroying this business but pissing off people who'd skin me alive if they ever suspected I was involved... I'm not that stupid."

"But you think Chip is?"

"He's not stupid, but he's no saint either. Like I said, risk brings its own rewards."

There was a pause. Slovak sat back and folded his arms.

"Is there anything else I can help you with?" he asked.

"No, Scooter. That's enough for now. Thanks."

"Well, thanks for dropping by," he said, getting to his feet and putting out his hand. "If I can help anytime feel free to give me a call."

"Will do."

"Cliff will see you out," he said without looking back. Cliff was already at the gun rack.

At the scanner, I lowered by head.

"Seems to me you didn't like what Scooter was saying back there," I said to Cliff quietly.

Cliff said nothing.

I moved through the scanner and turned back to see that his face was as impassive as it was when I first entered the building.

I heard a click behind me as Cliff released the lock from where he stood.

"Good day, Mr. Madison," he said, his voice cold as stone.

16

I got back to the office around three. I was two steps into the foyer of my building when I heard my phone ping with a text message. I fished it out of my pocket to see a message from Bella.

"Hi Dad. Back at Mom's now. Miss you xx"

My heart melted. I had my thumb poised to reply when a booming voice filled the room.

"Madison!"

I didn't need eyes to tell who was addressing me. I instantly recognized the voice and its owner's fondness for deploying it at full volume.

The one and only Wes Brenner was striding towards me. "Striding" was putting it favorably. A man Brenner's size doesn't stride so much as stomp. There are fatter men than Brenner, but he was snout-in-the-trough politician fat. Fat cat fat. He looked like there was never a free meal he'd turn down, never a hot dog he'd refuse on the campaign trail, never a burger he was too full to demolish. And the thing was, he seemed pleased with his bulk. To him, it was part of his power. Occupying more space in the world than most people was something he felt entitled to.

Another thing he felt entitled to was to reclaim his seat in the State Senate.

As he stepped toward me on the carpeted cement floor, I could swear I felt the ground shudder. That was the thing with Brenner: he disrupted the very earth around him.

"What do you want, Brenner?"

He stopped a yard in front of me, panting. "I should have known you'd take the case."

"Is there something you want to talk about?"

He nodded. But of course, there was no way he just wanted to talk. He wanted to give me a piece of his mind.

"You're defending a man who murdered his friends and stole a million dollars. What a life you lead."

"I know it means nothing to you, Brenner, but what you are referring to are allegations. My client is entitled to his day in court, and I mean to see that he gets it, and that he is treated fairly. It's a fundamental citizen's right. But that's not something you're too concerned with, is it?"

"This state's cannabis laws are a travesty," he yelled, as though he was addressing people in the mall outside as opposed to me three feet in front of him. "I warned everyone against Proposition 64. I said it would foster a nefarious industry ruled by lowlifes. And that's exactly what's happened. And we have you liberal bedwetters to thank for it."

Brenner had always been a staunch anti-drugs campaigner and the spate of cannabis-related crime had put extra wind in his sails. He took one step closer and shoved a finger into my face.

"Let me tell you, Madison. When I get back in the Senate, things are going to change. I'll be shutting down the scum like your client. Kicking them out of business."

"Is that so?"

"You mark my words. I'm going to clean house. If I can't get a repeal of the cannabis laws altogether, then I'm going make sure the only companies that can operate in it are those of tried and tested standing."

"Brilliant. A policy of idiocy and misunderstanding glued together with misinformation. Let me guess, those companies you speak of. Big pharma, am I right?"

"It's the only way to clean up this mess."

I tapped Brenner on his fleshy upper arm. "Good for you, Brenner. How much are they paying you to champion their cause?"

"They're not—"

"It'll be interesting to get a close look at who's funding your campaign," I said as I made for the stairs.

"Just good-hearted people who are sick of woke liberals turning this country to the dogs," he called out at me.

"Okay, Brenner. Lovely chatting with you."

As I passed the elevator, I stopped and pressed the up button.

"That's for you," I said. "I'm guessing you're not taking the stairs."

17

The banter flew thick and fast as the players bustled around the court. It may have been just another meaningless game of streetball, but to these guys it was all that mattered right now.

A shirtless black player took possession and paused outside the three-point line, dribbling the ball with smooth, casual confidence as he weighed up his options. He then dummied a snap pass to a team-mate before driving hunched over for the hoop. His first opponent was left clutching air. The second, though, checked him hard inside the paint. The dropped ball was snapped up by another opponent who raced to the other end, leapt high and slammed the ball through the netless hoop.

As he trotted back down court, high-fiving his team-mates, that's when Cliff, the guard who'd greeted me at HardShell, saw me. Immediately, his happy grin evaporated. His brow furrowed in annoyance.

He called for a player to sub for him and marched straight for me. I stayed where I was, leaning against the black chain-link fence.

"What the hell are you doing here?" Cliff demanded.

"Really, Cliff? As good as you guys are, I didn't come here to watch a pickup game."

"How did you find me?"

"What can I say? I'm resourceful."

"Did you follow me here?"

Cliff stepped even closer, looking like he wanted to punch me. I ignored his question. But for the record, yes, I did follow him.

"We need to talk."

"Like hell we do," said Cliff. He spun his back around to see who was watching us. All his friends were paying no mind to us at all. They were absorbed in the game. "I got nothing to say to you."

"What's with the hostility? Don't you want to help your friend Chip?"

"I can't do anything for Chip."

"Is that so. You can't or you won't?"

Cliff didn't answer. One of the other guys called him back to the court. Cliff waved him off.

"I just need a few minutes," I said.

"You can wait all day. I ain't staying, and we ain't talking."

I pulled out my phone. "You got the job at HardShell through Nate Reed, right?"

Cliff made a point of keeping his mouth firmly shut.

"That was a rhetorical question. I know you did."

Cliff just stared, jutting his chin out at me.

"You, Cliff Loda, and Nate did basic training together. Nate went on to join the 5th Infantry Regiment and got posted to

Iraq. And you were there alongside him. All the way. Or so the story goes, right?"

Cliff began grinding his jaw.

"But you and I both know that that's bullshit, don't we?"

Nothing. Standing dead still. Nostrils flaring.

"You never deployed with Nate."

I could almost see the panic erupt within.

"You never went to Iraq, Cliff Loda. You never got posted anywhere. Because you never finished basic training. For the ten years prior to joining HardShell, you were posted to stand guard over nothing more hostile than a parking lot. Isn't that right?"

Fear had now seeped into Cliff's eyes.

"Now, I understand if you don't feel up to talking with me. I'll just take that to mean you're okay with me setting Quinn straight about the bullshit artist he's got working for him. If I'm any judge of character, he's not going to be happy about being lied to. Especially not now, when he's in the thick of a crisis, and he doesn't know who to trust."

Cliff turned his head around, looking over his shoulder as if checking whether Quinn was in the vicinity.

"You're scared of him. No shame in admitting that. If he's anything like me, he hates guys who go around impersonating a soldier. Someone who completely fabricates their military record. Someone who's never fired a single shot in defense of his men, his unit, his country."

Cliff bowed his head and his body sagged.

"I needed a job. You pretty much have to be a vet to get the gig, so I stretched the truth, with Nate's help. Quinn didn't even interview me. And Scooter was so busy he just took Nate on his word."

"I'm sure you don't need to be a war hero to do your job, Cliff. But is that the extent of it?"

"What do you mean?"

"I mean, are you one of those weasels who goes out on Memorial Day wearing a uniform they bought from a surplus store and fake medals they got off eBay? If I find out you are then, I promise you, I will bring the four walls of Hell down upon you."

"Shit, Mr. Madison. I don't do stuff like that. I don't go around telling people I served. It was just to get the job. And even at work I keep my mouth shut. I never talk about anything to do with the military. I can do the job. It's not that hard."

"But it entails a significant degree of risk, and your co-workers are counting on you to know what to do if and when bullets start flying."

"Yes. That's true. But it hasn't come to that. And I'm no coward."

"Just a liar."

Cliff's head dropped.

"That's right. And I'm in good company there at HardShell."

"What's that supposed to mean?"

Cliff exhaled, kicking himself for speaking without thinking. "It's a good company in that it pays well..."

"But?"

"But it's not good in other ways."

"Like what?"

Cliff paused, trying intently to read me. "Why should I tell you anything? Why should I trust you?"

"Listen. You don't have to. But what you do need to understand is that I don't give a damn about what you do, so long as your military role-playing bullshit is limited to HardShell. My one aim is to defend my client. I'm out to clear Chip's name. I don't think he committed this crime and something tells me you don't either. Am I right?"

Cliff nodded. "Yes."

"Okay. You said the company wasn't any good in some ways. I'd like some specifics."

Someone from the court called out Cliff's name. The game had finished and they were getting ready to leave. One guy came up and asked Cliff if he was coming for a beer. He declined. Cliff's friend got the feeling I wasn't someone Cliff wanted to introduce him to, so he went on his way. When the guy had gone, Cliff turned around and gazed over the court.

"Nate and me were buddies long ago but he changed a lot, man."

"How so?"

"He was wild. Out of control, sometimes. I mean, there were a lot of stories flying around, some were hard to believe but other shit rang true."

"What the hell are you talking about?"

"I heard he'd killed some dude. Him and Bo."

"Who?"

"Don't know. It was over money. A shit load of money."

125

"When was this?"

"Not too long ago. A few weeks. But it was grapevine chatter that I didn't take much stock in. But those two guys, they were always up for some mad shit."

"What can you tell me that they actually did?"

"They hit a couple of dispensaries."

"They what?"

"They robbed them. The cops never found out it was them, of course. They hit these places at night and left no trace. I saw in the news the cops described one as a military type hit. They said they thought professionals were responsible."

"Did they admit this to you?"

Cliff nodded.

"How do you know they weren't lying?"

"They took photos. That's how cocky they were."

"And they showed them to you?"

"Nate did. We were both drunk and I guess he wanted to tell someone."

I took a moment to consider this news.

"Do you think they were part of the HardShell heist but were double crossed?"

"Yeah."

"Why?"

Cliff shifted around on the spot. He looked down at his feet.

"Nate told me to change shifts."

"What?"

"I was supposed to be driving on that run, not Chip. But Nate told me to swap with Chip, and he was always eager to pick up some extra cash."

"I see. Did Chip take part in these robberies with Nate and Bo?"

"I don't think so. My understanding was that it was just Nate and Bo, but hell, you never know. It would have been a nice side hustle for Chip, working as their driver."

"Okay, let's just say Nate and Bo were part of the heist but someone double crossed them. Who would that be? Who would be in on it with them?"

Cliff paused.

"I don't want to say what I think."

"Why not?"

"Because if I do, I'm a dead man. I won't just lose my job. I'll lose my life."

I grabbed Cliff's shoulder and turned him to face me. "Cliff, do you consider Chip to be your friend?"

"Yes," he nodded solemnly.

"Well, he could go to prison for the rest of his life for something he didn't do. Don't you want to help him?"

"Of course I do, man."

"Okay. Then who do you think Nate and Bo might have been working with?"

Cliff looked over my shoulder and let out a heavy breath.

"Look, all I know is that they were pretty tight with a couple of guys from Bravo Security."

"Really?"

"Yeah."

"And?"

"And well if you think things are wild at HardShell, well, those Bravo dudes fly way faster and way looser."

"How so?"

"They've got all sorts of shit going on, from what I hear. They even got cops in on it, using fake search warrants to seize drugs and cash."

"You're shitting me?"

"Nope. It's out of control."

I was starting to think Wes Brenner had a point. Legal cannabis was giving some very dangerous men the license to run amok.

"What about Quinn? Do you think he'd be involved?"

"No, he hates those Bravo guys."

"Yeah, I know that. But take Bravo out of the picture for a minute. Could you imagine Quinn pulling off something like this?"

Cliff shrugged his shoulders.

"The only reason I could see him doing it would be to get the insurance. You know, double his money."

"Not just his money. It would double his clients' money too."

I thought about it for a moment and shook my head.

"No, the way Quinn's been acting, he's not at all comforted by the fact that he's paid his premiums."

"Really? That's interesting," said Cliff.

"Can you think of why that would be?" I asked.

"Hell yeah. Maybe some of the stuff that was stolen, he can't tell the cops about."

"Such as?"

"Could be anything. Black market weed or cash from the black market. Or even..."

"What?"

"Look, this is what I heard but I've never seen it. Nate and Bo once said that Quinn would do anything to build his empire and crush Bravo. They believed he was considering getting into meth."

"What?"

"Plenty of it's being made up in Humboldt. Maybe that van had a secret stash of meth that's been stolen. That would mean Quinn is not just out of pocket, he's got a very unhappy client."

I didn't have to think too hard to guess who that might be.

18

Jack texted me that he'd found some juice on Rollins, and that he'd have a report written up for the morning. It was just after seven and I was about to leave the office for home. I wanted to hear what he had right away.

"Obviously, it can't wait till the morning," he said by way of a greeting. "Or else, you're sitting in your lonely little office with no one to talk to so you thought you'd pick on me."

"That smug thing you've got going on with your voice? It makes me want to puke, but I'm prepared to put up with it to hear what you've got on Rollins.

Jack laughed. "Don't give me that. You've just nothing better to do."

I could hear voices and music in the background. "Where are you?" I asked.

"Vinnie's. It's a bar on Sunset. You know? Live music? Drinks? Good times? Remember when you used to partake in a little fun, Brad? That kind of bar. Which means, not your kind of bar."

"Oh, and you're the party animal now? Having spent the past six months establishing yourself as the world's most devoted and sexiest dad."

A few weeks back, Megan had shown me a story that a prominent lifestyle blogger had written about Jack, his wife Chanel, their babies, and their idyllic Calabasas home. Most of it was Chanel singing the praises of dreamboat Jack. How hands-on he was, how devoted he was, how lack of sleep never dented his humor, what a great cook he was, how he'd given up drinking during her pregnancy, how he'd... No, I can't go on. Anyway, the story became something of a viral hit with women all over the world who swooned over this divine specimen of modern-day manhood. They were particularly taken by the photo of the family by the pool, with Jack's chiseled six-pack snaring the limelight.

"You saw the blog," Jack said, his voice tinged with unease.

"Unfortunately, yes. I did see it, and now I can never unsee it. So, world's best dad, I guess you've earned enough brownie points to have a night out."

"Yeah, there's this kid, Marcus King. Sings like Janis Joplin and plays guitar like Albert King. I'd ask you to come down but I know you hate the blues. You're more a Carpenters guy."

"Asshole." Jack knew full well I was a massive Stevie Ray Vaughan fan. "I'm coming over now."

"Really? You don't want to go home first, do your hair and put on a frock?"

"No, I'm good. And keep your fantasies to yourself."

"I guess chicks do love a suit. But it's not very rock and roll. I guess you could pass as some kind of A and R guy."

"Suits make the world go round, my friend."

"Well, get over here and prove it. I'll be your wingman."

Women were the furthest thing from my mind when I called. Now they were not so much.

Half an hour later, I was walking into Vinnie's, one of LA's best live music venues. I weaved through the crowd and found Jack at the bar with a stool waiting for me.

I ordered a beer and we clinked glasses.

"You came by yourself, I see," I said. "Guess that shouldn't come as a surprise."

"There's nothing wrong with that. I don't need company to enjoy myself."

"That's news to no one," I said deadpan before laughing. "So I'm curious. What have you got on Rollins?"

"I'll get to that. Have you eaten? I've just ordered the house burger."

"Sounds good to me."

Jack caught the bartender and placed the order. That done, he turned to me. "This Quinn Rollins dude, his story gets more interesting the deeper I go."

"That doesn't surprise me at all." I gave Jack a quick rundown of what Chip and Cliff had told me. From both accounts it was clear that no matter how much money Rollins was making it was never enough. What was not yet certain was exactly how far he was prepared to go to build his empire.

"The thing is," said Jack, "everyone thought HardShell was on this unstoppable roll when it wasn't."

"What do you mean?"

"Look, when Proposition 64 happened, it triggered a green rush. It was like what happened in '96, when California made medical cannabis legal, but on a much bigger scale. All of a sudden, everyone wanted in, from Mexican mafia to big pharma to college kids with start-up stars in their eyes."

"And Rollins' timing was perfect."

"True. And instead of production or retail, he went for the service sector. They say the best business to be in during a gold rush is pans and spades. All the wishful thinkers out digging are just buying into a lottery, you're supplying them with the tools they have to have. So yeah, he got the timing right and the position right."

"And HardShell went gangbusters."

"That's right. But then it started to come off in a big way."

"What do you mean?"

"It was thought that illegal growers would go legal under the new law. But it costs a lot of money to go legit. You've got high taxes, compliance costs. You've got to have seed money and business plans. The expense is prohibitive for most growers. So guess how much of the cannabis market is still illegal?"

I shrugged my shoulders.

"Eighty percent. Instead of stamping out the black market, the laws have kept it flourishing. It's cheaper to buy on the street than to buy in a shop, so these fancy new dispensaries are struggling to survive."

"So where does that put Rollins?"

"Even before he got rolled, his business was hurting. And from what I hear, he wasted no time hedging his bets. He's been setting himself up to play both sides of the law. On the books, he's the world's biggest legal cannabis courier. Off the books, he's servicing the black market. And for both, he turns profits into digital assets that are as easy to access as an ATM."

"So, he's laundering the proceeds of illegal cannabis while he's handling the legal cash."

"Yes. But that's not all. I heard he's handling meth too."

"I was told the same. Why take such massive risks?"

"Because the rewards are so massive."

"Ambition's one thing. This to me sounds like pure, rampant greed."

"Greed's only one of his prime motivators. There's also revenge and hate. You ever heard of Bravo Security?"

"As a matter of fact, I have. It's run by a guy named David McClean. He's a fierce rival of Rollins."

"That's right. They used to run a business together—a security consultancy serving mining and construction companies in Iraq. They fell out badly, each accusing the other of syphoning off funds. They actually came to blows inside the US base at Abu Ghraib. Had to be pulled apart. They were fit to destroy each other. And that's been their mission ever since."

I told Jack I'd heard Nate and Bo might be up to no good with a couple of Bravo guys.

"Well, it works any way you want to twist it. One way is that McClean planned the heist to deal Rollins a critical blow. And if Rollins caught wind of it, who's to say he didn't drop the two employees he thought were traitors and frame Chip to cover his tracks."

"So, Chip was his sacrificial lamb?"

"Could be. But that's just one way to look at it. The whole thing's as murky as a Louisiana swamp."

"How do you know Rollins is into meth?"

"Let's just say a not-so-little birdy told me."

"Jack, it's me asking. I want to know where you got this info."

"Why?"

"For all I know, it could just be lies spread by McClean."

"Could be. But I don't think so."

"Who are you getting this stuff from? A reporter?"

"If I tell you, you have to promise me you won't..."

"Brad?"

A woman's voice came from my right shoulder. It was a voice I recognized instantly. A warm voice, slightly husky. A voice I wasn't ready for.

19

"Abby," I said as easily as I could summon, as though the sudden pulses of disquiet and delight running through my body at the sight of her didn't throw me in the slightest.

How long had it been since I'd laid eyes on that stunning face, those alluring eyes? How long since I'd inhaled her scent?

Oh yeah, that's right. It was seven years ago. When Hollywood darling Abby Hatfield told me she'd decided to call time on us because she'd met someone else. She added that she felt I wasn't ready for a serious relationship so soon after splitting up with Claire. That was news to me. Anyway, the someone else she dumped me for turned out to be Tommy de Franco, one of her co-stars in the monumentally huge blockbuster *Sister Planet* franchise. So ended my foray into the fold of Hollywood celebrity. I was pretty bent out of shape by it all, as I was under the impression that we were very much into each other. Turns out· I was wrong. Later, I saw somewhere that they got married.

"Nice to see you," was the next thing that came out of my mouth, and it lacked conviction. It was both a truth and a lie.

Suddenly, in the middle of having a rational work chat with my buddy, I was compelled to deal with the kind of emotions that refused to yield to logic, the kind that bore a will of their own, no matter how many times over the years I thought I'd bashed them into submission.

Before I could come up with another brilliantly smooth line, Abby jumped in. She didn't look awkward in the slightest. She just looked perfectly pleased to see me in a platonic way, as though that was the natural state of the world.

"Are you here to see Marcus King? Oh my God, isn't he amazing? Are you a fan."

Abby and I had never reached the stage of exchanging mixed tapes, or Spotify playlists, or whatever the done thing is these days.

"I don't know yet, to be honest," I said. "I'm just tagging along with Jack. He's the fan. You remember Jack?"

"Of course," she said. "So the dynamic duo is out on the town?"

"Well, I was until he decided to gatecrash," said Jack. "He didn't come here for the music. He came to talk shop."

Abby looked at me fondly and put her hand on my shoulder. "Of course he did. Lawyer man's never off the clock."

I felt her hand linger. And the way she looked at me laughing, there was no pretending from her end that we were not once close, that there was a time when we could not keep our hands off one another. Her expression was so warm and candid, I had to almost scream at myself that there was no way she was flirting with me. She was just being nice. She was being a grown-up.

Since I was too stupid to do so, Jack offered Abby a drink.

"I can't stay," she said. "I'm with a friend. But what about later?" she said looking at me. "I know it's a school night, but do you want to meet up after the show? I can get us backstage."

"Are you in tight with the band?" asked Jack.

"My friend is. He and Marcus went to school together." I looked to where Abby's head had turned. There was a good-looking guy in his mid-twenties at a table. That didn't look like the co-star Abby had married.

"Thanks but I've got a big day tomorrow," I lied. It was just a normal day. A normal twelve-hour day that I was only happy to put in to keep myself occupied. I might as well have said, no thanks, I need my beauty sleep.

The brightness of her smile dimmed a little. It wasn't that I felt I couldn't be platonic with Abby. The stronger feeling was that I just didn't trust myself to be around her, to enjoy her company and make the mistake of thinking that it might be something more. At once I wanted to pull her close and walk away. And the smartest option in my mind was to do the latter. Say goodbye, leave, and hopefully never see her again for another few years.

"Well, maybe we could grab a drink on a non-school night?"

There was a moment's pause as I stopped myself from agreeing instantly. The question, "Aren't you married?" came to mind but to ask it would have been presumptuous, not to mention prudish.

"Sure. Why not?" I said with a distinct lack of commitment.

"Uh, okay then," Abby said, almost officiously. "Good seeing you, Brad. You too, Jack. Enjoy the show."

With that Abby left and walked back over to her friend. I watched as she got there. It looked like he asked something along the lines of, "Who were those guys?" I saw her shake her head and pick up her drink.

A surge of anger welled up inside me, directed at no one but myself. With some effort, I pushed all thoughts of Abby out of my mind and turned to Jack. He gave me a quizzical look and shook his head.

"What were you thinking, dude? She's still into you," he said.

His words were nice to hear but unwelcome as well.

"No she's not. She's married. We were done a long time ago."

"I didn't see a ring," Jack said.

"I didn't even look. And that doesn't mean shit."

"You're an idiot."

This was a well-meaning jibe but it gave me the opening to direct my anger elsewhere. I took a big swig of beer.

"Listen, these biker friends of yours," I said sternly. "The ones who told you all about Rollins."

"I never said they were bikers."

"You didn't have to." I was bluffing, running off what could best be described as a calculated guess. "Which gang, Jack?"

Jack stood straighter. He shook his head soberly. "You know I can't tell you that."

"Yes, you can. You just don't want to."

"You're half right. I don't want to because you'll go and do something stupid."

"It's the Iron Raiders, isn't it?"

Jack's face went blank. He picked up his beer. I was right.

"And you know, don't you?"

"Know what?"

"That they paid me a visit."

Now Jack looked genuinely confused. "They said nothing about you."

"They warned me off Chip's case. Basically said they'd kill me if I took it on."

"Why would they do that?"

"I have no idea. I can only think they don't want Chip to get off. They want him left hung out to dry with some useless judge-appointed lawyer."

"Like I said. They said nothing specific about you."

Thinking about the bikers, an idea came to me. Call it an idea. Call it inspiration. Call it leverage.

Or it might just be a dumb impulse that could get me killed. I drained my beer.

"Come on, let's go," I said.

"Go where, exactly?"

"We're going to go see them."

"No way. I'm not taking you there. They'll beat the shit out of both of us."

"No they won't," I said as I got to my feet. I stood there waiting to see if Jack was going to follow suit.

"What about the band?"

"Fuck the band. We've got work to do. A guy's life is riding on me, on us, doing our jobs."

Jack threw the remainder of his beer down and got to his feet.

"Shouldn't you be wearing a cape or some shit? Let's go, Batman."

As we made for the exit, I saw Abby's head turn in my peripheral vision.

To hell with her.

20

I guided my Mustang GT eastward along the Ventura Freeway. It not only felt good to open up the throttle of my pride and joy, it felt good putting distance between me and Abby. It was like I'd left my confusion back there in that bar with her, while I proceeded elsewhere charged with renewed focus. Jack and I didn't speak for the first ten minutes of the trip, save for him confirming the Raiders' clubhouse was in Ventura. I did wonder if the biker who crushed my neck would be there, and what he'd do if he laid eyes on me.

"Jack."

"Yup."

"How many Raiders did you get that info from?"

"Just one."

"What's his name?"

"Jeff."

"What's he look like?"

Jack looked at me. "He looks like a fucking Calvin Klein model. Waxes all over. Just the way you like it. Nutsack and all."

I kept my eyes, which had started to water, on the road. "Dude, I'm serious."

"He's average. Average height. Average weight. Long black hair with some shit tattooed on his face."

Well, that wasn't one of the guys who paid me a visit.

"Will he be there at the clubhouse, you think?"

"Probably."

"Do you want to let him know we're coming?"

"No."

"Why not?"

"Because no one knows he's my contact. And all he's going to do is tell me to stay the fuck away."

I thought about it for a moment as I changed lanes to overtake a semi-trailer. "Okay," I said. "Just thought I'd ask."

"We're going to get the shit beat out of us. You know that, right?"

"That's not part of the plan, Jack."

We spent the rest of the trip in silence, during which I made mental notes to prepare myself for some fast, persuasive talking. Of course, I questioned the wisdom of my idea, but I was convinced I had to go through with it.

I needed to know if something illegal was stolen in that fatal robbery. I needed to know if there was a huge angle to this crime that the cops had missed.

If that turned out to be the case, then I needed to prove it.

The clubhouse was marked by the perimeter wall with a large Iron Raiders coat of arms—a helmeted skull in front of two crossed Harley Davidson pistons and rods—painted over a black, sheet-metal door.

The muffled strains of Deep Purple's "Highway Star" came from within. I figured if we had to knock, I'd better make it loud.

I banged my fist on the door four times and waited.

Twenty seconds later, someone inside slid the Judas window open and a pair of mean eyes filled the rectangular frame.

"What the fuck you want?"

"We need to speak to the boss."

"Is he expecting you?"

"Not exactly."

"Then fuck off."

I saw the biker's fingers grab the grill to shut it.

"Look, I'm a lawyer," I said. I didn't have to look at Jack to know he was rolling his eyes.

"No shit," said the biker.

It dawned on me I was still in my suit, about ten o'clock at night outside the headquarters of one of America's most feared outlaw motorcycle gangs.

"I've got a proposition," I continued. "It's urgent. Tell him it's about Sonny."

"Sonny Cromer?"

"That's right. I can get him out."

I looked at Jack now, who clearly thought I'd lost my mind.

The grill slammed shut. The doorman didn't tell us to leave, so I figured we'd wait. A minute later, the door opened and in its placed stepped a barrel-chested biker wearing a greasy blue tank top and jeans.

"What did the boss say?" I asked.

The guy took a step forward, close enough for me to see the deep pores in his ugly, fist-weathered face, and close enough for me to get a dank waft of his Jack-and-Coke breath.

"He said the next word I don't like that comes out of your mouth, I got permission to punctuate it with your broken teeth. Got it?"

"Understood."

"This way."

The biker led us through a courtyard and into the clubhouse proper. The place was just like any old smoke-filled bar with leather booths, pool table, pinball machines, and now AC-DC blaring out of the sound system.

As we walked through the bar, a dozen pairs of eyes were fixed on us. *Who the fuck's the suit?*

My eyes scanned ahead to the drinkers at the bar. To my horror I saw that the Bear was perched there. He turned around to see what his drinking companion was looking at. I kept my eyes ahead. As we passed by him, he shot his arm out to block me.

"I thought I told you to stay clear of Chip Bowman," he growled.

"I know you did. But I'm hoping you and me and the boss can come to a new agreement about that."

The boss. I didn't know who was in charge of this chapter. I just said "the boss" like I knew him, and I'd deliberately avoided referring to him as "your boss." The Bear looked like he answered to no boss.

"What if I like our agreement just as it is, fuckface?" With this, the Bear downed a shot of bourbon and got off his seat. The scowl on his face made it clear I was about to die, or near enough.

"Randall," a deep voice cautioned from across the bar. The tone was calm, almost affectionate, like a doting dog owner commanding his cheeky Rottweiler to drop the neighbor's cat.

The man who spoke came and stood between us. He was not your typical biker, appearance wise. He was clean shaven. The jeans and t-shirt he wore looked like they'd been washed at least within the past few days. He had a narrow face and his light brown hair, up top, was thick and combed back while the sides were cropped short. Put a suit on the guy and he wouldn't look out of place in court. He looked young, too. Thirty-five tops. He looked fit, but not a soft city gym fit. I'd bet he was pretty handy at some form of martial arts, and that he could put Bear in his place with more than words. His eyes were sly and skeptical. Something told me this was one street-smart individual.

"Who are you?"

I told him my name and introduced Jack.

"I'm Ace," he said. "You look like a couple of Leos." That meant Law Enforcement Officers. To rid him of that notion, I pulled out my phone to show him my website.

"My sister's a lawyer," he said as he looked at the screen. Then he handed my phone back. "We don't talk much."

Ace walked toward the booths. Jack and I followed. The Bear turned back to the bar and grabbed a bottle of bourbon to refill his glass.

When we were seated, Ace laid his hands flat on the table. "So. About Sonny. You can get him out?"

"I can get him out."

This was my bright idea. Back at Vinnie's, the details of Sonny Cromer's case came back to me. He was arrested on an aggravated assault charge and the prosecutor went hard and got Cromer put away for ten years. The lawyer Sonny had was useless.

How did I know this? It was three weeks ago, and I saw it with my own eyes. I had the next case listed after Sonny's, and I got there early. My ears pricked up when I heard it mentioned that Sonny was high up the command chain of the Iron Raiders motorcycle club. The way his lawyer fumbled his defense, it made a mockery of our profession. I was insulted. Bob Housman was the lawyer's name, and he was living proof that you can pass the Bar and still be an incompetent idiot.

"What do you mean out, exactly?" asked Ace. "And how?"

"Sonny should never have been convicted. I know his case, and I can file and prosecute a successful appeal."

I wasn't certain that Sonny's lawyer had made an error that could form the basis of an appeal. I just had a hunch that he did. Actually, it was less a hunch and more of a wing and a prayer. The thing was, an appeal had to be launched within sixty days of conviction. With the time that had elapsed since Sonny's conviction, it was closer to forty.

"But you want something in return, right?"

"That's right. I want to know who asked your friend over there to pay me a visit."

Ace had to think about what I said. Then the penny dropped.

"Ah, you're *that* lawyer."

"Yes."

"I'm not going to tell you that. Next question."

"I want to know if it was Quinn Rollins."

"I said, I'm not telling you that. Anything else?"

"I understand you lost out in the HardShell heist."

"That's no secret. We had some weed in that van, and all of it was stolen."

"Yeah, I know that. And that will be covered by insurance, right?"

"It's already done."

"What do you mean? Rollins has paid you out?"

Ace nodded. Obviously, it was understood the Raiders were not prepared to wait for an insurance company investigation to recoup what they lost.

"My understanding is that you might have lost something that wasn't covered by insurance."

Ace's eyes hardened into a glare.

"What the fuck are you talking about?"

"I think you know."

Ace leaned in threateningly. "You're skating on thin ice, lawyer. You want me to call Randall over?"

"No. All I want to say is that my client is innocent, and that I intend to find out who killed those men." I held Ace's stare. "And I intend to find everything that was stolen that night. Everything."

Ace nodded once.

"I thought you'd be interested to know who the real perpetrators were and what they did with all the goods that they stole."

Ace didn't blink. "I'd be very interested."

Neither of us spoke for a few seconds.

"You'd best leave," said Ace.

"Don't you want to know how I plan to get Sonny out?"

"Nope. But I know I'm going to keep you to it."

Jack and I said nothing until we got back to the car. I wasted no time in firing up the engine and hitting the road.

"So," said Jack. "You just had Ace confirm your suspicion that Chip's van was carrying meth that belonged to the Iron Raiders."

"That's right."

"And you've told him that not only will you get Sonny Cromer out of jail, you'll tell him who stole his meth?"

I gripped the wheel a little tighter.

"Yep. That's about it in a nutshell." *And I've got less than forty days to do it*, I neglected to add.

"How do you suppose you're going to find this meth?"

"I was hoping we'd find it together."

"Too easy, Sherlock. All we have to do is search the entire city of LA."

I shook my head. "Nope. That's not where we're going to look. My guess is that it's a long way from LA by now. But I know where I want to look first."

"Where?"

"I'll drop you off home now then I'll swing by tomorrow afternoon to pick you up. I need you to pack all your surveillance gear. Especially your drone."

"Where the hell are we going?"

"Santa Barbara."

21

"What is that they're growing, anyway?" asked Jack, pointing to the rows of squat, leafy trees spread out below us. We'd just pulled off the road that offered a good view of Rollins' five-acre property in Toro Canyon, a hilly stretch of coastland in Santa Barbara County. I'd had to go see Chip at MCJ earlier in the day. Calls to inmates weren't permitted, and so to find out if he knew the location of Rollins' property, I had to ask in person. Fortunately, he did. He'd never actually set foot on the property, but he'd looked it up online when he heard Rollins had purchased it. Chip helped me find the listing, and from there the address. From the prison, I went straight to Jack's house. We jumped into his Ford Ranger and headed up the coast. Now the setting sun was over the Pacific, about ninety minutes from being swallowed whole.

"Coffee," I said. "Apparently, it was all the rage around here a few years back. Then a price slump hit and a few growers went to the wall. Chip says Rollins pounced on this place eighteen months ago. Got it for a steal."

From where we were positioned, the land fell away sharply into a valley. Rollins' orchard straddled the valley with rows of dark green plants climbing up both sides. Near the upper part of the estate were three buildings: a main house, a smaller cottage, and a green house.

We'd spent thirty minutes scoping the vicinity of the property before choosing this position, which was ideal for us to go about our work undetected. There were two ways out if we had to leave fast, and dense trees concealed the truck.

Squatting down among some scrub, we'd counted a total of seven men on the property, mostly standing around. Rollins, though, was not among them.

"Let me have a look," said Jack, taking the binos from me.

"You know a thing or two about cooking up meth, I suppose?"

"As a matter of fact, I do," he said, pressing the glasses to his eyes. "Don't feel bad that all you know comes from *Breaking Bad*. I got real-world experience in these matters."

"Really?"

"A year ago, I had a client who thought his tenant was acting sus. He was not what you'd call a cleanskin himself, so he wanted to find out what was going on without getting the cops involved. At first, at least. Turns out his tenants had converted his investment property into a cook house. So, he made an anonymous call to the authorities and, presto, problem solved."

"Did you just make that up?"

Jack shrugged. "You'll never know."

"I'm calling bullshit."

"You see, Madison. That's what that suit does to you. Turns you all cynical."

"I'm not wearing a suit. And cynical and skeptical aren't the same thing."

"I think in your case they are... Hello."

"What?"

"They're loading up."

"Give me that."

I took the glasses back and trained them on the men. They'd started carrying various items from the guesthouse to the main dwelling. I couldn't tell what they were holding. One guy lugged a small green duffle bag that looked packed.

"Something tells me that's not coffee."

Another three duffle bags followed. Then the activity ceased for about fifteen minutes. Then a black van emerged and moved up the driveway, followed by another.

We watched as the cars wound down the road toward the Pacific coast.

Jack stood up.

I stayed where I was.

"We going to follow them?" he asked.

"No. I need to know what's going on inside that guest house. Let's get your drone down there."

"Whatever we get, it won't stand as evidence," said Jack.

"You think I don't know that? It's not the point. Like I said, I need to know what Rollins is into. And I'll take anything we can get right now. It may not be legally obtained evidence, but it might prove powerful leverage."

I'd ruled out casing the property on foot. Rollins and his men were experts in turning homes into fortresses. This place would be rigged with more than just security cameras and alarms. They'd have the place booby trapped with grenades, most likely. Possibly, even claymore mines.

Jack had the drone ready in minutes. He'd told me this wasn't his most expensive drone, but it was the quietest. Unfortunately, no drones are silent. He launched the device with a hand-held console, steered it up over the road to clear the trees then sent it out toward Rollins' estate.

"Keep an eye on it, would you?" said Jack. His focus would be on the console.

"Sure," I said and moved forward and crouched. The drone was hovering almost directly above us. Then it shot upward with a high-pitched whir and within a few seconds it was a speck in the darkening sky.

"Stay high," I said. "Get over the guest house then drop straight down on my call."

"Got it," said Jack.

We had done repeated head counts during our watch. All seven men had gotten into the vehicles and left. This could be our only chance to get a closer look at what Rollins was up to.

"How long can this thing stay out there?"

"Fifteen minutes."

After two minutes of seeing no movement whatsoever, I told Jack to bring the drone down. The sun had set but there was ample natural light, at least for another half hour.

"Got it," said Jack. The droned dropped onto the guesthouse like it was sliding down a steep zip line. It stopped in front of a large window.

Jack came and crouched beside me, allowing me to see the drone's field of view on the screen. As the device hovered dead still, the aperture of its lens adjusted to the light. When the interior became clear, there was nothing to see besides a large steel vat.

"Move to the left," I said.

Jack steered the drone sideways. It didn't present anything new.

"Keep moving left. Around to the next window."

The drone shifted sideways and rounded the corner. It was out of sight now. All we had to go by was the screen.

"Easy," I said.

Jack slowed the drone down to walking pace.

"I'm going to have to pull back a bit to see what's on this side," said Jack.

As he did, the end of the guest house came into frame. There was a large wooden door with a window on either side, both blocked by blinds. There was a small window near the apex of the roof. I pointed my finger upward. Jack steered the drone to the top window, moving in close. From this angle, we could see what lay behind the vat. There was a large bench strewn with chemistry equipment.

"Well, well, well," said Jack. "That's interesting."

I could see there was another large window on the far side of the building, and it wasn't covered.

I tapped the screen. "Can we get a look through there?"

In a few seconds, Jack had the drone hovering right in front of that window. The vision presented to us was convincing. This was a clan lab if ever I saw one.

"This is recording, right?" I felt I had to ask the obvious.

"Of course, it records everything as video but if you want stills, I can get those too."

"But it's recording to your device, the one you're holding, right?"

"Yes. If we lose the drone, we'll still have the data."

That was reassuring. For a split second anyway. If Rollins and his men somehow seized the drone, they might be able to identify us, or Jack's car, in the footage.

"Super careful. Take it in close. See if you can zoom in on what's on that bench."

Jack had to judge the drone's distance from the window solely via the screen. He inched it closer and closer to the glass. Suddenly, the vision jolted.

"Damn!" said Jack.

"What?"

"Too close. I made contact. It's okay."

Jack positioned the drone outside the window again, and then zoomed the lens in on the bench. There were various chemicals there. I pointed at a plastic bag with a label on it.

"What's that?"

"Let's have a look."

The camera lens zoomed in closer.

"I can't read it."

"That's as far as I can go. I'll take some high-res photos. We can blow them up later."

The console replicated the sound of a camera shutter firing.

Suddenly, the screen went dark briefly. Something moved across it.

"What was that?"

Jack pulled the lens back to wide and there at the window was a man's face looking straight at the camera. He was shouting.

"Abort, Jack!"

I didn't really have to ask. Jack tweaked the toggle and the drone soared high.

As it did so, a shot rang out. Then another shot. I had the drone in sight now. Jack had it in evasion mode, zig-zagging through the sky. Only an extremely lucky shot could take it down.

I turned my eyes to the guest house. Two men were now outside shooting at the drone. Then came the sound of a motor. An ATV appeared beside the men.

"Jesus. There are three of them. They must have been inside the whole time."

As one shooter keep firing at the drone, the other got on the back of the ATV. The driver wrenched the throttle and came straight for us.

The drone was now above us. Jack stood up and backed away to his truck as he brought it down.

I saw the gunman on the ATV tap the driver's shoulder. The ATV stopped and the gunman levelled his weapon at us.

"Down, Jack!" I shouted and as I did, the shooter let go five rounds in quick succession. The bullets flew so close I could just about feel the air move.

"Fuck!" Jack shouted through clenched teeth. He hit the ground with his hand clutching his side. "Grab the drone," he said.

Jack had managed to ground the drone ten yards from the truck.

"You okay?"

"I'm fucking hit."

"Can you get to the truck?"

"Yeah. Get the drone."

I crawled as fast as I could and regathered the drone. I could hear the engine of the ATV revving as it climbed the ridge below us. I raced to help Jack into the passenger seat before rounding the front and getting behind the wheel.

"Where are the keys?"

"Shit. Hang on."

Jack twisted his body to try and extract the keys from his left jeans pocket. It seemed to take forever. Finally, he retrieved them and reached over to me, his hand slick with blood. I slotted the key home, brought the engine to life, then shoved the stick in reverse and hit the gas. The rear wheels churned up a cloud of dust that welled up all around us. Through it, though, I saw the ATV mount the road a hundred yards back. I spun the wheel, put my foot down, and steered the truck onto the road. As I did, I saw the shooter stand and take aim at us.

"Down Jack!"

A burst from the semi-automatic came at us, three bullets hammering into the back of the truck.

I cursed as I saw the road ahead was dead straight for another two hundred yards. Even with the fading light, we were an easy target. The shooter began emptying his magazine at us, spacing his shots as he took more care with his aim. I kept my head as low as I possibly could.

The back window exploded just before we entered a bend. Thankfully a series of bends followed. I raced the truck through, cutting corners and hoping like hell nothing was coming the other way.

"Where's your gun?" I shouted.

I didn't need to ask. Jack already had his Smith and Wesson in his bloodied hand. He swiveled around and fired through the now open window, sending five shots their way. Through the rearview mirror, I saw the ATV slow down, both driver and shooter ducking.

Around the next bend the road opened up and I was able to put five hundred yards between us in no time.

"They're done," said Jack.

I saw the ATV had stopped.

"Fuck," Jack said through clenched teeth as he lifted his shirt.

"How bad is it?" I asked.

"Could be worse. It's just caught the oblique muscle. It hasn't lodged but it's taken out a chunk of flesh," he said grimacing with pain.

"Hang tight," I said. "I'll pull over as soon as I can."

"Just keep driving," said Jack. "We'll sort it out at home."

We both knew going to a hospital was out of the question. Any physician presented with a gunshot wound was required by law to notify the cops.

"You got a first-aid kit in the truck?"

"Yeah."

"Okay, then. I'll find somewhere to pull over and I'll put a dressing on. Then we'll get you home."

"Great," said Jack, sarcastically. "Chanel's going to kill me."

22

I pulled off the 101 at Rincon Point, dashed around the back to grab the medical kit and opened Jack's door. I figured if Rollins' men had decided to give chase, they'd only be a few minutes behind. Jack swung his legs out slowly, grimacing with pain. The shirt he'd used to stem the blood was soaked through.

"Give me a look," I said.

Jack took his hand away. It wasn't pretty but I've seen worse. The bullet had grazed his left flank about half an inch in, ripping out a divot of flesh. The bleeding had slowed, and Jack was awake, alert, and breathing almost normally, so I knew he wasn't suffering a critical loss of blood pressure.

"You're damned lucky," I said as I packed dressing against the wound. "Hold this."

Jack put his hand on the wound while I wrapped a bandage around his waist.

"If that guy's aim was a fraction right that bullet could have gone through your stomach, not to mention your spine."

I used two elastic clips to secure the bandage. "It's going to need a few stitches. You trust me?"

"Do I have a choice?"

"No."

"That'll do. Let's go," said Jack. He popped the glove compartment open, took out a box of bullets, and began reloading the clip. I was already back behind the wheel when he jammed the full clip back into place.

"They may have got the plate," Jack said when we were back on the freeway.

"Maybe. It might have been just dark enough. At that distance, my bet is that they wouldn't have."

Jack took out his phone and tapped a contact. "Wish me luck," he said as he put the phone to his ear. It wasn't every day of the week you rang the wife to tell her you were coming home shot, and that his buddy was going to have to stitch you up in the bathroom. He spoke with Chanel for a couple of minutes before hanging up.

We made it back to Calabasas safely and as I swung his truck into the driveway, Jack aimed the clicker at the garage door, and I pulled in.

Before I could shut the engine off, the side door to the garage opened and Chanel appeared. She rushed up to Jack. He opened the door and Chanel gasped at the blood.

"Oh, my God," she said. "Look at you! How bad is it?"

"It's not as bad as it looks. Just a big scratch, really. Brad's going to put some stitches in and it'll be fine."

Chanel put her arms around Jack and then released him to look at me.

"Chanel, I'm sorry," I said. "This is my fault."

"That, I'd believe," she said. "What the hell happened?"

There was no point trying to spin Chanel some bullshit story. I told her about the case and that I asked Jack to come and surveil the property.

"So the aim was to get footage of this lab?" she asked.

"I suspected a lab was there and as it turned out I was right. We thought everyone had left when we sent the drone in. We were wrong."

"Did you get some good footage?"

"Yes, we did," I said, trying to make out that in some sense it was mission accomplished.

"Footage that you can't possibly use as evidence because you were trespassing," said Chanel coldly.

I didn't expect this line of questioning from her.

"That doesn't mean it won't prove vital to the case," I diverted. "Look we should get Jack stitched up."

Chanel looked at me with unrelenting eyes. For all the time I'd known her she had every reason to like me. I was a decent enough, smart enough guy who was a good friend to her husband. That view was being radically revised as we spoke.

Jack and I moved to the main bathroom. Soon after, Chanel appeared with a bottle of bourbon and three glasses.

"Thank God the girls are in bed," she said, handing me a glass. "You'd better know what you're doing."

"I've done this before. The wound's clean, in that there's no dirt, so getting it sterile won't be a problem. Then I'll do a bit of sewing," I said, holding up the needle and suture thread I'd taken from the first-aid kit. "I think he'll need eight stitches. That's it."

"I'll help," said Chanel. She removed the bandage and dressing and put her hand over her mouth in sympathy. She'd suffered terrible injuries during her career as a ski racer, so she wasn't one to be squeamish. She cleaned the wound and dabbed it as dry as she could, then held the skin together as I inserted six stitches.

After ten minutes the job was done, the sealed wound about two inches long.

Chanel handed me my drink.

"Thanks," I said.

"Brad, let me be clear. If you ever take my husband along with you on a job that has even the faintest chance of him getting killed, I'm going to kill you. Do you understand?"

I nodded. "Yes, of course, Chanel. I apologize."

With that, Chanel drained her glass and went to check on the girls.

"She's right, Jack," I said. "I can't keep asking you to do this kind of shit. You're a father."

"What are you talking about? So are you, you moron."

"I know, but it's different."

It wasn't quite the same for both of us. Jack could and should stay clear of this case for the sake of his family. I couldn't. I'd never back out and leave Chip's fate to some other lawyer. If I didn't stick with it, an innocent man would be sent to jail for the rest of his life. An innocent man with two young daughters, just like Jack.

I'd always needed to have faith in this case, and now I believed with all my heart that my client was innocent. There was something dark and dirty about HardShell and it wasn't

Chip Bowman. The trial would be upon us in a few months, and I intended to see it through to the end.

But if Rollins found out it was me who spied on his clan lab, there was every chance I wouldn't live to deliver my opening statement.

"I'm going home," I said, patting Jack on the shoulder. "Thanks for your help. Send me the bill for your truck."

23

I took a laptop with me to Men's Central Jail the next morning to show Chip the drone video. I opened the computer in front of Chip and brought up the file. I played the clip and hit the space bar to pause when the first man appeared.

"Do you recognize him?"

"Yes," said Chip. "That's Kenny Sutherland. He's worked for Quinn for years."

"He works for HardShell?"

Chip nodded.

I grabbed a pen from my inside jacket pocket, pulled out my notebook and wrote the name down. We continued on until all ten men had been identified. All of them were vets, all former private military contractors.

Chip pointed to the bag that one of the men was carrying. "What's in the bag?"

"I don't know. But I think it's meth."

Chip's face dropped. "Are you serious?"

"Couldn't be more so." I showed Chip the rest of the video, including the clan lab.

"I can't believe it," said Chip, flopping back in his chair. "I mean, I knew Quinn didn't mind pushing the boundaries, but I never thought he'd go that far."

I closed the laptop and sat down again at the other side of the table.

"Chip, I'm putting the pieces together here because the cops won't. All they're focused on is you. I'm convinced there was meth on that run you did." I didn't want to tell Chip that Ace had practically confirmed that there was. "And if that's the case, it was somehow loaded while you weren't there or you weren't looking."

"But I saw what we were carrying. There was nothing but legal cash and weed in that van. I'd checked it all on the manifest."

"Maybe it was hidden in the van somewhere."

Chip was lost in thought. "I can't for the life of me figure out where."

"Did you ever say anything that might have worried Quinn enough to get rid of you?"

Chip folded his arms and gave it some thought. "Well, I made it pretty clear to the other guys that I wanted nothing to do with any illegal carries."

I shook my head. "I can't imagine that would put a target on your back. Was there anything else you said?"

Chip thought some more. After a few moments, a recollection came to him. "The only thing I can remember was... Look, I mean it was nothing. It was silly. I was drunk and just having a joke."

"What did you say?"

"I told Nate and Bo that there was no way I was going to put my family's future at risk by getting into anything shady. To be honest, I was joking and I wasn't. I really wanted nothing to do with anything like that. I wanted to do my job and do it well and get rewarded well for it."

"What was the joke?"

"I said something like I might end up like the guy from *Goodfellas*, you know the Ray Liotta character? I said I might have to expose the whole deal to the feds and go into witness protection. It was a stupid thing to say, but I can say some dumb stuff when I've had a few beers."

I can only imagine how such a remark would have gone down.

"I think we may have found our trigger. Would Nate and Bo have told Rollins what you said?"

Chip shrugged his shoulders. "I don't know. But if they thought I was a threat, why didn't they just kill me?"

"Maybe because you are more valuable to them alive. Look at you. Sitting here in jail. Maybe this is exactly what they wanted. They wanted you to take the fall for their crime. You have no answers. You have no explanations. You can't talk your way out. And you can't betray your supposed co-conspirators. You get sent to jail. Case closed. And they get back to business as usual."

"But why are Nate and Bo dead?"

I shook my head. "That I don't know."

24

It's been said that it's not the evidence that counts in a trial but how you use it. Often, but not always, whoever tells the most compelling story with the given evidence wins. From the outset, I knew Dale Winter had the jump on me in that regard. He'd have no problem casting Chip as a desperate schemer who thought he'd gotten away with the perfect crime.

Winter sent me an updated list of his witnesses, and I was not surprised to see Quinn Rollins' name included. To counter the barrage Winter had planned, I had to focus on deflection and discredit strategies: lead suspicion away from Chip and undermine the credibility of Winter's witnesses. I had to somehow find a way to turn what I knew about Rollins against him.

"Mr. Madison," said Megan after buzzing me. "Mr. Scott Slovak is here to see you."

This was not a scheduled visit but it was welcome. I pressed the button. "Thanks Megan. Please send him in."

The door opened and Megan ushered Scooter Slovak into my office. He declined her offer of coffee or water and took a seat in front of my desk. His demeanor was very different to the upbeat vigor I saw at the HardShell compound. He looked nervous, lacking in confidence, and uncomfortable.

I wasn't surprised.

I'd left him a message immediately after visiting Chip at MCJ but I didn't hear from him for several days. When he did finally call, I told him Chip needed all the help he could get.

He needed more than a friend. He needed someone to stand up for him. I asked Slovak if he'd come in to discuss the prospect of him testifying. He said he'd think about it. I hoped that him coming to see me meant he'd decided to help, but I was prepared to be disappointed.

I had to ease into the proposition gently. The last thing I wanted to do was to scare him off. If my powers of persuasion failed, the strength of my case could be halved. I would be at Winter's mercy.

"How are you today, Scooter?"

"I'm good, Mr. Madison. It's all getting a bit crazy."

"I understand. It's often the way with cases like this. There are so many unanswered questions, so many allegations and theories. Then there are the lies and misinformation. It's hard to know what's what."

"Tell me about it."

Something told me we were not exactly on the same level.

"Scooter, you look bothered. Is there something I should know?"

He was reluctant to speak. After a few moments, he finally found his voice. "Things are getting way out of control, sir. I don't know what to make of it."

"Make of what?"

"HardShell. There's some crazy stuff going on. Crazy stories flying around."

"What stories? Stories about Chip?"

Scooter shook his head. "No, nothing about him, but it could be connected. Who knows?"

"Scooter, I don't know what you're talking about."

Slovak was wringing his hands and rocking slightly in his chair.

"There was an incident up at Quinn's farm."

A chill ran through my veins. It took a lot for me to act calm and oblivious.

"His farm?"

"Up near Santa Barbara. He bought a coffee estate up near Santa Barbara. It just got raided by the DEA."

My jaw just about hit the desk. "What?"

Scooter looked at me like he was just as surprised as I was. "Yeah, I know."

"Hang on, Scooter back up. You need to unpack this for me. Piece by piece."

"Yes, of course. Well, you know he's got the farm up there?"

"I do now."

"Recently, the teams have been using it as a stop-off point to break up the LA-Humboldt run. Quinn even put in a couple of vaults there. And apparently last week these two guys sent a drone in to spy on the place."

"Who would want to spy on Quinn's farm?"

"No one knows for sure. There's a lot of speculation but Quinn's in a state. Even more so than before. He's freaking out. But those guys could have been DEA. Or they could have been Bravo guys. No one knows for sure. But two days later, the DEA turned up and raided the place."

"Did they find anything?"

"No. Nothing. Quinn's tried to get them to tell him who called them in on him but they refused to say."

My blood pressure eased a little.

"And Quinn thinks David McClean sent his guys to spy on him?"

"Yes."

"And then they gave the DEA a tip-off?"

"That's what everyone thinks. It's a cut-throat business manned by some pretty intense dudes. Quinn and McClean both kind of have their own private armies. And they want to take each other down."

"I thought HardShell was doing much better and bigger than Bravo."

"It is, by a long shot. But Bravo is growing and McClean's always ready to pounce on Quinn's mistakes. Since the robbery, he's been contacting all our clients, saying we can't be trusted. And if HardShell was doing anything illegal, McClean would let the cops know, for sure."

"Scooter, is there anything that Quinn wants to keep hidden from the authorities?"

Scooter shifted.

"Maybe."

"Maybe what?"

"Well, you know how Chip was super uneasy about HardShell handling illegal goods?"

"Yes."

"Yeah, well, I think maybe he had good cause to worry."

There was a pause. This was my cue.

"Scooter, do you believe Chip is a good man?"

"Of course, I do."

"Do you believe he's guilty of killing Bo and Nate and stealing all that cash?"

"No. I just don't think Chip was like that."

"That makes two of us. Listen, Chip needs someone who can essentially say what you just told me in court. The jury needs to know that he is a good man."

A spark of fear hit Slovak's face. He began shaking his head.

"No, Mr. Madison. I can't."

"He needs you, Scooter. I need you."

"Quinn won't like it. He'll think I'm a traitor and that I'd be dragging HardShell's name through the mud. And I know Quinn. He's been fighting like hell to keep his business going. He'll do anything to protect his company. He's at war now and I don't want to appear to be on the other side."

"This is not about taking sides, Scooter. Don't think of it like that. All I'll be asking you are questions about your colleague and friend. You count yourself as a friend, don't you?"

"I guess, but we're not close."

"But you got him the job?"

"Yes."

"Because you felt like you owed him."

"Yes."

"Because he saved your life?"

"Yes."

"Well, now you can help save his life. I can't put it more plainly than that. And all that's required of you is to simply state the facts about Chip's employment, his job performance, and your assessment of his character."

"You want me to talk about how he saved my life, don't you?"

"No. I don't. Let me be clear: I don't want you to talk about that at all. You'd appear completely biased, and it would ruin your testimony."

"I don't know. I'll have to think about it."

"Chip's got no one in his corner, Scooter. No one."

"He's got you."

"That's not enough."

"But if Chip didn't kill Nate and Bo, then who did?"

"That's not what this trial has to resolve. This is about countering the effort to hang this crime on Chip. What I need to focus on, what we need to focus on, is making damn sure he gets his day in court. Can I count on you to help? Can Chip count on you?"

Slovak nodded.

"Yes. Okay, Mr. Madison. I'll do it. I'll testify."

I had to refrain from doing a fist-pump. Something had gone right in this case for a change.

25

After Slovak left, I sat in my office to contemplate the turn of events. Who had called the DEA on Quinn? And how did they clean up the lab so quickly? Maybe after the drone incursion, they thought a bust was imminent. Whatever the case, the raid was something I could raise in court when Rollins was on the stand. It provided an in to exposing HardShell's seedy underbelly.

My door had been left open after Slovak left. I lifted my head at the sound of soft knocking to see Megan standing there.

"This just came for you," she said, coming forward and handing me an envelope with a knowing smile. "I think I know who it's from."

I dug my finger in and tore it open, all the while looking at Megan with my eyebrows raised. It was a good luck card from Abby. She must have been following the case in the news, and knew the trial was coming up fast.

Caught off guard, I put the card right back in the envelope and placed it on the desk.

"Now I definitely know who it's from," said Megan. "Abby, am I right?"

"Wrong, it's from my mother," I said flatly.

I leaned back in my chair and looked at my watch. It was almost five on a Thursday afternoon but suddenly it felt like the weekend.

"Hey, why don't we go for a drink?" I asked Megan.

"Normally, I'd say yes but I've got to pack. Remember?"

It had slipped my mind that Megan was off on a mini break. One of her close friends was getting married in New Orleans, and she was taking Friday and Monday off. When she mentioned the wedding to me initially, she didn't ask for any time off. But after she told me she was the matron of honor, I insisted she take a long weekend and enjoy herself. Her boyfriend Sam was going too, and it was not hard to tell she was smitten. I was happy for her and hoped like hell that he didn't break her heart like the last prick she got serious about.

I'd processed the fact that I'd be without Megan for two working days, then promptly forgot all about it.

I must have looked a little bummed that she turned me down for a drink.

"Brad, you could use a break yourself."

Megan hardly ever said this to me. I think she admired my work ethic and knew that I tended to lose myself in cases.

"Don't be absurd. I'm preparing for a trial, Megan. I can't afford to take time off."

"I don't mean go on vacation. I mean you need to get your brain off the job for a while. A night even."

"You know that's impossible," I said, tapping my tight temple. "This thing doesn't have an off switch."

"Sounds to me like you're just making up excuses."

"I'm not."

"Why don't you call Jack? You do know the Lakers are playing tonight?"

"Yeah, of course I do."

I was lying. It had totally slipped my mind.

"And you do remember that Mrs. Lindstrom said she would get you courtside seats whenever you wanted, don't you?"

She was right. As part of her thank you for settling her divorce so quickly and favorably, Nina had offered me use of her Lakers season pass whenever I wanted.

"No, I'd actually forgotten all about that, Megan. I guess I could call Nina."

"And then give Jack a call."

"Ah, yeah. About that. Jack won't be allowed to come out and play any time soon. I can tell you that right now."

"Why not?"

I didn't want to go into the fact that he'd been shot. "He's busy being super daddy."

Megan sat herself on the edge of the desk. She picked up Abby's card and waved it in my face.

"Then call someone else," she said. "You need to go let your hair down, and something tells me that the ideal person for you to do that with is reaching out to you."

"I told you. That card's from my mother."

Megan cocked an eyebrow.

"Perfect. Then pick up the phone. Call your mom," she said, air-quoting the last word. "And take her to the frickin' game."

She slapped the card back down on the table, got off the desk, and headed for the door.

"All this will still be here when you get back," she said, standing in the doorway. "But it's going to do you no good to sit here and stew. You need some perspective. And a date with your mom is just the ticket."

"You're sick, you know that?"

"Yes, I do know that. Go show your mom a good time. Maybe she needs it just as much as you."

"Yeah, I don't think so."

Megan marched back to my desk, placed both hands on the edge and leaned in toward me. "Brad, you do know she's split from her husband, don't you?"

Megan's words jolted me. There was no way to hide it. Megan smiled as she read my furrowed brow. She took out her phone, tapped away, scrolled and tapped then showed me the screen. I took the phone from her hands. She was right, if the story could be believed. Abby and her husband were spending time apart. I felt so stupid, the way I acted that night in Vinnie's.

Megan took her phone from my hands and began gathering her things to leave. She stood in the doorway as she pulled her coat on, watching to see if I took action before she left.

"Go," I said to her, picking up my phone. "I'm calling. You can go now. I'm doing it."

"You'd better."

I began searching my contacts.

Megan reached for the handle to close the door.

"Say hi to your mom for me," she said with a wink.

26

"Hi, Brad. What's up?"

The tone of Abby's voice was cool. Not cool as in hip. Cool as in, "maybe me answering this call was a dumb idea, and I'm going to make a fast exit."

I cleared my throat. "First, I just wanted to apologize for the other night, if I was being rude."

"If? I came over to say hi, I asked you back stage, and for all your lack of enthusiasm you basically told me to fuck off."

"I'm sorry, Abby. You were the last person I expected to see that night."

"Seemed like I was the last person you wanted to see."

"That's not it at all. I was glad to see you. And if I'm being honest, maybe I was trying too hard to hide it."

There was a pause. I heard Abby take a drink. A few seconds passed before she spoke. "In case you didn't realize, this silence here is an invitation to keep talking."

"Right," I said as I tried to choose my words carefully, walking a dreaded line that threatened to expose my vulnerability. "Seeing you was a nice surprise. I just wasn't ready for it. And the way you were so open and friendly... it just took me back to how I used to feel about you. And the problem with that is that it's inappropriate now."

"It's inappropriate for you to like me?"

"You know what I'm saying."

"I think so, but only one of us knows what you mean."

"It's inappropriate because you're married. That's what I was wrestling with."

"Jesus Christ. You men. It's hard to tell who you're at war with—yourselves or the people you care about."

Abby didn't take this opportunity to even hint that her marriage was on the rocks. So maybe the article Megan showed me was just another made-up Hollywood story. Whatever Abby's status was, now was not the moment to probe.

"Well, I'd like you to know that I can wear my big boy pants and be friends with you if that's what you want."

"I don't know what I want. I was just happy to see you. But you did your best to show me you didn't feel the same. And then you just up and left. Your loss, Brad Madison. Marcus King is fucking amazing, and you blew the chance not just to see him but to meet him."

I leaned back in my chair. "I'll kick myself over that, for sure."

I opened my drawer and pulled out a bottle of Talisker 10 and a glass. Abby must have heard the soft pop of the cork.

"Oh, good. You're fixing yourself a drink. I hate to drink alone."

Her voice. Her humor. Her no-bullshit approach. This was everything I liked about her all those years ago.

I took a sip of my scotch. "Thanks for the card. That was sweet of you."

"Well, I know you've got that trial coming up. And I know that's what your mind will be on twenty-four-seven."

"I'm really behind the eight-ball on this one."

"You've got to win this one, Brad. I couldn't bear to see Wesley Brenner use it for his own political gain."

Her words surprised me. "Have you been following the case?"

"As a matter of fact, I have."

"I'm starting to think you showing up at Vinnie's was no coincidence. I'm picturing a crazy stalker wall—you know, covered in cut-outs and photos and freaky messages scrawled in red."

Abby laughed. "Let me stop you there before that swelling head of yours breaks a window. I'm following the case because Wesley Brenner is using it as a platform to get back into the Senate."

"You're not a fan, I take it?"

"The man's revolting. He groped me at a charity event a few years back. I gave him an earful and you should have heard what came out of his mouth. It was a hateful, disgusting rant littered with the c-word. So, no, I'm not a fan."

The thought of Brenner attacking Abby like that made me furious. I thought it best I change the subject.

"How's Hollywood treating you?"

"Good. I've had a great run, but I don't know how much longer I'll keep doing it. You know, one day you're on top of everyone's leading-lady list, next the only offers that come your way are for lame rom-coms."

The conversation veered to my own life, then to Bella, and Claire. I told Abby that Claire had remarried and that Bella wanted to spend more time with me.

"Do you still love Claire?"

"No, not in that way. Not like I used to. It took a while but it's not there anymore. I want her to be happy, but from what Bella's said all is not well between Claire and Marty."

"When we were together you were only just getting divorced."

"I know."

"I was sure you were the perfect man for me, but then I wasn't. There was something that always bothered me."

"What was that?"

"Like it was too soon for you."

"You're probably right. But I don't regret it. How's married life for you?"

"Tommy and I are separated," Abby sighed and took a swig of wine. "It's not malicious or anything, we just realized we're not on the same path."

"Sorry to hear that. Are you seeing anyone or is that off the cards?"

Abby hesitated. "Yes and no."

"What does that mean?"

"It means mostly no."

"Is there a chance we—?"

Abby shushed me quietly. "Don't Brad."

Suddenly I was confused again.

"Look," she said. "I don't know where I am at the moment. I like you a lot. So much so that it makes me feel I need to be guarded. Like you were with Claire, I'm not in the best emotional state, and I can't just grab onto another relationship to steady me. You know what I mean?"

"Sure, it's about timing."

"Yes. And to be totally honest, I wasn't happy with how things went the other night. I mean I was happy to see you—"

"Like I said, I thought you were married."

"I know. I don't hold that against you at all. It's just that it reminded me of how committed you are to your job. You eat, live, and breathe being a lawyer. And that's why I sent you the card. I really admire that about you. But I'm not sure how much room there is for other stuff. Other people."

"Abby, I'm not a machine. I have actually held down a job and a relationship before."

"I know, Brad. I'm sorry. See? This is what I mean about my emotional state. I'm making out like it's you, not me. I'm sorry. I don't feel like I've got my sea legs yet, if you know what I mean."

"I get it."

"I'm really sorry how things ended between us. I do care about you. I don't want you to hate me."

"I don't hate you. But I hate Wes Brenner even more after what you told me."

"Well, you'd better make sure you don't give him the satisfaction of seeing you lose."

"That's easier said than done."

"Brad, you were born to do this. You'll find a way, I'm sure. You're a brilliant lawyer. I'll be rooting for you."

"Thanks."

"I've got to go. Goodnight."

"Night," I said.

I put the phone down on the desk, my head in a haze. I took the bottle and poured myself another belt.

And another.

27

The next morning my office smelled of stale whisky. I picked up the glass from the night before and the wastepaper basket and walked to the breakroom. I emptied the trash and got a new plastic liner from a drawer and fitted it. I then washed the glass, grabbed a bottle of water from the fridge, and headed back.

It was odd to not have Megan there to greet me.

A recollection of my conversation with Abby came to mind. Not so much the words as the feel. The sound of her voice, the ease of our rapport. The thought hung there for a few moments then I just let it go. Observing it like that, it didn't make me feel anything other than a resignation to fate. Life and love is so much about timing. If Abby and I ever had a time, it had passed.

I sat down at my desk and surveyed the files placed there. All were related to Chip's case. I thought of Scooter, hoping he wouldn't pull out. I couldn't blame him if he did. I knew full well the courage it would take for him to speak in Chip's defense. Before he left, I reassured him we'd have ample time to prepare before he took the stand. Still, I know from experience that he was likely to try and pull out.

As I was thinking, my eye fell on my journal which was still open on the page where I made notes during my meeting with Scooter.

I leaned forward and picked up the book. Immediately, I was drawn to a sentence I'd underlined. It was something Scooter had said about Quinn: *He'll do anything to protect his company.*

I couldn't remember why it was that I'd underlined it. I mean, it wasn't like I didn't know Quinn was willing to break the law to keep his empire growing.

Henry Tuck then came to mind. Him sitting in this office, telling me he was having a hard time getting his money out of HardShell. That his partner was resisting Henry's wishes, telling him to hold off for a year.

But what if Rollins didn't want Tuck to cash in, period?

He'll do anything to protect his company.

Henry didn't look like a man who'd soon be blowing his brains out. Quite the opposite. He had everything to live for.

Yet Pete Chang felt differently. He said Henry's girlfriend had dumped him, and that his scorned wife was unwilling to take him back. The consensus was that Henry was heartbroken, alone, and so lost that he decided to kill himself.

Could the Henry Tuck I spoke to become such a vision of despair so soon?

I turned to my laptop and searched my inbox for the email Henry sent me via his girlfriend's account. When it came up, I felt like a dormant clue had just been revealed to me. It was a Gmail account, and it looked for all the world like she had used her full name as a prefix: fernortega.

I didn't want to contact her via email. At best, it would waste time. At worst, it would be too easy for her to ignore me.

I had to find out where she lived.

Within two minutes of searching online, I had an address. I grabbed my keys and made for the door.

28

An elderly Latino woman peered warily through the gap offered by the chain-lock. She must have been expecting someone she knew, as it was clear she regretted opening the door and was in half a mind to shut it without a word.

"Yes?" she said, politeness getting the better of her.

"Good morning, ma'am. I'm really sorry to bother you but I've come to speak with Fern Ortega."

The woman's dark eyes studied my face. She frowned and shook her head.

"She no live here," she said firmly and went to shut the door. I deployed the old salesman trick, sticking my shoe in the gap. This both alarmed and annoyed her.

"Mister. You go now."

With that, she kicked my toe several times but my foot didn't budge.

"Ma'am, please. I am no threat to Ms. Ortega. I promise. I'm a lawyer." I pulled out a card and flashed it at her. She made no attempt to look at it.

"Go away, or I call the police."

She started kicking my toe again harder and managed to nudge my shoe back a fraction.

"Por favor, señora," I said, pulling out my elementary Spanish. "Soy amigo de Henry. So su abogado. Es muy importante."

The woman was not about to change her mind. She raised her foot and was looking to see how she could stomp on my toe when I heard a younger woman's voice from within.

"Mama. Retrocede, por favor."

The older woman huffed and shifted back out of sight, and the face of a younger woman appeared.

"What do you want?"

"Are you Fern Ortega?"

"Who are you?"

"My name's Brad Madison. Henry Tuck came to see me about some matters before he died. I think he used your email account to send me some information. That's how I found you."

Fern bowed her head and a look of great sadness came over her. It seemed to me that even if she did break it off with him, it was not without pain on her side.

"Ms. Ortega, please. I'm defending a man who used to work for the company Henry was involved in. I'd be so grateful if I could ask you a few questions. Some things about Henry's situation don't make sense to me. I was hoping you might be able to help me understand."

Fern nodded. The door closed briefly as she unhooked the chain. She opened the door and looked behind me.

"Come in," she said. "Quickly."

29

The mother had moved into the kitchen and was placing vegetables on the counter next to a large pot. She kept an eye on me as she went about her business, clearly uncomfortable with my presence.

Fern offered me coffee. I wanted to take my time and get her to relax as much as I could so I said yes. She nodded to her mother who shuffled across the kitchen, took a cup out of a cupboard and filled it from the coffee machine.

"Leche?" the mother asked gruffly without looking up.

"No, gracias," I said.

The coffee was ready in seconds. The mother shuffled over, handed me a cup, and spun around before I got my thank you out.

"Please," said Fern, motioning for us to sit at a small glass-topped dining table.

"Fern, the reason I'm here is I'm trying to understand what happened to Henry," I said after we were both seated. "Were you helping him to prepare the documents he needed to give me?"

Of course, I remembered what Pete had told me, that he'd heard Fern had broken it off with Henry, that he was found clutching a photo of her, and that she'd dumped him via text.

But I needed to tread very carefully on the relationship issue as I was sure she'd be bearing a lot of guilt.

Fern gave me two quick nods but kept her mouth shut. It was not hard to see that she found the prospect of talking about Henry difficult. But she'd let me into her home. Something told me she wanted to trust me.

Wearing a pretty green floral dress, Fern held herself with stoic poise, her knees together and her interlaced hands resting in her lap. Her fingers pressed against her own flesh, massaging out some of the stress she obviously felt.

"Ms. Ortega, Henry came to me for help not just with his divorce but with getting his money out of HardShell Security. He promised to send me his contract and financial statements. All I got was a basic list of assets he sent me though your account, or else you sent it."

"I sent it," Fern said.

I paused, studying her reaction. She looked uncomfortable, as though expecting to be fiercely interrogated.

"Ms. Ortega, I don't want to make your life more difficult than it already is. But I suspect that Henry's situation might have some bearing on the case I am working on. I'm hoping that you might have some information that could help me."

"I'm not sure how I can help," she said.

"Ms. Ortega, I don't mean to be rude but I just want to understand things better. Henry was on top of the world when I saw him. He was clear-eyed about spending the rest of his life with you, but he wanted to do right by Laura. I just don't understand why he would kill himself."

She kept her mouth shut. She hadn't told me to shut mine so I ventured to think I could explore the subject a little more.

Careful not to lay the blame at her feet, I started with some other theories.

"He might have been ill. Was he ill?"

She shook her head. "No."

"Was he worried about anything?"

"No."

"Was he really as happy as he seemed to be?"

"Yes."

"Can I ask when you saw him last?"

Fern bowed her head, then lifted it again to address me. "The day before he died."

Tears were filling her eyes.

"Excuse me," she said. She got up and went to the kitchen and came back with a box of Kleenex. She pulled out two sheets and dabbed her eyes. She was trying hard to keep herself together.

"Ms. Ortega, if you don't mind, what was the nature of your conversation with him that day?"

"What do you mean?"

"I mean, was everything okay? Was it a happy conversation? A normal conversation that couples have?"

Fern let out a little moan as tears fell from her eyes. She dabbed them once more, as well as her nose. "No. It was not like that."

"It wasn't?"

"No. Why are you asking me this?"

"Ms. Ortega. Something is not right here. It just doesn't add up. And I'd like to know the truth about what happened to Henry. There, I said it. This is not just me sticking my nose into your business, I assure you. What you tell me could help save another man's life."

Fern straightened herself again and swept her right hand over her thighs. There was a steel about her now.

"I broke up with him," she said resolutely.

"Can I ask why?"

"I thought he was being foolish. I'd told him many times that I felt things were moving too fast. I felt uncomfortable, and I didn't think he really cared about what might happen to my mother."

"He wanted you to leave her and move in with him?"

"Yes. But he knew I could never leave my mother by herself."

"He didn't talk about living somewhere with both you and your mother?"

"No."

"And so you broke it off?"

"Yes."

"Were you in love with Henry?"

Her head went dead still as she directed her words at me. "Yes. Very much so."

"Couldn't you have worked something out?"

Fern's lips began to tremble. Then her next words came rushing out. "Mr. Madison. I'm so scared. I just don't know what to tell you."

I leaned forward.

"Ms. Ortega, you have nothing to fear from me, I promise. I'm not judging you. If you wanted to break up with Henry, that's your business. But to tell you the truth, I'm not sure you're being totally honest with me."

She bowed her head again. Then she took a sip of coffee. The drink seemed to give her a modicum of comfort.

"I did not want to break up with Henry," she said ruefully. "I was forced to."

"Forced? Who forced you?"

"Some men came to my house. They were ugly men. Very rude and very rough. They told me they were Henry's friends and they were not going to let me ruin his life. They said nasty things to me. They said I was a whore and that all I wanted was his money. Then they told me I must never see Henry again. If I refused, they said, they would kill both me and my mother."

"They threatened to kill you?"

"Yes. They made it very clear. They said they could make me disappear, just like that." She snapped her fingers.

"What did you say to them?"

"What else could I say? I told them I would obey. They made me write a message on my phone. They read it. They told me it wasn't enough. I had to write other things. Cruel things."

"Like what?"

"That I never loved him. That I'd realized what a fool he was and that he was too old for me. They made me send it."

"Henry would have been devastated. But he would have tried to call you, wouldn't he?"

Fern nodded. "Yes. I'm sure he did. But they took my phone with them. So I'll never know."

Fern then broke down sobbing. After collecting herself, she resumed. "The next thing I heard, Henry killed himself. And it was all my fault."

Fern hunched forward, her shoulders wrenching with the force of her sorrow. Her mother came in, bent down and put her arms around her.

Fern gently shrugged her mother off. She straightened her back and looked at me. "You see, Mr. Madison. It's all my fault. I am the reason Henry killed himself."

"Ms. Ortega. I don't think you should believe that." I took out my phone and showed Fern a photo of Quinn Rollins. "Is this one of the men who came to see you?"

She shook her head. "No."

I then pulled up another photo.

"What about him?"

"Yes."

I flicked through to another photo I had on file.

"And him?"

"Yes."

"These are the two men who came here and threatened you?"

"Yes, that's them."

Fern looked surprised. I wasn't.

"Ms. Ortega. You are not responsible for Henry's death. I don't believe that Henry committed suicide. And nor should you. He was murdered. And I think I know exactly who killed him."

The photos I'd shown her were of Nate Reed and Bo Hendricks.

30

With the trial looming fast, Megan and I commandeered the conference room. It was time to take stock of the case. We laid everything out on the huge table. In one corner were photos of all the key players including Chip, Rollins, Scooter, Nate, Bo, plus a photo of a Harley Davidson to represent the Iron Raiders. In the opposite corner, we had the crime scene photos. In between were piles for witness statements, police records, forensics, and exhibit lists.

"I think you should tell him," said Megan, as she neatened all the piles. She'd returned from New Orleans feeling refreshed and ready to hit the ground running. After commenting on her glow, I asked how the wedding went. She described in some detail how wonderful it was, and how particularly sweet Sam had behaved. I immediately imagined that another wedding might be in the air, but kept my mouth shut. I didn't want to jinx her.

I'd followed Megan's New Orleans debrief with an account of my visit to Fern, and how I was sure Henry had been murdered by Bo and Nate on Rollins' order. Megan thought I should take it to Detective Frierson.

"The only reason I'd do that would be if I actually wanted him to laugh in my face. And I'm no masochist. Ed Frierson is not interested in anything that either waters down his line of inquiry or deviates from it."

"That's just wrong."

"Not from Frierson's end. At this stage of the game, he's like a freight train on a track: hard to stop and impossible to change course. I can just see his reaction as I try to explain why I think Henry Tuck was murdered and that it could be linked to the HardShell heist. He'd laugh even harder when I admitted that I had no hard evidence to back my theory. Same with the prosecutor Dale Winter—he's locked and loaded too. He would never deviate from his position on my account. So, no. I'm not feeling up to being their court jester."

We stood at either end, surveying the material.

"Winter may pull a surprise, but I think his strategy will be straightforward. He's got strong evidence, and a compelling story to tell."

I paused for a moment and moved over to the crime scene photos.

"What?" asked Megan upon seeing the expression of my face change.

"Winter's going to tear Chip to shreds. Our case is so feeble by comparison. I mean, look at this."

I picked up the photo of Nate Reed's body, two neat holes in his forehead, his eyes frozen open. While I saw a bad seed who'd basically killed foreign civilians for sport, who'd murdered Henry Tuck, and robbed dispensaries all over the city, the jury would see, with the help of Winter, a man of honor, a brave soldier whose only mistake was to trust his wicked colleague Chip Bowman.

"It's going to be hard to argue against the fact that these two guys died with Chip's bullets in their brains. I can't deny that to the jury. And as much as I might try to make my own story plausible, my fundamental flaw will always be there."

"Your fundamental flaw?"

"That I'll be asking them to believe that an invisible man, a mystery figure, is to blame. Winter just has to show them this," I said waving the photo, "and point to Chip and his gun, and it will make perfect sense. The jurors will join the dots to get a simple, compelling truth."

"They might believe you, Mr. Madison."

"I wouldn't be too sure. They'll see through my story, and what an effort of construction it is. It will come across as a story that's striving to be the truth."

Megan looked worried. "You're not giving up, surely?"

I shook my head. "No, of course not."

"Well, you sound like you've lost before the trial has even started. That's not like you at all."

Megan walked up to me. "You still believe Chip Bowman is innocent, don't you?"

"Yes, of course."

"Then he needs you. And he's lucky to have you. You're not just the only chance he has to get his life back. You're his best chance. Believe me, if Dale Winter is feeling complacent, he's a fool. He knows what he's up against. I expect he's working this case like his life depended on it. Beating him won't be easy. But if anyone can beat him, you can."

"Thanks Megan," I said. "There's so much that I know, so much that I can't prove, so much that I can't take into that courtroom, I feel like I'll be fighting with one hand tied behind my back."

"Then it'll be a fair fight, won't it?" Megan smiled. Then her face displayed a pride in knowing that her words had lifted me.

A loud banging on the conference room glass window broke the moment. I spun my head to the source to see Wes Brenner standing there with a big, knowing grin on his fat face and his eyebrows arched high in delight.

"Sorry to disturb you both," he said in a derisive tone. "I just wanted to drop something by. A gift for my favorite lawyer."

With that, Brenner stepped into the room and tossed a package onto the table. As it landed with a thud, he was already on his way back out.

"I'll let you get back to work," he called out as he walked away, laughing at whatever he'd conjured up in his sordid mind.

I picked up the package. It felt like a book. I tore the envelope open and, sure enough, it was a paperback entitled *How to Save California From Itself*. My eyes ran down to the bottom of the cover to see Brenner's name there.

"I didn't know he'd written a book," I said.

"Maybe it's new."

I turned the cover to check the publication date.

"You're right. It's just come out," I said. I turned another page and saw Brenner had written a dedication in blue ink.

Thanks in advance for your help, Loser.

Wes.

PART II

31

It was late spring when the trial began, but summer was muscling its way in. At 8:15 in the morning, the Downtown temperature was getting toward ninety. But it wasn't the weather that got me hot under the collar, it was the sight and sound of Wes Brenner standing at the entrance of the Criminal Courts Building, spouting his two-cents' worth of bullshit for the assembled media.

I heard him clearly from thirty yards away, ranting about the blight of legal cannabis and what he thought should be done about it.

I felt the strong urge to walk up to him and plant my fist into his face, but I sucked it in, skirted the media scrum and made for the glass entrance doors.

Taking the elevator to the ninth floor, I passed through security, and made my way to courtroom 311.

A few people had arrived before me, including prosecutor Dale Winter and his two assistants. As I reached the defendant's table, Winter was deep in conversation with his team. I assumed he was giving his day's strategy one last run-through.

Winter and I, overseen by Judge Clinton Birch, had completed jury selection the day before. Of the twelve jurors and four alternates chosen, I had no major concerns. You can never feel too presumptuous about the sympathies of any given jury, but on balance I had no misgivings. My overriding sentiment was that the verdict would ultimately reflect my performance. I either managed to counter Dale Winter's villainous portrayal of Chip Bowman or I didn't.

Over the next few minutes, the courtroom began to fill and soon, right on nine o'clock, Judge Birch took his seat on the bench.

If trial lawyers had a similar say over judges as they do jurors, I'd have struck Judge Birch from contention without hesitation. As much as judges must base their decisions on law, their leanings show. And Judge Birch, a tall rake of a man just a few years off retirement, had shown himself to be a willing combatant in the War on Drugs. Other than that, he was just about impossible to read. His eyes, underscored by puffy bags, were often kept hooded, so he usually appeared bored or immune to your argument.

Judge Birch asked the bailiff to bring the jury in, and once they were settled, he turned to Winter.

"Mr. Winter," he said, and paused for a moment to turn away from the microphone and clear his throat. "Is the State ready to get us started with opening statements?"

"Yes, Your Honor," said Winter, and he got to his feet, pulled his jacket over his belly, and, after a little wrangling, succeeded in buttoning it.

He looked very much at home standing at the lectern. Giving the jury a modest smile, he clasped his hands in front of him and let his arms go slack. His relaxed, reasonable demeanor exuded confidence, no doubt, but it also hinted at his ease of conscience. Without uttering a word, Winter conveyed to the jury that he was on the side of good.

"Ladies and gentlemen, I'd like to start by expressing thanks on behalf of the State of California for taking time out from the important duties of your own lives to serve your fellow citizens. And when it comes to taking care of the members of our community, few things are as important as justice.

"Sure, that's the sort of thing you'd expect to hear from a lawyer, but I actually believe it to the very core of my being. And you, for the duration of this trial, serve as the conscience of all Californians.

"We are here to seek justice for the deaths of two men: Nathaniel—or Nate as his friends knew him—Reed, and Bo Hendricks.

"And I'll tell you from the outset that this is a case of cold-blooded murder and cold-hearted greed. These two men, Nate and Bo, are the victims of a most treacherous, heinous crime. Two brave veterans dedicated to their jobs, gunned down like dogs in the street. Two close friends, whose deaths have brought untold grief to their loved ones, family, and friends.

"Yes, Nate Reed and Bo Hendricks were veterans. They took up a gun and faced the worst of our enemies far from our shores. They put their lives on the line to defend the democracy that we enjoy here in America.

"When they came home, they found honest work as security guards. Sure, there were risks involved in these jobs, but these men felt confident that the dangers were small by comparison to what they'd been through.

"But whatever the risks, they had every right to feel safe amongst their fellow workers.

"Sadly, they were not.

"One day they got dressed, kissed their kids and partners goodbye, and left home for work. They probably said something like, "See you later." But not long afterward, both men were dead.

"Nate Reed and Bo Hendricks transported money and legal cannabis around the state, and someone killed them in order to steal the fortune they guarded.

"The evidence tells us they were shot at close range. It tells us one of them drew his weapon in self-defense, but he was too late.

"How could this happen? How could someone get the better of two armed, battle-hardened vets? How could they approach these men and shoot them at close range? The answer is clear: they were murdered by someone they trusted.

"The bullets that ended the lives of these two men came from the same gun. And that gun belonged to the defendant, Nate and Bo's trusted co-worker.

"Bo Hendricks didn't raise so much as a finger before he was shot. No defensive wounds. No unholstered weapon. He never saw his execution coming.

"Nathaniel, on the other hand, did manage to draw his weapon and fire one round in his defense.

"Where did that bullet land? It ended up in the body of the defendant, Nate and Bo's trusted co-worker. Nate did all he could, as fast as he could, but he didn't stand a chance.

"Three victims were found at the scene of this violent robbery, ladies and gentlemen. But only one survived. Only one survived to tell his version of what happened. And that's the defendant. The sole survivor of this brutal attack.

"He says he had nothing to do with the deaths of Nate Reed and Bo Hendricks.

"But thankfully we don't have to rely on his version of events to know the real story of what happened that fateful night. You will hear the real story as it is told by forensic evidence. A story told clinically and impartially. You will hear a story that tells us who ambushed these two battle-hardened men and how. And this story, the one the evidence tells, does not match what the defendant would have us believe.

"There can only be one truth here, ladies and gentlemen, and it lies in the power of facts and evidence.

"As this trial proceeds, I urge you to keep justice front and center in your minds. I urge you to place logic above sentiment, to commit yourselves to distinguishing fact from fiction. Because that's what you must do. You must set aside all appeals to your emotions, all desperate attempts to counter what we know to be true. You must listen to the truth of evidence and find the defendant guilty as charged. Thank you."

Looking quite satisfied, Winter returned to the prosecution table. His team members, who'd lapped up his every word and marveled at his every gesture, received him with silent but vigorous nods of approval.

"Defense, Mr. Madison?" asked Judge Birch in his deep, dry voice.

"Thank you, Your Honor," I said, already stepping over to the lectern. I then turned to the jury.

"Ladies and gentlemen, as with my colleague, Mr. Winter, I too would like to thank you for fulfilling a vital role in our justice system.

"But why are you here? What is your purpose? If everything is as Mr. Winter claims, this trial is a complete waste of time. You are here because Mr. Winter and I see things very differently. By that I mean the parties we represent are completely at odds over what happened that terrible night.

"In the wake of a terrible crime, there were three victims who were shot. But why is one of them, the only one who survived, now the accused?

"He's on trial here today because the police and Mr. Winter have settled on one theory about how this crime went down, and they have stuck to that theory with the tenacity of a pit bull.

"You, ladies and gentlemen, are under no such obligation to absorb their theory. I urge you to consider this case to be open, to consider that we have here an innocent man, a victim of the very crime he is accused of committing. And I urge you to consider that whoever killed those men and stole the property they and my client were protecting, is still at large.

"Taking Mr. Winter's cue, I'll remind you that, just like Bo Hendricks and Nathaniel Reed, Chip Bowman is a war veteran. He's a man of honor, a hero who risked his life to protect people like you and me. Like Nathaniel Reed and Bo Hendricks, Chip too took a job with HardShell because it fit his skill set, it paid well, and it came with an element of risk— something that appeals to a lot of vets.

"And like Bo and Nathaniel, Chip left home that day not knowing how dreadfully momentous it would become. He kissed his two daughters—Tracy, age four, and Hannah, age two—goodbye. He kissed his wife Carrie. And he went to do his job, only to find himself thrown into a complete nightmare.

"His day's work would end with him lying unconscious with a bullet in his leg. And from the moment he awoke under the care of a paramedic, Chip Bowman has not only had to cope with the death of his two colleagues, he's had to live with the hell of being blamed for their murder.

"Now, I need to stress that it's not up to me to prove that Chip Bowman is innocent of all charges. It's up to the prosecution to prove to you beyond all reasonable doubt that Chip is guilty. In the end, you'll have to weigh all the evidence shown to you, all the arguments put to you, and ask yourselves: does this stack up? Does this make sense? Really? Did Chip Bowman, a hero soldier, a loving father, a devoted husband, decide to risk everything to steal the treasure he was tasked with protecting?

"Where's the payoff? Where's the sense? I'd argue that there is none. There is no reason for Chip Bowman to take such an absurd risk and throw his life away. That's the prospect he now faces: a life in which he cannot kiss his beloved girls goodnight.

"I will be holding the prosecution to account. I will scrutinize every piece of evidence they present to you because justice is not about convenience, it's about truth. I say to you again: whoever killed those two men is not in this courtroom.

"Chip Bowman should not be on trial. It is only fair, right, and just that you acquit him so that he can return to the loving arms of his family."

32

The first witness Winter called to the stand was a man named Irving Kovel, a mid-thirties hipster who sported a back-and-sides buzzcut, a slicked-back thatch up top, and about half a foot of pampered beard hanging off his chin. He described himself as a coffee entrepreneur. Kovel said he was collecting beans from the storage unit he leased on Boyd Street, right near where it intersects with Mission Street. He was loading a bag into his trunk when shots rang out. In no doubt as to what he'd heard, Kovel called 911 immediately.

With the basics established, Winter started in on the particulars. "Mr. Kovel, how well do you remember those gunshots?"

"They're etched in my brain," said Kovel. "It's like I can just hear them at will. I can replay the exact sound in an instant."

"I see. How many shots did you hear?"

"I heard five shots."

"Are you absolutely sure?"

"Like I said, it's burned in my brain. There were five. Not one more. Not one less. I can replay exactly how they were spaced out."

"Is that so?" asked Winter, like he'd never suggested to Kovel pre-trial that it was exactly the kind of thing the jury should hear.

Kovel shifted in his seat and straightened his back. His eyes were wide with the earnest will to oblige. "Well, the first two were close together. Like this... Bam. Bam."

Kovel smacked his hand down twice on the rail of the witness stand, the beats less than a second apart.

"Then there was a break of about two seconds. Then bam, bam. Another two shots came. But they were spaced out a little further than the first two. Like this."

Again, he slapped his hand twice on the rail. This time the gap was about a second and a half.

"And then?" asked Winter.

"There was nothing for five seconds before the last shot."

Winter looked fascinated. "What did you think when you heard these noises?" He gestured with his right palm for Kovel to speak.

"I knew exactly what they were. And I knew they weren't far off. I don't mind admitting I was scared."

"That's understandable, Mr. Kovel. What did you do next?"

"I called it in. I rang 911 right away."

"And then what did you do?"

"I walked down the street a little to my car. It was closer to where the shots were coming from. And I waited there, crouched beside my car."

"What were you waiting for?"

"I wanted to see if I might be of use to the cops."

"Did you hear anything else?"

"No."

"Could you see the crime scene from your position?"

"No. It was around a corner."

"Did you see any other activity in the area?"

"No. The next thing I heard was the sound of sirens approaching. It was coming up to ten minutes after I'd placed the call."

"You heard the police sirens approaching?"

"Yes. That's when I got in my car and drove slowly toward the corner to see if I could see anything."

"What did you see?"

"I came up to this lot, and there was a van parked there with its rear doors open. And then I saw three bodies lying on the ground."

Kovel ran his hand over his mouth and down his beard, unsettled by the memory of that night.

"I see," said Winter. "Other than those three bodies on the ground, did you see anyone else in the vicinity?"

"No, not a soul."

"Mr. Kovel, did you hear or see anyone leave the vicinity after you heard those gunshots?"

"No."

"Did you hear or see a vehicle leave the vicinity?"

"No, I did not."

"So, if someone left the crime scene during those ten minutes at that time, they did so very cautiously."

"Objection," I called. "Calls for speculation."

"Sustained," said Judge Birch.

"I'll rephrase," said Winter without missing a beat. "Mr. Kovel. Did you hear the sound of screeching tires or revving engines?"

"No, I did not."

"Did you hear any shouting?"

"No, I did not. It was eerie how quiet it was."

"When you got to the crime scene what did you see?"

"I parked my car on the street and walked into the lot," said Kovel. "I saw one of the guys move his leg. He didn't get up or lift his head or anything. His leg just twitched."

"Was that man you describe the defendant?"

"Yes."

"Okay. What happened next?"

"A police car arrived."

"What did you do?"

"I approached their car but they drew their guns and told me to raise my hands. I said I was the one who placed the call. They approached me and made sure I wasn't armed. One of them checked my ID then asked me to wait. Then they went and checked the lot."

"Did more police arrive?"

"Yes. But the paramedics were next. Then a bunch of bikers."

"A bunch of bikers??"

"They're members of a motorcycle gang. There were seven of them."

"Do you know what gang they belonged to, Mr. Kovel?"

Kovel looked very uncomfortable, as anyone would.

"They were Iron Raiders, I believe."

"And what did they do?"

"They all got off their bikes, and three walked over to where the paramedics were at."

"How would you describe their demeanor?"

"They looked concerned. Pissed off." Kovel cast a quick apologetic glance at Judge Birch for having cursed in court.

"What did they do?" asked Winter.

"They began shouting at the guy on the ground."

"The defendant?"

"Yes."

"What were they saying?"

"They were saying... Well, they were cursing. They were asking him what happened. They were asking him where their money was."

"To be clear, these questions were directed at the defendant, were they?"

"Yes. Then the cops stepped in and told them to step back."

"What did the bikers do then?"

"They called out that if their stuff was gone, that he was in trouble."

"Mr. Kovel, can I ask you to repeat word-for-word what the bikers said?"

Kovel again glanced at Judge Birch who nodded his permission.

"They said, 'If our shit's gone, you're dead, motherfucker.'"

"So, they were blaming the defendant for the robbery?"

"Objection," I called out. "Leading the witness. And hearsay."

"Sustained," said Judge Birch.

Winters didn't seem to mind. He knew the court reporter would wipe his question from the record, but what no one could change was that the jury heard it, and that it was sure to stick in their minds.

"No further questions, Your Honor."

"Your witness, Mr. Madison," said Judge Birch as Winter returned to the prosecution table and I got to my feet. My first order of business was to rip out the seed that Winter had placed in the jurors' minds.

"Mr. Kovel, I'd like you to clarify something. At any stage, did you hear anyone at the crime scene accuse the defendant Mr. Bowman of being involved in this fatal robbery?"

"No."

"More specifically, did you hear the bikers directly accuse Mr. Bowman of robbery?"

"No. They thought he had messed up."

"Objection," cried Winter. "Speculation."

"Sustained," said Judge Birch. "Mr. Kovel, you must restrict your answers to the factual. What you think someone may have intended is speculation, which is why I've sustained Mr. Winter's objection. Do you understand?"

"Yes, Your Honor," replied Kovel.

"Did the bikers say anything else to the defendant?"

"Yes. As they walked away, they called him stupid and useless. Not to mention motherfucker."

"Nothing further, Your Honor."

33

Detective Ed Frierson walked to the stand with almost a skip in his step, like he was coming upstage to receive an award. There was always an energy about him; a sprightly man trapped in a heavy man's body. He took the oath and then adjusted the microphone to his liking. He fixed his gaze on Winter and waited with confident ease. It was like he'd called us all here, and that he was only too happy for Winter to kick things off.

Winter spent a few questions establishing Frierson's credentials. Then he moved on to the case at hand.

"Detective Frierson, when did you arrive at the crime scene?"

"We got the call right after the first squad car arrived. I was off duty and at home at the time. I wasn't Downtown, so I ended up getting there about an hour after the first squad car."

"Please describe the scene for the court."

"There was an unmarked black van with its rear doors wide open. Both driver and passenger doors were closed, as was the side door. About ten feet in front of the van, there were three men down. Two dead and the third being treated for a gunshot wound to the upper right thigh."

"Did you question the defendant at the scene?"

"Yes. Briefly. I asked him what happened, and he said he did not know. He said he couldn't remember anything."

"What else did you ask him?"

"I asked him what was in the van."

"What did he say?"

"Cash and legal cannabis. That was about it."

"Did he ask you anything?"

"No."

"Did he ask if the money and cannabis were still there?"

"No. And I didn't think I needed to tell him the van had been cleaned out. I think he'd figured that out."

"Detective, did you inspect the bodies of the dead men?"

"Yes. Both of them were shot twice in the head."

"Detective, what was your early take on what had happened?"

"It seemed all three guards had been shot by bandits who'd cleaned out the van and fled. But once we started the investigation proper, the evidence began to tell us that we were off track."

"I see. Did you have any suspects?"

"Not right off the bat."

"Did you have any clues about who might be responsible?"

"Yes. Over the past fourteen months, there have been many robberies targeting the cannabis industry. Most were dispensaries but other vans have been hit. But a few growers who'd opted to transport their money and cannabis themselves were robbed too."

"These crimes were carried out by armed men?"

"Yes, but there were also ram raids. You know, when no one is in the store late at night. Three dispensaries were robbed in this manner."

"Were you investigating these crimes?"

"Yes. I was trying to see if they were related."

"And were they?"

"I can't say right now because it's still an active investigation."

"But you can say that the armed robbery of a van containing cash and cannabis was part of a broader investigation?"

"Yes. Another security team was robbed at gunpoint a month before this case but, as I said, I'm not at liberty to discuss the nature or findings of an ongoing investigation."

"I understand. Was anyone killed in those cannabis crimes you mentioned?"

"No. This was the first fatal cannabis robbery I've come across."

"Did you have a suspect?"

"Yes. From very early in the investigation, the defendant was a person of interest."

"When did the defendant become a suspect?"

"When it became clear that it was an inside job."

"How did you reach that conclusion?"

"The owner of the company told us no one other than staff members and clients knew where this van was."

"No one?"

"That's right. Whoever committed this crime knew exactly what they stood to gain. It wasn't random or opportunistic. No one would confront three armed guards and be prepared to shoot them if they were just taking a chance on the reward."

"Are you saying that the perpetrators of this crime were prepared to do whatever it took to get their hands on the contents of the van?"

"Yes."

"But the defendant was shot. How could he be one of the perpetrators?"

"As soon as I looked at the two dead guards, I knew they were the victims of a fragging attack, in that they were killed by someone on their own side."

"Could you please explain your reasoning, Detective Frierson?"

"These guys weren't jumped by a bunch of armed robbers. They didn't die in a shootout. They weren't caught in crossfire."

This was Winter's cue to bring the crime scene photos up on the monitor. The first screen showed close-ups of Nate Reed and Bo Hendricks. Both staring open-eyed into the night sky, both with two dark red entry wounds—Reed in the forehead and right cheek; Hendricks in the forehead.

"The victim on the right of the screen is Bo Hendricks," said Frierson. "He never drew his weapon." Winter flicked to a photo that illustrated Frierson's point. "See there. His gun's holstered. Reed, on the other hand, did manage to get his weapon out and he fired one shot."

"What do these facts tell us, Detective Frierson?"

"These men were executed at close range by someone they knew. It was like one moment they were just standing around chewing the fat and then bam, bam, bam, bam. Down they go."

"What evidence do you have that the defendant was the culprit?"

"Okay so we know the killer knew the victims. He was able to approach them without causing any alarm whatsoever. And the gun used to kill Nate Reed and Bo Hendricks belonged to the defendant."

"I see.

"Why would the defendant commit such a treacherous act?"

"The obvious motive is greed."

"Do you have evidence the defendant had such a motive?"

"Yes, we do. A couple of telling facts came to light as we pursued our investigation. The first was that the defendant had recently been part of a failed business venture. He'd lost just over half a million dollars in this scheme."

"Does that make him willing to commit this robbery?"

"No, on its own it doesn't, but he had spoken openly with his co-workers about his financial struggles. He told them that he wanted to get rich as fast as he could."

"Has the money and the legal cannabis from this robbery been retrieved?"

"No. But in the process of our investigation we discovered the defendant received a suspicious payment of five-hundred thousand dollars. It was placed into an account that he thought was secret. And it is not possible to determine the source of that money."

"There's no way to find out where that large deposit came from?"

"No."

"And the defendant has provided no explanation for that money?"

"No."

"How long after the robbery did this money enter his account?"

"Five days."

"You say it was a secret account. How did you find out about it?"

"The company the defendant worked for—HardShell—cooperated with the investigation. They gave us access to every file relating to the defendant. We then got a warrant to pursue some of this information ourselves and we discovered his digital currency account."

Winter scratched his chin. "But hang on, detective. The defendant was shot too."

"Forensics can explain it to you, but it's not clear what happened."

"I don't understand. Where did the bullet in the defendant's leg come from?"

"The bullet matches the weapon of Nate Reed."

"But doesn't that mean that Nate Reed reacted to the attack, shot at the defendant, and hit him in the leg?"

"Yes, that's one possibility."

"Are there others?"

"Well, yes. It's equally possible that the defendant took Nate Reed's gun and shot himself in the leg to enable him to play victim."

"Are you saying it is possibly a self-inflicted wound?"

The court gasped.

"While his partners in crime made off with the money?"

"We believe he and his fellow perpetrators thought this would cast the defendant as a victim and hence avoid suspicion, and that the case would be almost impossible to solve."

"The perfect crime?"

"The perfect crime."

"I have nothing further for the witness, Your Honor."

"Mr. Madison?" asked Judge Birch.

"Yes, Your Honor. Of course," I said and made my way to the lectern.

"Detective Frierson, can you prove that that money in my client's account was linked to the robbery?"

"Not exactly."

"That's a no then?"

"Yes, it's a no."

"So, it's purely your theory that this money was his share of the loot, isn't that right?"

"He couldn't tell us where it came from."

"But as you said, the source was untraceable. It's possible that he himself doesn't know where that money came from?"

"That's ludicrous."

"No, it's not. You said it yourself, the source of that money is untraceable. Isn't that right?"

Frierson huffed. "Yes."

"The way you tell it, my client planned an audacious, cold-blooded crime in which he killed two of his co-workers, shot himself in the leg, and let someone else run off with the money. Are you convinced that there can be no other explanation?"

"Yes. It was an inside job. He had help planning that robbery but only he got caught."

"And your theory is that he shot himself to fool the authorities?"

"Yes. If he'd just run off, all the suspicion would have fallen on him immediately. We allege he volunteered to be a victim precisely to avoid suspicion."

"Detective Frierson. Is it possible that my client was framed?"

"That's most unlikely."

"I didn't ask you if it was unlikely. I asked if it was possible."

"Yes. It's a possibility."

I was happy to have that minor concession from Frierson, so I moved on.

"Detective Frierson, you told the court earlier that there had been a spate of robberies targeting cannabis retailers, growers, and security transport services, right?"

"Yes, that's right."

"And you were involved in investigating those crimes, were you?"

"Yes. Still am. We have three detectives working on those cases."

"Detective, were any of these robberies carried out with the sort of military precision as the crime my client is accused of?"

Frierson shrugged his shoulders and looked non-plussed. "What do you mean?"

"I mean is it your belief that any of these other crimes your team is investigating were carried out by military veterans?"

"I can't possibly say, these matters are still in the process of investigation."

"You Honor," I said, appealing to Judge Birch.

Birch looked down at Frierson. "Detective Frierson, you cannot tell me that answering Mr. Madison's question will compromise your investigation."

That was exactly what Frierson had wanted the court to believe. "We do think it's possible that vets may have been involved in some of the cases we are looking at."

"Right," I said. "Detective Frierson, were Nate Reed and/or Bo Hendricks persons of interest in any crime you're investigating?"

I heard murmuring behind me. I was not surprised that my line of questioning would be taken as me smearing the memory of two vets whose murder we were seeking justice for in this court, and whose grief-stricken families were present.

Frierson could not hide his annoyance. He tried to head off Judge Birch. "You Honor, I don't think that question is appropriate or relevant, and to supply Mr. Madison with an answer would compromise our ongoing investigations."

Birch placed his elbows on the bench and leaned a little more Frierson's way. "Detective Frierson," he said. "I understand that there are sensitivities to be considered here. But Mr. Madison's questions are not for you to sanction. And I cannot see how providing Mr. Madison with an answer would spoil your chances of advancing your investigations of Nathaniel Reed and Bo Hendricks. With due respect to their families, these men are dead, Mr. Frierson. Please answer the question."

Frierson arched his neck and held me with a hot glare. "Yes, they were persons of interest."

"Are you telling the court that both Nate Reed and Bo Hendricks were persons of interest in the armed robbery of cannabis-related businesses?"

"Yes."

"So at some point you suspected that these two men had committed similar crimes?"

"That's what persons of interest means, Mr. Madison."

"Thank you for clarifying. One last question, Detective Frierson. Was Chip Bowman ever a suspect in any of these crimes your team is investigating."

Frierson stared at me, grinding his jaw. He then shook his head. "No."

"I have no more questions for the witness, Your Honor."

34

Dale Winter's next witness was forensics officer Christopher Gemmell, a thin, unassuming man who wore dark pants, a gray jacket, and yellow tie. As he took his seat, I saw he kept two pens and a small notebook in his shirt pocket. His brown hair fell down at the front to form a thick fringe, and he peered out across the courtroom with an alert expression of curiosity.

Winter established Gemmell's credentials as a ballistics expert who moved into crime scene investigation three years after graduating as an LAPD officer. He invited Gemmell to regale the jury with accounts of the more notable crimes that his work in the Firearms Analysis Unit had helped solve. I felt that Winter lost a little ground with the jury here because Gemmell spoke in a droning monotone that clearly stupefied some jurors and irritated others. I counted four yawns and three watch checks as he spoke.

"Officer Gemmell," Winter began. "Could you please tell us the key pieces of evidence found at the crime scene, and what they revealed?"

"Certainly," Gemmell replied. "In short, the evidence tells us it was a double murder by fragging. The two dead men were caught completely unaware by their assailant. They were shot from the front, not behind. No one snuck up on them. So they saw their killer, and they were comfortable in his presence, that is, until the lethal weapon was drawn."

"Officer Gemmell, does the evidence tell us who killed these men?"

"Yes, it does. The killer was the defendant, Mr. Bowman."

"How did you reach that conclusion?"

"First, the ballistics tests we conducted on the bullets and the casings were conclusive. The bullets that killed the two victims came from the defendant's weapon. Not only that, there were no other fingerprints on his weapon besides his own."

"No one else took the defendant's weapon and used it to kill the victims?"

"No. Also, the police who attended the scene first reported that the defendant was found with his gun by his hand."

"Is that so?"

"Yes, and our tests found gunshot residue on his right hand, which we have ascertained to be his shooting hand."

"I see. Is there any other evidence that supports your conclusion?"

"Yes. We studied the positions of the victims and could see where they were standing in relation to each other when the shooting started. Bo Hendricks, who was standing nearest the shooter, would have died instantly. As you have heard, Nathaniel Reed drew his weapon, so we must conclude the lethal weapon was now trained on him. He did fire his own weapon but he was hit in the forehead by a bullet that, like Mr. Hendricks, would have killed him instantly."

"That's three shots," said Winter.

"Yes, the last two were to finish the victims off. But, as I said, they would most likely have been dead by then already."

"Where did he shoot them?"

"In the head."

"No further questions, Your Honor."

Gemmell took a sip of water as I readied to put my first question to him.

"Officer Gemmell, you've told the court that the ballistics evidence supports the conclusion that the defendant shot both victims, haven't you?"

"Ah, yes. That's correct."

"And that's the only conclusion you can draw, is that right?"

"The evidence points to that conclusion emphatically."

"Okay, but your ballistics analysis cannot be taken in isolation to draw a conclusion about what happened that night, can it?"

"No, it is one part of forensics analysis. But when the other scientific analysis was taken into account, my conclusion was all the stronger."

"I see," I said. I picked up a piece of paper, held it up and addressed Judge Birch. "Permission to approach the witness, Your Honor?"

"Granted," said Judge Birch.

I walked up to the stand and handed Gemmell the document.

"Officer Gemmell, do you agree that what you are holding is the medical report conducted on Chip Bowman when he was admitted to the hospital on the night of the crime?"

"Yes."

"What does it say about Chip Bowman's injuries?"

"It says he has a gunshot wound in his right thigh, and a subdural hematoma on the back of his head."

"Thank you, Officer Gemmell. Now that medical record makes note of the fact that the paramedics found Chip Bowman unconscious, doesn't it?"

Gemmell ran his eyes over the text and in time nodded. "Yes, it does?"

"And it suggests the subdural hematoma is the reason why he was unconscious, doesn't it?"

"Yes."

"Does the medical record state which injury Chip Bowman suffered first, the blow to the back of the head or the gunshot wound?"

"No, it does not."

"Officer Gemmell, can you conclusively determine whether Chip Bowman was shot first or passed out first?"

"It stands to reason that he was shot, fell down, and knocked his head."

"With all due respect, that is pure speculation on your part."

"No, it's—"

"Isn't it just as possible that the defendant was shot while he was lying unconscious on the ground?"

"Yes, but it is a fanciful notion. You do know that we found gunshot residue on his hand? Did he shoot those men in his sleep?"

Gemmell was giving me a smartass check-mate kind of smile.

"I thought you might say that, Officer Gemmell. How long does gunshot residue last if left undisturbed?"

"A long time," Gemmell answered, somewhat reluctantly, the air of triumph seeping away.

"A long time? How about forever?"

"Well—"

"You don't have to answer that. As you know Chip Bowman was a security guard in a high-risk field. Your Honor, I'd like to enter the terms of Chip Bowman's employment at HardShell."

Judge Birch looked at Winter as he read over the copy I handed to him.

"Mr. Winter. Any objections?"

Winter shook his head. The document appeared harmless, but he knew that I would push to get it submitted and would likely succeed, and he chose not to fight this battle.

"Permission to approach the witness, Your Honor?"

"Granted."

I handed Gemmell the contract.

"Officer Gemmell, as you can see, under the terms of his HardShell contract, Chip Bowman was required to spend two hours a week at the firing range to keep his shooting skills sharp. You can see that, can't you?"

"Yes."

"So my question is this. Could the gunshot residue you found on Chip Bowman's hand have gotten there days earlier, if not weeks?"

Gemmell's mouth flatlined grimly. "It's possible."

"Right, so the gunshot residue you found on the defendant's hand actually tells us nothing whatsoever of value, does it?"

Gemmell stammered. "You should not dismiss—"

"Gunshot residue, or GSR, is very easy to transfer, isn't it, Officer Gemmell?"

"Yes, it is."

"So if I had GSR on my hand I could easily transfer it onto yours, isn't that right?"

"Um, yes."

"So it's possible too that the GSR on Chip Bowman's hand was planted there?"

"It's very unlikely."

"I'm not asking if it's unlikely. I'm asking if it's possible."

"Yes, it's possible," said Gemmell through gritted teeth.

"One last question. Does the GSR you found tell us for certain that it was Chip Bowman who used his gun against his co-workers with his firearm?"

"Like I said, there is other evidence."

"I'm not talking about other evidence. There is no ironclad proof that Chip Bowman fired his weapon that night, is there?"

"Yes. There is. The ballistics tests."

"They are one-hundred percent conclusive, are they? There is no room whatsoever for doubt in your conclusions, is that right?"

"Of course, there's room for some doubt but it's negligible."

"You may deem it to be negligible, Officer Gemmell. Your life is not on the line here. But my client and I see things very differently. Is it possible that Chip Bowman did not fire his weapon that night?"

Gemmell breathed in deeply. His chest sagged as he exhaled. "Yes, it's possible."

"Thank you, Officer Gemmell."

35

I had the evening to revise how I'd go about cross-examining the next witness. Winter was calling Quinn Rollins, and I aimed to use him to expose his company for what it was: a modern-day pirate ship of cut-throats. The risk was that I'd be tarring Chip with the same brush. I felt confident that I had seeded doubt into the collective mind of the jury, but I needed to find a way to show that Chip was the black sheep in a white flock gone bad.

I hadn't spoken to Rollins in a long time, not since he'd authorized my visit to HardShell. Since then, he'd made no effort to contact me, so I figured I was right in thinking his initial offer to help me was just a way to keep tabs on Chip.

I had managed to keep tabs on Rollins, however. I'd kept in contact with Cliff Loda, who remained my helpful if nervous insider at HardShell. He'd reported that ever since the fatal robbery, Rollins had practically been working around the clock. He'd met with all his clients and persuaded most to stay. He was micromanaging to such a degree that he sometimes manned the vans himself. He'd upped the internal monitoring, and he'd become intolerant of any mistakes. He'd fired half a dozen staff members for indiscretions he claimed were breaches of trust. Cliff assured me he knew of no illegal activity but to my mind Rollins sounded like a Scarface figure, a man who was an utter slave to his own manic ambition.

Every time I spoke with Cliff, I touched on the fact that I wanted him as a witness. I never pushed it because I knew he was terrified about the prospect of testifying.

He'd told me Rollins had made it clear to all staff that Chip was the enemy and that anyone who did anything to help him would be shown the door. Cliff believed if he testified, Rollins wouldn't hesitate to have him killed.

Someone else I stayed in touch with was Jack, of course. He'd long since recovered from his injury, and I'd managed to get Chanel's permission for him to do some low-risk work—he didn't have to leave the house. I wanted Jack to dig deep on Reed and Hendricks in their time at Fortis, the private security company. I wanted details on their apparently hasty departure from Iraq.

I sent Megan home from the office at seven, feeling I was as well prepared for my cross of Rollins as I could be. I never believed you could plan everything in advance. A cross-examination is a fluid interaction. No matter what strategy I took in, I had to be prepared to be responsive.

I made my way home around nine, and was disturbed to find Ace and two lesser Iron Raiders waiting for me outside my apartment building. They'd ridden their bikes up on the pavement and had remained in their saddles. Upon seeing me, Ace dismounted.

"You could have called, Ace. Not that I'm unhappy to see you."

My attempt at disarming humor fell flat.

"Where the fuck have you been, lawyer?" demanded Ace. "And what the fuck have you been doing?"

"What are you talking about?"

"We had a deal. Remember? You said you were going to get Sonny out."

"It's in the works, Ace. It's going to take some time."

"Bullshit. Sonny says he doesn't know what the fuck's going on."

"He said that?"

I was more than a little peeved but I wasn't surprised. I'd visited Sonny in prison soon after I saw Ace—well, about a week after Jack and I got shot at in Toro Canyon. I'd explained to Sonny that I'd examined his case and that his useless defense attorney had screwed up. First, he failed to object when the prosecution produced harmful inadmissible evidence. Second, he failed to investigate the case satisfactorily, which meant he missed out on finding a key defense witness. A week later I filed an appeal under California Penal Code Section 1237 with twelve days left on the sixty-day clock.

"I explained to Sonny what was going on. I did it face to face. I've filed for appeal"

"When did you see him?"

"Months ago."

Ace frowned. "And yet he's still inside."

"These things take time. All the briefs have been filed. I'm just waiting on a date for oral arguments."

"Oral arguments?"

"It's when I argue the appeal before a judge. The prosecution does the same, then the judge makes a call."

"When's that going to happen?"

"It usually takes a year. Sixteen months tops. Again, I explained this to Sonny."

Ace nodded. "Well, his memory's always been pretty shit."

"Seriously, there's nothing I can do."

"Get your phone out and take this down."

I did so and Ace gave me a number. He then motioned to his friends that it was time to go. "Call me as soon as that date is set."

"Will do," I said, adding Ace to my contact list.

I went up to my apartment, pulled open the fridge, and took out a beer. As I took a swig, I considered how much I'd love to get out of LA for a while. The thought soon led to my mind wandering off to a better place. Sunny weather. Bright sand. Blue water. Great surf.

Then and there, I resolved to make that daydream happen.

I went over to my dining table, took out my laptop and checked Bella's school term dates. I checked out some accommodation at one of my favorite getaways: Hawaii. Then I texted Bella.

"Hey sweetheart. How does surfing in Hawaii for a week in August sound? Just you and me. Unless Mom's got something planned? But maybe it's the worst idea in the world."

Of course, I was kidding. Bella loves surfing, loves the beach, and she has told me once or twice that she loves me.

Less than a minute later, my phone pinged.

"Are you kidding??? That would be AMAZING! Yes, yes, and yes!!! Mom's cool with it."

"Fantastic. Booking now."

"YESS! Thank you daddy xxx"

Within a minute, I'd booked an ocean view suite at Turtle Bay. Now I had something special to look forward to once this trial was over: a week away with my favorite girl in the world. I looked at the photos on the website and let my mind wander to a stunning place far from LA.

I was a happy man.

36

Quinn Rollins looked like a man running on adrenaline, or some artificial stimulant; cold and composed yet wired at the same time. Immaculately dressed in a gray tailored suit and blue silk tie, he was calm in his movements but there was a manic intensity to his gaze. Staring out across the courtroom from the witness stand, he bored right through everything his eyes fell upon.

I wished it was him that was on trial, that I'd unearthed evidence to expose his duplicity, to lay bare the fact that this seemingly successful, if troubled, entrepreneur was in fact a drug trafficker. He was not the one on trial, but discrediting him was key to my strategy.

I caught Rollins' eye for a second or two and I offered no greeting. He stared at me as though I was an unfamiliar object. His gaze then fell on Chip and his face turned sour. It was clear who he blamed for his unwelcome burdens.

The movement of Winter to the lectern broke Rollins' attention away from Chip.

I knew what to expect from Quinn and I was ready. Or so I thought.

"Mr. Rollins," Winter began. "Could you please explain your business, HardShell, for the court?"

"Certainly. We are a security firm manned by professionals, most of whom are military veterans. We offer a specialized service for businesses in the cannabis economy. Because of a non-alignment between state and federal cannabis law, the businesses involved face a rather unique problem. Most banks won't accept their money, because in the eyes of federal authorities they'd be handling the proceeds of an illegal substance. So there's a lot of unsecured cash that we offer to transport and store in our compounds, which are as safe as banks. Then we help our clients get their money into credit unions, and then into electronic funds and digital currency."

"What was the job assigned to Nathaniel Reed, Bo Hendricks, and the defendant Chip Bowman the night of the crime?"

"They'd made a run from Humboldt County to Los Angeles. It was a four-day job. They drove up to Humboldt, collected over a million dollars' worth of legally grown cannabis, and some cash that needed to be transferred."

"Is your business successful, Mr. Rollins?"

"Very much so. It's the biggest cannabis security company in California, which makes it the biggest in the world. No one else comes close."

It seemed Rollins couldn't help having a dig at his rival David McClean, even though his rival wasn't in the courtroom.

"I guess the night your company was robbed changed all that."

"Yes, it did. It was a horrible, tragic event for the families of Nate and Bo. But it made life very difficult for me and the rest of my staff."

"Did you know Nate Reed and Bo Hendricks well?"

"Yes. Very well. Both of them have worked for me for the better part of ten years. They were part of my team in Iraq when all three of us worked for Fortis."

"What's Fortis?"

"It's a private security contactor. It's a very large organization hired by the US Government to perform various tasks in conflict zones. Anything from bodyguarding politicians to training Iraqi police."

"What kind of men were Nate and Bo?"

"They were the tough, loyal, and brave kind. I had a lot of respect for them. That's why I hired them in Iraq and back home. They were two of my best men."

"Do you believe the robbery which cost them their lives was an inside job?"

"Yes, I do. It had to be. Only the personnel involved in the job knew the details of what they were assigned. Part of our security protocol is to restrict, or compartmentalize, the specific information about where a team is going and what they are tasked to do."

"Who knows?"

"Well, there's me. There's our chief financial officer Scott Slovak, and there's the men rostered on."

"No one else?"

"The clients whose assets we are shipping are kept in the loop."

"I see. How does that work?"

"We provide our clients with a tracking service, an app, that lets them monitor where their assets are."

"Like tracking a FedEx package?"

"Exactly, but it's not real time. We put a delay on that information, for the mutual security of all clients. They have our schedule and they know within thirty minutes whether their goods have reached point A, point B, and so on."

"Before this crime, had HardShell been robbed before?"

"No, never."

"Why do you believe it was an inside job?"

"Well, like I said, very few people know the exact, real-time whereabouts of our teams. For one, the attack took place in a new compound that had no security cameras in place yet. Then as you have heard, Nate and Dan were shot like sitting ducks. These guys are highly experienced soldiers with combat experience. Detecting even a hint of danger is a sixth sense to them. There's no way an armed stranger could have gotten anywhere near them."

Rollins then turned and looked at Chip. "Whoever shot them was someone who had their deep trust, the kind of trust they depend on when fighting shoulder-to-shoulder on the front line. They never knew what hit them."

I had to hand it to Rollins, for a man who headed what was, at least in part, a criminal enterprise, a man who quite possibly planned this whole robbery for his own gain, he did a damned fine job of playing the victim scorned.

"What about Chip Bowman?"

"What about him?" Rollins was staring back at Winter now.

"What kind of an employee was he?"

"I didn't know Chip before he started at HardShell. He was recommended to me by one of my most trusted employees,

Scott Slovak. I interviewed him before hiring him and he seemed like a good man, and he proved to be a solid worker."

"Was he loyal?"

"Yes. At least he seemed to be. And he showed promise and was good with people, so I gave him a leadership role and had him on client liaison. When he was on runs, he was in charge. He'd be contacting clients ahead of time, making the arrangements for pick-ups. He'd also boost our business by selling our financial services."

"Did he earn good money?"

"Very good money. And he got commission for any finance package he sold."

"I see. So you trusted him?"

"Yes. I came to trust him implicitly."

"Did anything about Chip make you reconsider the wisdom of hiring him?"

"No. If I did have, he'd have been out the door pronto."

"But you do believe that he has betrayed you?"

"Yes, I do, in the most egregious manner possible. I don't want to believe he committed this crime, I hate to believe it, but I live in the real world. I'm a realist. I need to be, particularly in my line of work."

"But did you ever doubt his ability?"

"Well, I did suspect he was unstable at one point."

"Unstable, how do you mean?"

"Well, I heard from some of the men that—"

"Objection," I called out. "Hearsay."

"Sustained," said Judge Birch. "Please stick to things that you know to be true, Mr. Rollins."

"Yes, of course, Your Honor. All I mean was that I spoke to Chip about things that got back to me."

I felt Chip shift beside me. "That's a lie," he seethed "Why's he saying that?"

I leaned over to Chip and levelled my voice to a whisper. "Easy, Chip. Just hold it together. I told you this would be tough."

Winter heard me talk, turned to me, and waited for silence. "Can you tell us what was discussed in that conversation?"

"I said it had come to my attention that he was talking loosely about how easy it would be to rob dispensaries."

A muffled stir ran through the gallery behind me.

"Really?"

"Yes. This was after there were two in quick succession. Naturally, the men talked about it—you know, breakroom chatter. I told Chip that it had come to my attention that he'd been suggesting to other members of my staff that they should rob dispensaries."

"Who told you this?"

"Nate Reed and Bo Hendricks."

"The two men he is now accused of killing?"

Chip jostled next to me. "He's lying!" he hissed to me. "That's total bullshit!"

I gave Chip a look that reminded him to cool his jets. *It had better be bullshit, Chip*, I said to myself.

"That's right," continued Rollins. "Now, I could have taken this as pure macho talk, but nonetheless I told Chip he needed to stop talking crap and focus on the job."

"Was this a warning?"

"An informal one; a piece of advice. He knew that if the problem persisted, he was gone. And I've been around enough vets to know that their heads can get a little crazy now and then. A lot of my men would not suit selling cars or waiting tables. They've been shaped by war, mentally and physically. The job I give them—to carry a gun, to guard these valuables with their lives, to work to a tight schedule, to follow plans, and obey orders—is what they're good at. It's their wheelhouse."

"Is there anything else you can tell us about why this was an inside job?"

"Well, the fact is that Nate and Bo were shot by Chip—"

"Objection," I said, getting to my feet. "Speculation."

"Sustained," said Judge Birch. "We are here to ascertain whether or not that is true, Mr. Rollins."

Rollins sighed and sought, with evident frustration, to rephrase his response. "They were shot with Chip's gun. But I believe there was more than one person involved in this robbery."

"You believe he had help?" asked Winter.

"Of course, he did. But no one knows who they are—not the cops, not me. I mean, for all I know some of the culprits are still working for me, the same men who I greet in the morning every day. That said, the cops tell me all their alibis check out."

"Do you have any idea what became of the stolen money and cannabis?"

"No. At least until five-hundred grand turned up in Chip Bowman's account," Rollins fumed.

"Objection," I called. "The witness is once again speculating."

"Sustained," said Judge Birch before ordering the court reporter to strike Rollins' last comment from the record.

Winter raised his palms out in front of his waist and smiled, displaying his contentment of where things were at.

"On that note, Your Honor, I have no more questions for Mr. Rollins."

As Winter spoke those words, my phone buzzed. I picked it up to see a text from Jack.

"Check your email. NOW. You can thank me later."

I only got to read the subject of Jack's email—"Reed and Hendricks"—when I heard Judge Birch's voice.

"Your witness, Mr. Madison...

"Counselor. Would you care to cross-examine the witness?"

I looked up and got to my feet. "My apologies, Your Honor. Some important information has come to hand. Actually, it's urgent. I'd like to request a short recess to digest this information."

Judge Birch shut his eyelids slightly and studied me. I got the point: he only just believed I was genuine. "You've got fifteen minutes, Counselor."

37

We resumed fifteen minutes later, and Judge Birch once more invited me to cross-examine the witness before adding dryly "assuming you're ready."

"Mr. Rollins," I began. "I understand that it has been tough going at HardShell since this terrible event."

"Yes, it has been but spare me your phony sympathy, Mr. Madison."

"I'm not here to indulge you in sympathy, Mr. Rollins. I'm merely trying to establish the fact that since your two employees were killed and your clients' cash and cannabis has disappeared without a trace, it must be hard to convince clients that what you offer is a safe and secure service."

"It was and remains safe and secure. But nothing can be one-hundred percent bulletproof to acts of treachery."

"I understand. Now, as you've already told the court, you hire a particular breed of man. Isn't that right, Mr Rollins?"

"No woman has ever applied for any position in my firm."

"Okay. I mean, HardShell is staffed exclusively by vets, isn't it?"

"Yes."

"They are warriors in your eyes, is that right?"

"Yes."

"*Your* warriors."

"It's not a private army, Mr Madison. It's a security company that operates in a high-risk environment."

"No, it's not a private army but the two victims of this crime served under you at Fortis, a private security firm overseas, didn't they?"

"Yes."

"Objection," called Winter. "Relevance."

"Where's this going, Mr. Madison?" asked Judge Birch.

"Your Honor, Mr. Winter opened the door on the character and caliber of men that Mr. Rollins employs, and it's important for the jury to understand the nature of the workplace Mr. Rollins presides over."

"I'll allow," said Birch. "Continue, Counselor."

"Thank you, Your Honor. Mr. Rollins, you said that Nate Reed and Bo Hendricks were two of your best men, right?"

"Yes."

I held a piece of paper in my hand. It was a bunch of printouts of newspaper articles attached to Jack's email.

"There have been numerous news stories about Fortis, the company you worked for, being the subject of complaints in regard to the conduct of its staff in Iraq. Is that right?"

"What's that got to do with anything?"

"Could you please answer the question?"

"There were things written about Fortis. But it was all just a bunch of fake news."

I waved the papers.

"These so-called fake news stories say that Nathaniel Reed and Bo Hendricks were whisked out of Iraq under a cloud of outrage about their conduct."

"That's not true."

"Which part? Being kicked out or them being guilty of grave misconduct?"

Rollins' face flushed with anger. "I'm not going to sit here and sully the memory of two fine men."

"Were they sent home?"

"No. They were reassigned. That's all. Relocated to Virginia."

"So it had nothing to do with them being accused of executing Iraqi civilians and planting weapons on the bodies so as to cast them as insurgents?"

This was not mentioned in the news articles I held. Jack had sifted through thousands of Wikileaks files leaked from military operations in Iraq. Several references were made to incidents involving Fortis personnel. But Jack dug deeper and through other channels not yet known to me, he'd managed to get hold of two internal Fortis incident reports that implicated Reed and Hendricks in the murder of Iraqi civilians.

Rollins' eyes glared at me but he sat himself back, assuming a more relaxed position for our confrontation. "The enemies over there lie, Mr. Madison. They'll say anything, do anything, to try and weaken us. What you just said is wrong. There were false accusations, and none was ever proven."

"These men were under your direct command in Iraq when those alleged incidents took place, were they not?"

"Yes."

"And as soon as you set up HardShell back home in the States they were the first two men you hired."

"I hired a bunch of men to get the ball rolling and they were part of that first batch."

"Chip Bowman wasn't, though, was he?"

Rollins remained silent, his arms now folded and his eyebrows raised. After a few moments' silence he said, "Oh, was that a question you actually want me to answer?" He scoffed.

I waited.

"Bowman was hired at a later date," he said finally.

"Did he ever come to you to air his concerns about company business?"

"No."

"But he told you he suspected some HardShell personnel were handling illegally-grown cannabis and illicit cash, did he not?"

"Oh that. Yes, I remember. And I thanked him for his concern and encouraged him to tell me if he saw anything untoward."

"But he was not the only person who was concerned HardShell was operating in the black market, was he?"

"I don't know what you mean."

"Mr. Rollins, isn't it true that the silent co-founder of HardShell, Mr. Henry Tuck, shared the same concerns that the company was involved in illegal activity?"

Rollins shook his head.

"No. He never said anything of the sort."

"Your Honor, I'd like to enter this email exchange between Mr. Rollins and Mr. Tuck."

"That was a misunderstanding on Mr. Tuck's part," said Rollins, as I carried copies to Winter and Judge Birch. "There was one employee who was skimming off some cannabis, and I got rid of him."

"But in that email exchange you're holding, Mr. Tuck told you he wanted to pull his money out of your company because he suspected something nefarious was going on. Isn't that right?"

"Yes," Rollins said wearily. "But Henry had no idea what was going on. And his suspicion was non-specific, and unfounded. That's why I dismissed it. I think Henry just wanted his money so he could go lie on a beach with his girlfriend."

"Right. One last question, Mr. Rollins. Was anything stolen from that van that we don't know about?"

"What? No."

"So, there was no illegal cargo being carried in that van?"

"No."

"So why did the Iron Raiders show up so quickly at the crime scene?"

"You'd have to ask them that."

"How much of the stolen assets was theirs?"

"Ten pounds of legal cannabis."

"But they know that they'll be compensated for that, don't they? I mean, once your insurance pays out."

"Yes, all our clients know that insurance will cover the loss of any assets they have entrusted us with."

"And yet they turned up right away. When they got to the scene, as the court has heard, they were very angry. If there was no contraband in that van, why would they be so furious?"

"I have no idea."

"Were they concerned that something else of theirs had gone missing? Something illegal? Something not covered by your insurance?"

Rollins looked at me fit to kill. "I don't know what you're talking about," he said dryly.

"Traces of meth were found on the defendant's hands, Mr. Rollins. How do you explain that?"

"I can't obviously. That's for Chip Bowman to answer."

"Are any of your vans fitted with secret compartments to stash contraband?"

"That's rubbish," he said, turning to the jury with a smile before addressing me again. "No, is my answer."

"So your business was totally above board?"

"One hundred percent."

"Thank you, Mr. Rollins. Just one more thing. You own a property up in Toro Canyon, do you not?"

"Yes."

"And wasn't it raided by the DEA on the suspicion that there was a meth lab on the premises?"

Rollins dropped his chin into his collar. He paused to figure out how to phrase his answer. "That's true. That was a hoax tip-off from a rival company that is desperate to take me down. But the DEA found nothing."

"Are you saying that suspicion doesn't matter a damn, right?"

"Right."

"What matters is irrefutable proof?"

"Yes."

"I see. Nothing further."

38

Rollins was Winter's last witness, so Judge Birch called time for the day and said the defense could call its first witness in the morning.

I'd decided to open with Chip. This was highly unusual for me, or any other defense lawyer. It's pretty much a golden rule for us to not let the client anywhere near the stand. To do so risks them saying or doing something that will sink their own case. The jurors might not like the sound of their voice, they might find them untrustworthy, too emotional or not emotional enough. Then there was the likelihood that the prosecutor would pick them apart with a sharp cross-examination, or coax them into a damning outburst that couldn't be undone. It's a potential minefield best avoided.

Despite the risk of exposing Chip to Winter's interrogation, I felt the jury needed to hear Chip speak. If the jury liked him, if they believed him, his testimony might just win us the case.

"Mr. Bowman. How did you come to work at HardShell?"

"Well, I wasn't happy where I was. I was working at a jewelry store. The pay was okay but it was a little slow. Then I got tapped to apply for a vacancy at HardShell. I liked the sound of the job and I jumped at it."

"Did someone recommend you for the job?"

"Yes. Scooter. Well, his real name's Scott Slovak but everyone calls him Scooter. We worked together in Iraq a few years back."

"Were you happy at HardShell?"

"Very much so. The money was great, it was interesting, and it was kind of exciting. You know, we were couriering millions of dollars' worth of assets around the state. There was always the very real prospect of facing a threat of some kind."

"You mean like being robbed?"

"That's right. At first, it was just something you told yourself could happen. Then it started happening for real."

"What started happening for real?"

"Teams were getting hit. Dispensaries were getting robbed. Pretty soon it felt like we were like modern-day stagecoaches. It felt like it would be only a matter of time before we were hit by outlaws."

"Outlaws," I repeated. "It's interesting you say that because you actually had to deal with people that society deems to be outlaws, didn't you?"

"Yes, that's true."

"Could you please explain that part of your job for the court?"

"Well, I was given what you might call a client-liaison role. I would deal directly with our clients on the day-to-day deliveries. You know, dispensary owners who ordered shipments of recreational cannabis, labs that placed orders for medical cannabis, growers who wanted us to transport their crop or their cash. There are all types of people growing cannabis legally up in Humboldt County. And some of those people are outlaw motorcycle gangs."

"You dealt directly with bikers?"

"Yes. Like any client, I ensured they got their tracking numbers for their shipments, that they knew how to work the app. And I would also explain to them the financial services we offered."

"The app. We heard from Mr. Rollins that there is a thirty-minute delay from real time. Is this why the bikers got to the crime scene so quickly?"

"Yes. They would have noticed there was some kind of delay and came to check for themselves that everything was okay, but it wasn't."

"Chip, can you tell me what you remember about that night?"

"Not a lot. I remember getting to the warehouse, and parking the van. I remember getting out of the van, and that's pretty much it. The next thing I knew I was waking up to a paramedic over me and learning I'd been shot."

"Why can't you remember?"

Chip shook his head. "I think it's because of the knock I got on the back of my head."

"The subdural hematoma."

"Yes."

"You have no idea how you got that injury?"

"No."

I took a moment to survey the jury. All eyes were on Chip. I sensed that they were taking him for his word. At least, they seemed open, receptive to him. At that moment I felt I'd made the right call to put Chip on the stand. But it was early days.

"Chip, were Nate and Bo your friends?"

"I wouldn't say we were friends. I didn't hang out with them outside of work. We got on okay, though. Worked together well enough."

"Did you ever have reason to think they were doing anything unusual at work?"

"Well, there was a real cowboy streak in both of them. They were super tight—best buddies through and through. They did everything together, even in their down time. They were pretty much inseparable. But I noticed a couple of things going on that didn't seem right."

"What kind of things?"

"Well, on a couple of runs we did up to Humboldt, I suspected they'd loaded something onto the van when I was not there. But I checked the van and went through all the items we'd loaded and everything was spot on. Nothing missing and nothing extra."

"Did you speak to anyone about it?"

"Yes. I spoke to Scooter about it."

"What did he say?"

"He said I should tell Quinn."

"And did you?"

"Yes."

"What was Quinn's response?"

"He told me he wouldn't tolerate any kind of underhand activity but he said that he knew those guys, he trusted them, and that I must be mistaken. He told me to let him know if I suspected anything else."

"Did Bo or Nate do or say anything to make you believe they were involved in illegal activity?"

"Yes. They said a couple of things that were pretty out there."

"Like what?"

"One night we were having a few beers after work and another dispensary had been hit a few days before. We were talking about it and I said the cops thought the robbery was done by well-trained professionals. Both Nate and Bo started laughing. It was like they knew something. I asked what their game was, and they just laughed. They said, 'You know, these dispensaries have such pathetic security. They're useless. Maybe we can help them with that.' And then they just laughed."

"No further questions, Your Honor."

39

The smug half-grin on Winter's face told me he was relishing the prospect of burying Chip with his cross-examination. I'd thrown everything at Chip in our rehearsals and he'd handled himself well. Court was a different ballgame, though. No matter how much you prepare, no matter how well you think you know your opposition, there was bound to be a few surprises. And on that front, Winter didn't disappoint.

"Mr. Bowman, it seems you were somewhat at odds with your colleagues Bo Hendrick and Nathaniel Reed. Is that a fair assessment?"

"As I said before, we were friends but not super close. We got along okay."

"There's no harm in admitting that you didn't like them, Mr. Bowman."

Winter was using seemingly innocuous candor to create intimacy between himself and Chip. A closeness that he hoped to exploit. Wisely, Chip offered nothing in response, keeping a distance in the exchange.

"But from what you have told the court today, it's clear they did not like you. Am I right?"

"I can't say."

"After you went to the boss to air your suspicions about their behavior, did they treat you differently?"

"No."

"Did they know that you'd aired your concerns with the boss?"

"I'm pretty sure they did, but I don't know how."

"Did they confront you, Mr. Bowman?"

"No."

"Did they threaten you?"

"No."

"So even though they knew that you'd claimed they were engaged in illegal activity, they treated you no differently?"

"Not in a way I could perceive. No."

"Did you ever put your suspicions to them directly?"

"No."

"Yet you were convinced they were up to no good, weren't you?"

Chip paused for a moment, then leaned closer to the microphone to answer. "Yes, I was."

"You must have been worried that such behavior, if it were true, would cost you your job. Is that right?"

"Yes."

"Given the inherent dangers of your job, did you ever think their behavior might cost you your life?"

"Yes, I did."

"Then it's fair to say that you considered them a risk to your livelihood. Is that right?"

"Yes, but—"

"They posed a risk to your family's future, didn't they, Mr. Bowman?"

I tried to get Chip to look at me. Winter was drawing him into a trap. But Chip kept his eyes fixed on Winter. It seemed he felt that being unreservedly honest, almost defiantly so, would help his cause, even though I'd warned him that such naivety could allow Winter to bury him.

"Yes," he said. "I wanted nothing to do with anything illegal. I wanted to work hard, earn my pay, and then go home."

"I see. Now, Mr. Madison has done his best to portray HardShell as a company run by pirates. Is that an unfair depiction, Mr. Bowman?"

"In some ways, I don't think it's far from the truth."

"So, in some ways, you believe Bo Hendricks and Nathaniel Reed were modern day pirates, do you?"

"They were mercenaries in every way. They'd been so for a long time. They didn't see fit to respect the rules of the game. You can see that in their track record."

"I'm not sure what track record you're referring to. Mr. Rollins speaks very highly of both men. He told this court that they were the first men he wanted on the team at HardShell. Despite Mr. Madison's attempts to slur their reputation, no allegations of misconduct against them have been proven."

"They were sent home from Iraq in disgrace," fired Chip.

"Oh, you know that for certain, do you? Were you over in Iraq working for Fortis then, were you?"

"No."

"Then what you are dealing with is no more than gossip, Mr. Bowman. Don't you think people are innocent until proven guilty, Mr. Bowman?"

"Yes, of course."

"But you have judged your two co-workers without proof. You have more or less accused them of being criminals in this court."

"They rode fast and loose."

"And you didn't?"

Chip's face went blank. He kept his mouth shut.

"Correct me if I'm wrong, Mr. Bowman, but didn't your boss see fit to reprimand you for shooting your mouth off about the rewards of robbing cannabis dispensaries?"

"I misspoke. I was foolishly trying to appear tough in their company."

"Oh, so it's different for you, is it, Mr. Bowman? Isn't it true that you're doing your utmost to cast your dead co-workers in the worst possible light in order to save yourself?"

"No. That's not true at all."

"It could be surmised that you are trying to blame them for their own deaths. Is that the truth, Mr. Bowman?"

"No, it's not. That's absurd."

"Even though they were shot dead—executed—with your own gun?"

"I can't explain that."

"No, of course you can't. Your memory has conveniently failed you just at the time when all the evidence tells us that you drew your weapon when Nathaniel and Bo were completely relaxed in your company, fired a bullet into Bo's head and then another into Nathaniel's."

"That's not what happened."

"How can you say that? You can't shed any light whatsoever on this diabolical act. Perhaps that's because you don't want to."

"If I knew what happened, I would tell you."

"Of course, you would, Mr. Bowman. But you were the one who planned that job. You were the one who had the most to gain by this crime. You got your two difficult co-workers out of the way and you made a fortune. Or so you thought."

"Objection!" I called out, getting to my feet. "Counsel is testifying."

"Sustained," said Judge Birch, but Winter spoke over him undeterred.

"All you had to endure was a bullet in the leg, fired by your accomplice, who made off with all the bounty for you to share."

"Counsellor!" said Judge Birch. "I ruled on the objection." To the court reporter he said, "Strike Mr. Winter's last outburst from the record," before addressing Winter again. "Watch yourself, counselor. I will not have you ignore my rulings in my court!"

"What he said is not true," said Chip.

Winter was unfazed by the drama he'd stirred up.

"Understood, Your Honor. Mr. Bowman, you have painted your co-workers as reckless men capable of doing anything. Isn't that a fair description of yourself?"

"No, it's not."

"Yet, you were the one found with traces of methamphetamine on your hands, weren't you?"

"For the life of me I can't explain that."

"Of course, you can't. But you'd have us believe that Nathaniel and Bo killed Iraqi civilians and planted weapons on them to cast them as armed hostiles, wouldn't you?"

"I happen to think that Bo and Nate were capable of doing such a thing."

"They were cut-throats then? Working in a cut-throat industry?"

"Yes."

"And what does that make you, Mr. Bowman? Do you really expect the jury to believe that you're the honest Joe of the bunch, a do-gooder who tried his darndest to behave himself while all around him chaos reigned?"

"I don't pretend to be a saint."

"No, you could never do that. No one would believe you. Mr. Bowman, Nathaniel and Bo trusted you with their lives, didn't they?"

"Yes, we all trusted each other like that. That's what we do as a team."

"Yet you shot those two men in the most cold-blooded manner possible, didn't you?"

"No, I did not."

"And Nate shot you."

"That I can't say, because I don't remember."

"Well, that's what the evidence tells us. That's what the forensic analysis tells us, and that's what those two men are telling us from the grave. You have offered nothing to make the slightest hole in the case against you. How can you expect a jury to swallow the lie that you had nothing to do with this heinous crime?"

"I'm innocent."

"That's what they all say, Mr. Bowman. Is that why you ran from the police when they came for you?"

Chip struggled to come up with an answer. The foolishness of that decision was back to haunt him with renewed force.

No answer came from Chip's mouth. Winter didn't even wait for a response. He just collected his documents off the lectern, tapped them loudly on the slanted wooden top, and turned for his desk.

Leaving Chip speechless, Winter no doubt reasoned, spoke volumes.

40

The next witness I put on the stand was Cliff Loda. As it turned out, his testimony added little to Chip's cause. The jury got to hear that Nate had asked him to swap shifts with Chip, and that Nate and Bo had all but confessed to robbing a cannabis dispensary, but it seemed to come across to the jury as an overplayed act of misdirection on my part. Thankfully, Winter didn't unearth the fact that Loda had lied his way into HardShell. All he did was argue that Loda's testimony amounted to yet more unfounded accusations against two dead men who weren't on trial.

Next up was Scooter Slovak, whose main purpose, from my end, was to vouch for Chip's character, and the improbability of him committing a serious crime. Winter had thrown a lot of shade on Chip during his cross-examination, and it troubled me that the jury seemed to buy the skepticism Winter was selling about Chip's standing, or lack thereof.

I was pleased to see Slovak show up to court looking the part. He was dressed in a smart jacket and tie, and he displayed a kind of naïve goodwill as he approached the stand, nodding a greeting at the court reporter, the bailiff, the foreman—whoever caught his eye. I was relieved he didn't include Judge Birch in his circle of welcome. Slovak's positive energy was there, in the way he walked, in how he sat and took in his surrounds with bright-eyed wonder. Not that he was flip. All of it, it seemed, was just him being pleasantly dutiful.

"Mr. Slovak, what is your role at HardShell Security?"

"I'm the chief financial officer. I've been there from the get-go. I'd worked with Mr. Rollins overseas, and when he told me his idea to start a security service dedicated to the cannabis economy, I thought he was really onto something. I never studied finance or anything, but I have a knack for figures. I came up with some financial services we could offer our clients, on top of taking their money and crops from point A to point B."

"What were they?"

"The main difficulty our clients face is getting the cash that they have earned into safe, secure accounts that they can access anywhere. Because of the federal laws it's actually very hard for legal cannabis businesses to do the kind of banking that the rest of us take for granted. You know, like being able to access your money via your phone. I set up a system that lets them keep their money safely tucked away yet freely available."

"Go on."

"I came up with the idea of getting these businesses into cryptocurrency banking."

"What do you mean?"

"It's essentially a financial system that exists outside the normal banking framework, and as such it's safe from any laws. It's accessible whenever the client wants, and it's completely mobile and costless. There are minimal service fees—apart from the extra that HardShell charges—and you can move your money anywhere in the world, whenever you like. No foreign exchange rip-offs, no ridiculous fees that banks will charge you for doing the equivalent of sending an email."

"It's cutting-edge banking?"

"Yes, but anyone can do it. Except it's not something everyone trusts themselves to do. And it takes time to learn it. That's where I, we, come in."

"And so you offer a cheap, secure alternative to banks and credit unions?"

"That's right."

"Now that we knew where you fit into the operation, what about Chip? It was you who sought him out to join HardShell, wasn't it?"

"Yes, that's right. We were growing fast and we needed someone to handle client liaison on a day-to-day basis. Quinn's time was being spent on higher level stuff, and I was more and more focused on the finance side of things."

"Why did you think of Chip for this job?"

"I knew he was a solid guy. And he was smart and personable. We needed someone to both deal with the clients and ride in the delivery vans."

"So you recommended that Quinn hire him?"

"Yes. And he did."

"But Chip was not a perfect fit, by the sound of things."

"Well, he was not like a lot of the other guys we had on board who were, what you might say, pretty spirited. He was more strait-laced."

"Which was why he was good for the client role?"

"Exactly."

"But what about the fact that he shot his mouth off?"

"When I say he was strait-laced, that's actually relative to the other guys. Chip was a risk-taker but he was also a family man. As much as Chip could talk crap like the rest of them, he also talked about building a future for his girls. We all knew he was intent on banking as much money as he could for their education. No amount of money was enough, it seemed."

As soon as he said these words, Slovak knew he had overstepped. We'd gone through this in our preparation. I'd told him to never mention Chip's hunger for money. And now he'd practically spelled out a compelling motive for Chip to carry out a daring robbery.

The jury knew, everyone knew, that this was an inside job. And if Chip wasn't the culprit, who could it possibly be? As much as I'd tried, I'd come up short. The bottom line was that I had to cultivate and preserve the image of Chip being the good, loyal employee. Now Slovak had just declared that he was both risky and ambitious. I needed to change tack.

"Mr. Slovak, do you think Chip was capable of committing the crime he is charged with?"

"No, sir. I do not."

"Why not?"

"Chip just didn't have the know-how to pull that off. I mean, why would he agree to be part of a plan that saw him get shot and risk taking the fall for murder and robbery?"

"Well, his accusers say he probably thought he could get away with it."

"I can tell you that this was not in his nature. And besides, he was smart but he's not smart enough to plan something like this. And he's not dumb enough to allow himself to be blamed for it either. I think someone wanted the money and thought this was a good way to get him blamed for it."

"What skills are needed for Chip's job?"

"The kind of skills that only men with military training and combat experience have."

"Chip has those, obviously."

"He has them in spades. He's a professional. Both as a soldier and as a HardShell employee. He's not a mercenary."

"What do you mean?"

"The rest of the guys at HardShell, I'm sorry to say, would sell their mothers and aunts for a buck. Chip was never so ruthless. He was an outsider at HardShell to some extent. And believe me, that's a good thing. It's a compliment."

"Do you believe this crime was an inside job?"

"Objection," said Winter. "Calls for speculation."

"You Honor," I said. "Mr. Slovak knows HardShell better than just about anybody. He knows all the systems and how the teams go about their work. He is not someone plucked from the street. He classifies as an expert witness, surely, and as such his opinion holds weight."

Judge Birch ran his hand slowly over his mouth and looked down at his notes. "I must agree, Mr. Winter," he said. "Overruled. The witness can answer the question."

"Do I think it was an inside job?" asked Slovak. "Yes, I do. But that said, I can think of one other possibility."

"What's that?"

"That it was carried out by personnel from a similar company who had inside help."

"What do you mean?"

"The rivalry between HardShell and Bravo is pretty fierce. I bet certain people from Bravo would do anything to see HardShell go down."

"Thank you, Mr. Slovak."

On that note, I ended my direct examination. The jury looked as though there was so much more to this case than they thought. And that augured well for Chip. Slovak had done his job after all.

41

Winter stood at the lectern with his hands clasped behind his back, staring pensively at Slovak. After a few moments, he released his right hand to dab a finger gently at the witness.

"Mr. Slovak, you think a good deal of the defendant, don't you?"

"Yes, I do."

"You say he's honest?"

"I do."

"Trustworthy?"

"Yes."

"Decent?"

"Yes."

"A man of principle and integrity?"

"Yes. I would say that."

"This court has heard of instances of the defendant's behavior being anything but principled. You do know what I'm referring to, don't you?"

"Yes. He shot his mouth off once or twice. But, like I said earlier to Mr. Madison, we are not all one shade of color. Chip has his flaws but he's as decent a man as I have ever known."

"A decent man, who declared that he would be inclined to hold up a cannabis store at gunpoint. You call that decent?"

"I—"

"Do you regard that as decent behavior?"

"Not really."

"I take it that by that you mean no?"

"Yes. I mean, my answer is no."

"And when the defendant tried to run from the police when they came to arrest him... That was the act of a man with integrity, was it?"

"That's not for me to say."

"You can't have it both ways, Mr. Slovak."

"You can't have it one way, either, Mr. Winter," said Slovak with an even, firm tone to his voice. His sudden steel jolted somewhat against the well-presented, amenable guy-next-door disposition he'd displayed to date. And the jury noticed it, big time. "It seems to me that you want to demonize him. I'm offering some balance."

Winter's face went red. I imagined it must have been a combination of fury and embarrassment at Slovak's challenge. He dropped his eyes to the lectern to consult his notes, or at least pretend to.

"Mr. Slovak, it would be fair to say that you are particularly loyal to the defendant, is it not?"

"He's someone who I think has a lot to offer."

Winter's question raised a small red flag. *Where was he going to take this loyalty line of inquiry?* I'd deliberately avoided any reference to the fact that Chip had saved Slovak's life. I wanted that to stay buried so the jury wouldn't be tempted to frame Slovak's praise of Chip as blind loyalty. I'd gambled on Winter not digging that deep.

"But you have done him a few favors, haven't you?"

And now I was about to lose that gamble.

"Nothing anyone wouldn't do for a friend," replied Slovak.

"Ah, but not everyone lends their friends a great deal of money."

I felt relief that Winter had taken a different tack, but I wasn't happy that Chip had failed to mention anything to me about Scooter lending him money, which, I was just learning, was not an insignificant sum.

"No, but it's relative," said Slovak. "What I lent to Chip I could afford to lose, and I knew he would pay me back."

"Because he was foolish with his own money?"

"He made a couple of bad investments. He's hardly Robinson Crusoe in that regard."

"The court has heard that the defendant was hungry for money, desperate even. We've heard he was out to make some fast money. That's true, is it not?"

"I don't think that's fair."

"We're not here to talk about what's fair, Mr. Slovak. We're interested in what's true. We are trying to ascertain the character of a man charged with committing a double murder. And he was driven by money, wasn't he?"

"I wouldn't say that."

"But when you approached him to join HardShell, you told him that the job paid extremely well, no doubt?"

"Naturally. Everyone wants to know the pay when they're talking about changing jobs."

"Did he tell you that he was in debt then?"

"He did mention an investment that went bad."

"Is that when you offered him the loan?"

"Yes."

Winter's confidence was way up now. He positioned himself beside the lectern, his hands now clasped in front, his body swaying ever so slightly back and forth as he rocked on his feet.

"Mr. Slovak. Did the defendant ask you if there was any extra money to be earned in the job?"

"Yes. That's when we talked about the financial services I'd put together to offer clients. I thought Chip, being a personable sort of guy, would do well as a sales rep. In that capacity, he could earn commission on every client he signed up."

"So you then trained him up on establishing crypto accounts and that sort of thing?"

"Yes. He needed some basic training so he could answer most of the things clients would want to know, and boost their confidence."

"That seems very generous of you, to offer him such an attractive package. No wonder he jumped on board."

"It was a win-win for him and HardShell."

"Mr. Slovak," said Winter, his voice ringing with confidence now that he had the cross-examination back under control. "We now understand that the defendant was heavily indebted to you. He owed you money and you gave him a job. But you were heavily indebted to him, weren't you?"

Shit. He knows.

I'd told Slovak I wanted to keep this out of the courtroom, and he understood why. Now, put on the spot by Winter, he wasn't sure what to say. He looked at me then addressed Winter.

"I'm not sure what you mean exactly," he said, unconvincingly.

"I think you know exactly what I mean. The defendant saved your life in Iraq. You were wounded and exposed to the enemy and the defendant dragged you to safety. I mean, that's putting it in a nutshell but does it ring a bell?"

"Yes. He saved my life."

"And you have remained indebted to the defendant ever since, haven't you?"

"Yes, figuratively."

"I'd suggest there's nothing figurative about it, Mr. Slovak. If not for the actions of the defendant, you would be dead. Are you telling the court you do not feel a deep sense of gratitude toward the defendant?"

"Anyone would."

"But a debt of such magnitude—you would never do anything to harm him."

"Is that a question?"

"No. But this is. Would you say you are truly able to testify without bias in this case, a case in which the man to whom you owe your life needs you to vouch for him?"

"I've said he wasn't perfect."

"Yes. But he could be reckless and take great risks, couldn't he?"

Slovak remained silent.

"Mr. Slovak? The defendant was desperate to make money, wasn't he?"

Slovak bowed his head. I watched him with dread. He nodded, "Yes."

"He had everything needed to commit this crime. The motive, the know-how, and the ruthlessness, didn't he?"

"You're twisting it—"

"Did you ever think that Chip Bowman was guilty?"

"What does it matter what I think?"

"Oh, it matters. Just as it matters that bullets from his gun ended up in the bodies of his co-workers, your co-workers. What about your loyalty to those men? What about your loyalty to their families and loved ones? Or do they not count?"

"No. I mean, of course they do."

"Do they not deserve justice? Do they not deserve the truth?"

"Yes."

"I think it's time you put justice for the victims of this heinous crime above personal loyalty, Mr. Slovak. Do you think the defendant killed those men?"

Slovak bowed his head. "I'd like to think not."

An excited murmur sprang from the gallery.

Winter stood silently for a few moments, letting Slovak's response hang there.

"Well, that's a ringing endorsement if ever I've heard one. Nothing further."

Winter gathered up his notes with an air of satisfaction and stepped back to his table.

With Slovak's testimony at an end, I rested my case. Judge Birch declared that the court would adjourn for the day and that closing arguments would begin the next morning, with the jury instructions to follow.

I barely heard the sound of the gavel after Judge Birch spoke. I was already thinking about my closing statement. The way I saw it, none of those jurors could have a resolute conviction about either Chip's guilt or innocence.

It was a such a close case. Not what I wanted, and now it appeared that my words could be the deciding factor.

More than ever, Chip's fate was in my hands.

42

Winter moved to the lectern, which was now pivoted to face the jury, and without pausing began to speak. He was itching to start, and drive the final nail home in the State's case against Chip. Like me, he would have taken nothing for granted. He would have reasoned that neither of us had put a lock on this case.

At this moment, I couldn't help but revise my take on the state of play. I told myself, again, that I must have seeded significant doubt into the jury's collective mind. Enough anyway to have them question deeply whether or not they could, in all good conscience, convict my client.

Could Winter now negate my gains with his words?

"Ladies and gentlemen of the jury, over these past days we have sought to present to you how two good men came to die. Two men who were executed in a brazen bid to steal a fortune in cash and legal cannabis.

"We have no idea where the stolen assets are, but that is where the speculation ends.

"The evidence I have presented, the evidence that was compiled by diligent, professional men and women, experts in their field, tells a tragic story of unchecked greed stampeding over every virtue.

"It tells the story of one man who was so out of his depth financially, who was so far from his material ambitions, so far from the life that he desperately wanted, that he stooped to plot against, to deceive, and to kill the people who trusted him the most.

"His co-workers Nathaniel Reed and Bo Hendricks, had put their lives on the line for their country. And at HardShell, while the risk was less than that of war but still very great and very real, they put their lives on the line for each other.

"And what did the defendant do? He used that implicit trust against them. He ditched the honor of duty and commitment.

"Driven by greed, he planned an audacious, murderous money grab. He waited until the most vulnerable moment to kill the men that he knew would stand in his way. He knew they were professionals of the highest caliber. He knew that they would carry out their job of keeping their cargo safe with unerring vigor. He knew that to get the money he needed to kill them in cold blood. And to kill them he had to have the advantage of surprise and the grace of trust.

"And so that's what he did. He waited until his two co-workers were close. They were probably just chewing the fat about what they were going to do after the shift. They'd just worked four ten-hour days. They were about to get four days off. Maybe go fishing. Hiking. Camping. Spend some time with their loved ones. But none of those simple plans would ever come to be. Because at that moment, the defendant drew his weapon fast and put a bullet straight through Bo Hendricks' forehead. Bo was no longer a friend, a co-worker, to the defendant. He was an obstacle. He was a life that had to be extinguished for the defendant's own gain.

"Quickly, the defendant swung his weapon at Nathaniel Reed. But as he did so, Nathaniel, who had just seen his best friend executed, was quick to respond. He drew his weapon, and seeing the defendant's gun now pointed at him, fired as soon as he could. The premature shot did not reach its desired mark. It struck the defendant in the leg, just as he fired into Nathaniel's face.

"But Nathaniel's bullet is akin to him pointing a finger at his killer. He succeeded in hitting his target, at least. He succeeded, then, in telling us who his murderer was.

"The defendant made sure of his cold-blooded work. He fired another bullet into each man's head. And then, as blood drained from his leg wound, he collapsed.

"This is not a scenario that required imagination to put together. All it required were the facts. Ladies and gentlemen, the facts tell the story here. They tell it without reservation and without wonder. There are no gaps here. As you have seen, the bullets, the fingerprints, the science have all built a rock-solid account of what happened that terrible night.

"How the defendant planned to get away with this horrific crime is not our concern.

"Our concern is the evidence presented.

"It's unequivocal. The bullets that killed Nathaniel and Bo were fired from the defendant's gun. No one's fingerprints other than his were on that weapon.

"We know the defendant was in debt, and that he had big plans for the future. But those plans required a lot of money. The kind of money that he didn't have. The kind of money he could not earn fast enough for his liking.

"So, he took a diabolical shortcut.

"And no, it does not look like he acted alone. But we are not here to find out who his accomplice or accomplices were. The defendant's not going to come clean and tell us now. He's lied to everyone.

"He's lied to his wife.

"He's lied to his boss.

"He's lied to his friends.

"He's lied to his co-workers.

"And he's lied to the court. To us.

"Well, those lies are no match for the truth of evidence.

"I have presented the case for the State as diligently and as thoroughly as I possibly could. Now, it's up to you.

"It's up to you to see that justice is done for the families and friends of Nathaniel and Bo.

"It's up to you to hear the loud and clear message the evidence is telling you.

"It's up to you to see that this heinous crime does not go unpunished.

"On the weight of such compelling and overwhelming evidence, the only verdict that will deliver justice here is guilty.

"Thank you."

43

"Good luck, Mr. Madison," said Chip quietly as I pushed my seat back to stand. Chip's words almost stopped me in my tracks. There was something about the tone—a humility, a sincerity—that struck me as being utterly selfless. Here, at his most critical moment of need, when no one could blame him for feeling overwrought with what might befall him, Chip was rooting for me like I deserved to excel, as though I'd earned it.

But how much was any amount of fine oratory worth if the man beside me was jailed for the rest of his life?

Nothing.

I had to reach the jury. I had to.

"Ladies and gentlemen, the nature of a trial is by its very nature adversarial. One side argues vehemently to get you to see things their way and the other tries equally hard to do the same.

"There is common ground, though, in that we are not assessing different evidence here. And as ridiculous, as astounding as it sounds, you can be asked to believe stories that are barely alike but which are borne of the very same evidence.

"How is this possible?

"It's possible because of this irrefutable fact—none of us knows exactly what happened that night.

"The prosecution rests their argument on the fact that the two victims were killed with the defendant's weapon.

"They say that this is how it went down. We had two shots here, then two more, and then one last shot. So this is how the defendant killed those men and ended up with a bullet in his leg.

"Now unlike my friend sitting at the prosecution table, I don't claim to know the exact order of those bullets being fired. No one can. Not even the defendant. He can't remember what happened. And the fact that he can't remember anything about the night has been attacked.

"It's an explanation, not an excuse. Chip Bowman can't remember anything because he was out cold. Now that blow to the head gave him the perfect excuse to lie, to feed the police details that he wanted them to believe. But he did no such thing. He did not seek to mislead. He simply couldn't remember. He told the police that, over and over again.

"Think about that.

"Remember: you owe it to this man to presume that he is innocent. Don't you ever forget that. It is your duty to hold fast to that principle until all doubt has been removed.

"You have to entertain the possibility that the blow to the back of Chip's head did not come from hitting the ground as he collapsed. He was knocked out by one of the robbers. If they were going to get their hands on that fortune, they needed Chip out of the way. Why? Because he's honest. He'd never allow it.

"And whoever struck Chip might have been known to Nate and Bo. Another colleague perhaps. Maybe the three of them had planned it together. And Nate and Bo were double-crossed. Maybe the killer didn't want to share after all. So he took Nate's gun and put a bullet into Chip's leg, letting him live so that he took the blame. After the killer shot Nate and Bo with Chip's gun, all he had to do was plant the gun in Chip's unconscious hand.

"Why shouldn't you believe that story? It's just as credible as the story the prosecution has proffered. Like I said, same evidence, different story.

"The victims knew their killer. Yes, we are certain of that. They were shot with Chip's gun. Yes, we are certain of that. And there's someone out there who has gotten away with murder. Yes, we are certain of that too.

"This story is no more far-fetched than the prosecution's. I would argue it is less so. Remember what you heard earlier in this court, how innocent civilians in Iraq were murdered and then had weapons planted on them so they could be classed as insurgents.

"Nate and Bo were accused of doing this exact thing in Iraq to escape the reach of the law.

"The other thing we're certain of is that it was an inside job. The person who killed Nate and Bo knew them well. They knew him, and on that night had no reason to distrust him. And this person, the real perpetrator of this terrible crime, is still out there, laughing at having set up Chip Bowman, and counting his piles of money and cannabis.

"You have heard about the ruthlessness of the men who are employed in this industry. You have heard of the robberies that have preyed upon cannabis businesses in recent times. You have heard that it has become as lawless as the Wild West.

"But as I have shown you, Chip Bowman is no cowboy. To judge his character, go by his proven actions. Go by the fact that he went to his boss to express his concern that there might be some illegal activity going on. Go by the fact that he did this because he wanted to do things right. Yes, he wanted to make money. But he wanted to do that the right way, the honest way.

"Chip Bowman worked hard. He did extra shifts, undertook sales work, to bring in more money.

"Yes, he had debts. But he had set about recovering them in the right way, the honest way. He put his head down and did the work.

"You cannot simply assume that his poor financial position makes him a desperate villain, a man who planned to kill to get his hands on a fortune. How many times have you heard of millionaires being broke at least once in their lives before going on to strike it rich?

"Members of the jury, if you buy the prosecution's argument that my client is guilty, then you must ask where was his out? How did he envision getting away with it? Because that has not been presented.

"The prosecution is happy to say Chip Bowman had debts, so he was desperate, and so he had motive. Well, if he was that determined, if he was that smart, then how did he end up unconscious with a bullet in his leg?

"The law says you must rid yourself of all reasonable doubt before reaching your decision. You cannot in good conscience tell me there is no room for doubt in the case against Chip Bowman.

"Unless you can honestly say there's no reasonable explanation other than the version presented to you by the prosecution, then you must find the defendant Chip Bowman not guilty.

"Thank you once again for your time."

44

"Will they let him come home?"

Carrie Bowman's voice was tinged with strained hope. We were driving from the court back to my office, where Megan was looking after Carrie's two girls. It wasn't the first time Carrie had sought my reassurance. Positivity from her husband's lawyer was a rope for her to cling on to, particularly after hearing Winter portray Chip as a cold-blooded killer.

Carrie's predicament was never lost on me. Her presence in court was a reminder that if I failed, her husband would never come home, her daughters, Hannah and Tracy, would never see their father anywhere else other than inside a prison.

"I can't say for sure, Carrie, but I'm optimistic."

I always spoke candidly with Carrie, never promised what I couldn't deliver. But I did promise to do absolutely everything in my power to bring Chip back to her. And, in the event of him being found guilty, I would be straight onto an appeal.

"Listen," I said, "I've looked at this from every angle. I watched the jury's response at every turn. And my sense is that there is genuine empathy there. I see them look at him like someone they've gotten to know. Now that doesn't mean they like him. What it does mean is that the prospect of finding him guilty will weigh on them all the more heavily. Juries never want to convict an innocent man—it's a very powerful thing; it's a real test of conscience. They are so much more invested in getting their decision right. I didn't see them looking at him coldly, or indifferently."

"I did," she said, staring out the window.

I'd asked that Carrie turn up at court so that the jury would see Chip not just as a defendant but as a husband whose wife was going through hell. I know that sounds manipulative, but you must use everything at your disposal to keep the jury thinking of the defendant as a human being who is loved, who is connected to society. A defendant can so easily be reduced to a two-dimensional figure, seen only through the funnel of one incident in their entire life. And Carrie had done that every day. Some days, the girls were left with her parents, on others she entrusted them to Megan.

"Okay, there were a couple occasions when a juror looked at him in a tangibly negative way," I conceded. "But this decision has to be unanimous. And I believe the bulk of those jurors harbor doubts about what went down. And if that's genuinely the case, then they'll have to acquit, because I can't see them all being talked into a guilty verdict."

"I wish I could be so sure."

"That's understandable. I know this is a nightmare but it will soon be over. Chip will be home soon."

I kicked myself. *Why did I say that?* Of course, I felt sorry for Carrie but to be certain of a future event typically invites a contradiction. I should know better. I do know better. But sometimes you just speak as a person who knows another person is hurting. It's hard not to say whatever you think will alleviate their pain.

Yet the truth was I actually believed my own words. After all my years as a trial lawyer, you learn to read a jury—what resonated with them, what touched them, what disgusted or offended them. And the way I read this particular jury, most of them were with Chip. For the most part, juries take a rational, commonsense, fair-minded path to reaching a verdict. But if their sympathies and reasoning led them Chip's way, you could be sure that this would be countered by the duty to the victims' loved ones.

The more I thought about it, the less sure I felt about anything.

"Do you mind?" asked Carrie, having reached for her pack of cigarettes.

"No go ahead."

I didn't smoke but I didn't take offense at those who did.

Carrie lowered the window after lighting her cigarette and kept the burning ember close to the crack, allowing the suction to drag the smoke outside.

"I can't just think it's going to turn out okay, Brad. I know I should but I can't."

"That's understandable. You've got no say in a decision that's going to affect you for the rest of your life. There's no harder place to be."

"Chip might be taken from us, and there's not a damned thing I can do about it."

"It's just a waiting game now, Carrie. Soon we'll know one way or the other."

"What am I going to tell the girls if they find Chip guilty?"

It wasn't a question that Carrie was looking to me to answer; it was more a spoken thought, one that must consume her, even in sleep.

"Hannah and Tracy think the world of him," he said. "How can I ever tell them that he's never coming home again?"

She took another drag, and spoke words that were addressed to herself more than me. "Well, if that's the way it goes, that's the way it goes."

"And we will appeal, if that happens," I said.

"Who knows what else might come to light?"

"That's right."

"The police know that someone else was involved but they won't do anything about it."

"Yes."

"And if Chip is found guilty, they'll pat themselves on the back and not bother to give it another thought."

"I hate to say it, but I think you're right."

"They think the only way to find out is for Chip to tell them. And if he doesn't then he deserves to rot in prison for the rest of his life. And they call that justice."

"No, that's not justice."

Carrie looked at me, the brave talk was getting too much. "They're not going to find him guilty, are they?"

She turned away without waiting for an answer. It was now not a question but a simple expression of her life's profound uncertainty.

As I pulled into the parking lot in Santa Monica my phone rang.

The caller identified herself as Judge Birch's clerk.

"You need to get back here," she said. "The jury's reached a verdict."

45

Chip entered the courtroom looking dazed. The decision on his fate was imminent. Bearing the extremes of consequences, his verdict loomed with terrifying might.

As he took his seat next to me, I put my arm on his shoulder and spoke some encouraging words. They were inane words, really. Futile sounds that had no bearing on the outcome whatsoever. But that's what we do. We have to say something. We have to stay positive.

What I told Chip was that I thought it was a good sign that the jury had taken only a couple of hours, if that, to decide.

I found it extremely hard to believe the jury had swung so quickly and heavily against Chip. The speed of the deliberation meant there wasn't much debate at all, not a lot of persuading, not much arguing, and few, if any, rounds of showing hands. No, this was about as clinical as a jury decision gets.

Judge Birch entered and directed the bailiff to bring the jury in. After the jury members had taken their seats, Judge Birch cast his eyes in their direction and asked the foreperson to stand. The juror selected for this role was a plain-looking man in his late forties wearing a light gray suit. At first, I couldn't recall his name but then I remembered in jury selection that he declared, practically in the same breath, that he was Henry Ford and that he sold Toyotas on Hollywood Boulevard and that his wife's maiden name was Lincoln and she worked for General Motors in some capacity. This had gotten a laugh from all the jurors on the panel, and I think I even detected a grin on Judge Birch's face. Such mirth seemed a long time ago.

"Mr. Ford. I take it the jury has reached a verdict," said Judge Birch, his tone reflecting his surprise at such a fast turnaround.

"We have, Your Honor," said Ford.

Judge Birch turned to Chip. "Will the defendant please stand?"

Chip got to his feet, as did I.

The next words that came from Ford's lips were a stream of sounds above which key words and phrases porpoised—"first count"... "murder"... "Nathaniel Reed"... "We find the defendant guilty"... "second count"... "murder"... "Bo Hendricks"... "guilty."

"Oh, my God!" A muted scream erupted from Carrie as cheers rose from the other side of the gallery.

I was unable to hide my shock. I bowed my head and cursed, then I turned to Chip and grabbed his shoulder firmly. I turned to see Carrie, hand over her mouth, glistening eyes wide in shock, her cheeks caving in as she sucked air though her fingers.

The commotion behind us grew into a dull roar. I put my arm around Chip and pulled him in. His head rested against my shoulder. He didn't say a word.

"Chip," I said into his ear. There was a rage in my voice that stemmed from my soul. "This is not fucking over, Chip! This is not over." I grabbed both shoulders now and talked into his poor, dejected face. "This is just round one. It's a bullshit verdict. I promise you, Chip—the minute I leave this court is the minute the fight to overturn this travesty begins."

Chip was white, his breathing shallow and his eyes defeated.

"Thanks for everything, Mr. Madison," he said.

Chip turned to embrace Carrie. Two deputies approached the couple, one telling Chip he had to go with them.

"No," Carrie cried mournfully, holding on to Chip for dear life. "Please don't take him away. He's innocent."

"Keep telling yourself that, lying bitch!" a man shouted from behind.

The deputies led Chip to the door.

"Rot in hell, you fucking murderer!" yelled the same man.

"I love you, darling," she said, as the door was opened for Chip. Then louder: "I love you, darling."

Chip turned around and mouthed the words: "I love you. It's okay. It'll be okay."

Two seconds later, he was gone.

I walked up to Carrie and put my arm around her.

"How can it be okay?" she said tearfully. "It will never be okay."

Carrie shrugged me off and reached into her handbag for her cigarettes before realizing where she was. She shut up her bag and then glared at me coldly.

"How could you let this happen?"

"Carrie, I—"

"How could you? You said they wouldn't do this to him. You told me. You basically promised me they'd let him go."

"Carrie, I'm as stunned as you are."

"Are you? I can assure you, Brad. No one on God's earth is as stunned as I am right now. No one."

"Listen, Carrie. You have to believe me when I tell you this is not over. I told Chip I'd launch an appeal and that's exactly what I'm going to do."

"They're taking him to jail, Brad. He's going to fucking jail. They'll lock him up for life."

"I know you're angry. At me, and at pretty much everyone, and you have every right to be."

I tried to stay close to Carrie as we left the courtroom but she walked ahead of me. We said nothing to each other in the elevator.

As the doors opened on the ground floor, I saw the throng of media outside and grabbed Carrie's hand.

"Stay close to me, okay?"

Carrie nodded.

When we exited the building, Dale Winter was addressing the large group of reporters and camera operators.

"Of course, this was a fair decision," I heard him say. "The State placed its faith in twelve honorable men and women. We always thought we had a very strong case, and I'm glad that the jury agreed. I congratulate them. They've given the victim's families a small but significant consolation. It's called justice."

I put my arm around Carrie's shoulder and pushed through the crowd as cameras fired at us.

"Are you surprised they reached a decision so quickly?" I heard a reporter ask Winter.

"No, I'm not. The evidence was strong, and it told them all they needed to know. To not reach a guilty verdict would have required a ridiculous perversion of the facts in evidence."

I looked up and saw Winter. Standing beside him was Wes Brenner, ready to crow about the verdict being what the state of California wanted and needed.

I stopped, still holding onto Carrie. I had initially thought I'd bypass the press. Now I knew I could not let Winter go unopposed, nor could I resist the opportunity to take some wind out of Brenner's sails.

"The defendant Chip Bowman killed two men in cold blood," Winter said. "That was clear as day before this trial began and its most certainly clear now. We now look forward to sentencing—"

Winter was cut off by Brenner, who was now beside him and raising his voice to full pitch. "Life is too good for that despicable man. Chip Bowman deserves nothing less than the death penalty."

Winter took that as his cue to leave. He raised his chin and moved forward, parting the crowd before him.

With that, the press gathered around me, much to Brenner's disappointment.

"Mr. Madison," a reporter asked. "What is your reaction to this verdict?"

"I'm stunned, to be honest," I said. "This is a total miscarriage of justice. Simple as that. I have nothing bad to say about the jury members as individuals but collectively they got it wrong. They got it so wrong. There were holes in the prosecution case that you could drive a truck through. I'm at a loss to understand how this verdict was reached so quickly. It doesn't seem right, and it doesn't seem fair."

"Do you intend to appeal?"

"You bet I do. I'll be initiating an appeal immediately."

Over the flurry of several questions being asked of me at once came Brenner's voice. "You're just being a sore loser, Madison! You tried to defend a double murderer and you lost!"

I looked Brenner in the eye with a degree of relish. Among the tasks I'd asked Jack to do was to discover who was funding Brenner's campaign. When Jack delivered his findings, I was shocked but not surprised. Now was the perfect time to let people know a couple of home truths about Brenner.

"I see Wes Brenner is here trying to exploit this case for his own personal gain," I said, leaning a little closer to the ring of microphones, voice recorders, and smartphones in front of me. "And before anyone seeks Brenner's opinion on anything concerning the cannabis laws in this state, perhaps they should ask about his connection with Traxon Pharmaceuticals, the biggest corporate player in the cannabis industry. Ask Wes if Traxon is funding his campaign. Ask him if it's disingenuous for him to try and rework legislation in order to hand Traxon the lion's share of cannabis production in California. Ask him if him owning a sizable holding of Traxon stock is coloring his opinions."

As I spoke these last words, I fixed my gaze on Brenner. I'd never seen him look mortified but it was pretty to watch.

I turned back to the reporters. "Before you have a chat with Wes, let me just reiterate that the evidence in this case was far from conclusive. I'm not going to stand idly by and watch an innocent man be sent to prison for the rest of his life."

"You think he's innocent?"

"Yes, I do."

"Then why couldn't you prove it? You had your chance."

"It wasn't my job to prove anything. The State had to prove that my client killed two men and stole a lot of money, but as I said in court, they came up short. Their case was riddled with doubt."

"That's not what the jury thought."

"Well, what can I say? The jury and I see things very differently. That's their prerogative, sure, but it doesn't mean that they're right."

"What about the victims?"

"This is all about the victims," I said. "If their loved ones wanted justice, they don't have it. The people of California don't have it. My client Chip Bowman doesn't have justice. Nor does his family. If the State wanted the perpetrator of that terrible crime to be brought to justice, then it has failed. Everyone has lost here and the real killer is still at large in the community."

"You're a liar. You're defending a cold-blooded killer!" This voice came from behind the members of the press. It was a member of the public, a member of Nate or Bo's family, I assumed.

"I understand the emotions of a trial like this, and they're running super high. But I promise you this—it's not over. Not by a long shot."

"You're scum. You piece of shit." It was the same man. I said nothing more and began backing away from the media, with my arm around Carrie.

"Let's go," I said. "We've got work to do."

As we walked away, I heard several people calling out Brenner's name. I turned around to see him trying to walk away while swatting microphones away from his face.

On the way back to the car, I felt my phone buzz in my pocket. I fished it out and looked at the screen. It was a text from Abby.

"Just heard about the trial. So sorry x"

"Thanks but it's not over yet," I typed back.

After I sent Abby's text, I brought up the list of favorites and tapped a contact.

"Father of the Century, please hold."

"Jack, we lost. I'm just leaving court now."

"Lost what? The trial?" Jack said seriously, having noted from my tone that I was in no mood for humor. "You're shitting me."

I broke away from Carrie, holding my hand up to ask her to wait just a minute. I hunched over to ensure the conversation couldn't reach her ears.

"I wish I was. It was the Usain Bolt of juries. It was like they had nothing to discuss in the deliberation room. Buddy, something's not right here and I need to find out what. I need your help. As in drop whatever the fuck it is you're doing—not that fatherhood's not important—and get your ass to my office pronto."

"You know what Chanel's gonna—"

"Jack. Come on. They've just convicted an innocent man, a father of two young girls, for double murder. Jack, you've got to get a hall pass. I need your help."

"You sound convinced he's innocent."

"I am. Look, it's not my job to believe a client, but this guy? Jack, he's an innocent man facing life."

"Don't worry. I'll be there."

46

Jack walked out of the Hollywood Toyota showroom into the morning sun with Henry Ford in tow. We'd spent hours the previous night working up a plan. There are many grounds upon which you can lodge an appeal. I was going to focus on two: finding a legal error in the court proceedings and finding grounds to overturn the verdict.

The first option could only work if I proved that the error swayed the outcome. So I would have to go through everything: the court reporter's transcript, the clerk's transcript—which included all the exhibits, motions, documents—and all the briefs.

But the speed of the deliberation suggested that trying to overturn the verdict might be my best bet.

There was something rotten about how Chip's trial ended; it stank of jury misconduct, and my nose told me to follow the jury foreperson, Henry Ford.

The unsuspecting Ford was under the impression that Jack wanted to test drive a double cab Tacoma, and Ford, who had some keys hanging from his right hand, was only too happy to oblige.

I'd waited in the car yard. As Jack and Ford stood by the test-drive truck discussing specs, I approached.

Ford was clearly not pleased to see me. He knew exactly who I was. He knew my name, he knew the sound of my voice, he knew my fashion sense, he knew if I'd cut myself shaving. I was part of the slow-moving drama that he'd watched like a one-channel TV set, for days on end.

"Mr. Madison, I'm with a customer," he said. "If you just go on inside, Tom can help you with whatever you need."

Ford smiled with the hope that, by some extraordinary coincidence, I'd actually dropped in to talk Toyotas.

"It's okay, Henry. Jack here's with me. And I'm not here to buy a car."

"This is not right," Ford said, flustered. "It's not legal. You can't be approaching jurors after the verdict."

"That's not true, actually. If Judge Birch had expressly disallowed post-trial interviews with jurors, you might have a point. But he didn't. All I want to do is ask you a few questions."

"What for?"

"Due diligence, Henry. I lost. And I don't like losing. You can understand that. So I need to know if there's anything I can improve for next time."

"You did fine, Mr. Madison. The verdict was not a reflection on your performance. You shouldn't take it personally."

I nodded. "I suppose you're right. I do tend to take things personally. I should move on but, like I said, I can get stuck on things. Can't let them lie. My secretary actually tells me to my face that I'm too obsessive."

"Maybe she's right. But look, I really can't do this now. I've just gotten back to work, and I need to make up for lost time."

I ignored him.

"Man, you guys whipped through that deliberation like you all had a train to catch," I said. "I've never known a jury to reach a decision so quickly."

"I guess it was fast."

"Fast? It was extraordinary."

Ford was caught between the hope of seeing me off with chit-chat and the dread of knowing I wasn't going anywhere.

"I've never seen anything like it," I said. "And I mean that quite literally. Never in all my years have I seen a turnaround like that."

Ford put up his hands. "Look, Mr. Madison. I don't want to do this. I don't have to. I want to put the trial behind me and get on with my life. I did my duty. I'm done with it now. It's over."

"Not for me, it's not. Something's not right, Henry. What happened in there?"

"Look, I can't stand around talking, or my boss is going to chew my ass."

I gestured to the truck. "Let's go for a test drive then. Ten minutes, Henry. We'll take her for a spin, have a little chat, and then we're out of here."

Ford let out a big breath and then lifted up the keys and pressed the remote unlock. "Okay. Hop in."

With Jack driving the Tacoma and Ford in the passenger seat, I positioned myself behind Jack.

"Henry, I'm not going to cry if you tell me I screwed up. I just want to know how I managed to lose this case so big, so fast."

"Yeah, well maybe if you'd done a better job, Chip would be walking free right now."

"Are you seriously telling me it wasn't even close? Henry, I was defending a man who's now going to die in prison. I'm not worried about a stain on my resume. What could I have done better?"

Ford shook his head. "I don't know."

"Surely, you guys had some doubts you needed to work through in that deliberation room."

Ford said nothing. He looked out the window.

"I just struggle to understand how there was no hesitation whatsoever. I mean, sorry, but that was brutal."

Ford's right elbow was propped on the door frame, his fingers pinching his lower lip.

"I thought he was guilty, okay?" he said defensively. "I mean, his gun was the murder weapon. They were shot so close. Your story was the one that seemed more made up. Sorry, but that's the truth."

"Okay. I understand that. Thank you for your honesty. But, as I made clear in court, my story was not the stuff of fantasy. That kind of shit happened all too often overseas, by the likes of Hendricks and Reed. Chip wasn't like that, Henry. And something tells me you know that."

Ford took another deep breath and blew it out with an audible whistle.

"You were always up against it, Mr. Madison."

"What do you mean?"

"There were two jurors who were never going to acquit. We all knew that from the outset."

"What? Before deliberations even started?"

Ford nodded. "We all knew the rules. You know, that we were not to discuss the case with anyone. And these two guys were talking to everyone about how it was a slam-dunk case of murder and that we needed to put justice for the victims' families above all else."

"None of you should have been discussing the case with anyone until you got to the deliberation room."

"I know. I know," said Ford. "And when I said something about us being obliged to keep an open mind, things started to happen."

"What things?"

"Shit, Mr. Madison. They fucking followed me. I had my kids and they were following me."

"Who followed you?"

Ford rubbed his hand over his mouth as though his body was telling his mind to shut up. "Bikers," he said. "They tailed me, right after I picked my kids up from school. All the way home. I mean, they scared the shit out of me. And then they started with the calls. Always the same guy, same message. 'Henry, it's either guilty or you're dead.' Then he'd hang up."

"Were the bikers Iron Raiders?"

"I couldn't tell you. I've got no idea."

"So now there were three of you advocating for a guilty verdict?"

"That's right. But to be honest, there was not much persuading that needed to be done. Like me, most of the other jurors were leaning toward guilty."

I tapped Jack on the shoulder. "Jack, take us back to the lot."

Ford swung around and fixed his pleading eyes on me. "Mr. Madison, you can't say anything. They'll kill me."

I paused for a few moments. "Henry, what you've just told me is pure jury misconduct, not to mention tampering. And that will almost certainly give me grounds to have the verdict impeached. But don't you worry, I'm not going to come back to you until I've dealt with the men who threatened you, do you understand?"

"Yes, thank you, Mr. Madison."

Jack turned the truck into the Hollywood Toyota and pulled up outside the glass entrance doors.

"Henry, I'm going to need the names of those other two jurors," I said.

Again, Henry struggled to think his way out, but he'd lost the resolve to resist. He bowed his head. "I only know their first names. It was Rhett, number six, and Landon, number ten."

Jack cut the engine.

"Thanks, Henry," I said. "Now, I don't know when exactly but I'll be coming back to see you. And when I do, I'm going to get you to sign an affidavit that says what you just told me. And that's going to help me set my client free. Okay?"

Ford shook his head. "I can't do that."

"Yes, Henry. You can," I said. "And you will."

We all got out of the Tacoma, and Jack and I walked straight to my car without another word to Ford.

"Well, that went well," Jack said to me as we got into the Mustang. "You've got what you need for an appeal now, right?"

"Yes, what I'll have is reason to overturn the verdict on the grounds of jury misconduct. But that doesn't mean it's enough."

"How so?"

"Winter will oppose the appeal. He'll have his own affidavits that will most likely discredit Ford."

"So what now?"

I got behind the wheel and Jack took the passenger seat. I had my phone out, trying to find the document I was after. Within a minute, I had it: the records from jury selection. It contained the names and other details that the prospective jurors had given when they completed their qualification forms.

"These are the guys," I said. "Rhett Botula and Landon Chapel. I'll send you the document with their details."

"You want me to go see them?"

"Yeah. I need to know exactly who leaned on them. I need you to not just get an admission but a positive ID."

"Do you have some candidates in mind?"

"Yes. I'll send you a pic of Rollins for you to show them."

I tapped away at my phone until I'd sent everything Jack needed. Then I started the car.

"And what are you going to do?" asked Jack.

"I'm going to go pay Rollins a visit."

"Rollins? Why the hell would you go and see Rollins?"

"The trial's done and Chip's off to jail as far as he's concerned. His insurance payout is all but assured now. And my bet is he thinks it's back to business as usual."

"And you intend to tell him otherwise, I take it?"

"You've got that right. If he thinks he can just sail off into the sunset, he's got another thing coming. He's heading for an iceberg. He just doesn't know it yet."

47

The Santa Monica Pier was teeming with its usual summer afternoon crowd of people ambling between tourist stalls and street performers. A guy selling his own CDs tried to stop me but I brushed straight past him, my eyes scanning ahead as far as I could into the distance. There was a big swell, and the sound of crashing waves mingled with the screams of delight coming from the roller coaster.

At last, I spotted him. Seeing me approach, Quinn Rollins turned his back against the railing and cast an instinctive eye behind me to see if I had company.

"It's just me, Rollins," I assured him as I stopped before him.

When I'd called Rollins earlier in the day, he'd refused to meet me. He was happy to rub my nose in the fact that I'd lost the trial, that my faith in Chip had been stupidly misplaced, and that he could now move on with his business. "Go back to your cafe breakfasts," he laughed, his voice thick with hubris. "You and I have nothing to discuss." That was when I told him that Henry Tuck had made Fern Ortega the executor of his will, and that she'd asked me to handle the probate. Fern was only too happy for me to put the process on ice until the trial ended. That point had now been reached, and I intended to get Tuck's money out of HardShell immediately.

"Why do you want to interfere with my business, Madison? It's over. You lost. I'm happy to negotiate a time-frame for releasing Henry's money, but I urge you not to push me."

"I'm not here to negotiate, Rollins," I said. "I'm taking Henry's money out without delay, and if it's not there then I'm taking your business down. And my guess is that will give Bravo the perfect opportunity to take HardShell's place. There'll be no comeback for you."

"I don't take kindly to threats, Madison. You don't know who you're dealing with."

"I'm pretty clear about who I'm dealing with. You're a murderer and drug trafficker. You had Henry killed to avoid paying him out. That's what kind of man you are."

Rollins laughed. "Madison, I didn't expect you to be so pathetic. You lost the trial, fair and square. Chip tried to steal from me and he killed two of my men in the process, and now you want to try and take your anger out on me?"

"Fair and square? You threatened half the jury to make sure that Chip was convicted."

"Is this a joke? Jesus, Madison. Take it on the chin. Go and appeal, like you said you would on the news. Just get the fuck out of my face or, mark my words, you're a dead man."

"You rigged the jury to make sure Chip took the fall for a robbery that you set up."

Rollins laughed. "Wow. Really, Madison? I must admit, I'm surprised. You need to take some time off. Get some rest. Because you are delusional. Why would I set up the robbery?"

"To double your money with the insurance payout. And you framed Chip because he was onto your illegal activity."

Rollins shrugged. "What illegal activity are you talking about? Everything I handle is above board."

"Of course, it is. Like the meth you run for the Iron Raiders, and the meth you're cooking up at Toro Canyon."

Rollins shook his head like he was doing a double take on what I'd just said.

"I'm running meth now, am I?"

"Yes. I saw the lab with my own eyes."

Rollins looked hard into my eyes. I could almost see the wheels of his brain spinning. I figured he was contemplating when and how he was going to kill me and dispose of my body.

"You've seen my lab, have you?" he hissed. "The fucking DEA raided my property on some bullshit warrant and found nothing. Zero. Nada. It was all just an effort by David McClean to try and damage my company. He's like you, Madison. A spiteful, jealous man who blames me for his failures."

"I was there. I saw it."

Rollins' eyes narrowed. "You were at my property?"

"Yes. I've got video of your operation. Your goons shot my investigator."

"That was you?"

"That was me."

"You're shitting me?"

"No. Those assholes who work for you chased us down the road and shot up our truck."

"Is that right?"

It was like Rollins had taken a mental departure. The animosity he'd been projecting at me had seeped away. If I wasn't mistaken, he was intrigued by what I was telling him.

"So, let me get this straight, Madison. You think I framed Chip because he suspected my company was running illegal drugs. You think I planned the robbery to get the insurance. And, what was that you said about Henry? You think I killed him?"

"You had him killed."

"Henry killed himself, Madison. He got a Dear John text and put a bullet through his brain. It had nothing to do with me."

"Your guys forced Henry's girlfriend to send that text. They took her phone so he couldn't speak to her. Then they paid Henry a visit. And they made it look like a suicide. Because they were good at doing that sort of thing, weren't they, Rollins?"

"Who?"

"Reed and Hendricks. And my guess is that's why you killed them at the robbery. You didn't need them any more. They'd become a liability."

"Look Madison," Rollins said calmly. "When you feel we can have a conversation without you making baseless allegations, then we can arrange the release of Henry's money. And if you can't do that, then you should let someone else handle Henry's probate."

As Rollins turned and walked away, a cloud of sea spray whipped across the pier. Everyone ducked to shield their faces but Rollins didn't react at all. He just kept walking with his hands dug into his jacket pockets.

I felt my phone buzz. I had the screen in front of me in an instant. Jack was calling.

"How'd it go?" I asked.

"Do I ever not deliver? I got what you wanted. Both of them gave me the same story."

"You got a positive ID?"

"Yep."

"You showed him the photo of Rollins?"

"No. I didn't have to."

"How come?"

"They said the guy who threatened them was in court. They knew exactly who it was. He was a witness."

"Yeah, Rollins was a witness. I've just had it out with him. He denied everything."

"No. They weren't talking about Rollins."

"Who were they talking about?"

"Scooter Slovak."

Jack's words floored me. "What?"

"Scooter Slovak. He was the one who put the fear of God into these guys. Threatened all kinds of shit."

My mind was racing.

Scooter? How did this make sense? Was Rollins being straight with me just now? Did he really have no idea about any of it? And if that's the case...

"Jack, how long do you think it takes to set up a meth lab?"

"No more than a day. A matter of hours, if you really know what you're doing."

"Then it's possible Rollins had no idea about the lab. And he actually believes Bravo tipped off the DEA. Hell, Jack. I've got it all wrong. Listen, you have to tell those two guys to take cover. They need to gather up their families and lay low until we give them the all clear. I'm not kidding. Slovak will be mopping up now and they're on his to-do list."

"Got it."

"I'll call you later."

I hung up the phone and raced toward the shore to try and catch Rollins. As I ran my eyes over the parking lot, I caught sight of him. When I yelled out his name, he stopped and turned. I held up my arm for him to wait, then raced as fast as I could.

"Rollins," I said, between trying to catch my breath. "I owe you an apology. I'm sorry. I thought there was no way you didn't know what was going on."

Rollins held up his right palm. "I understand, Madison. Believe me, I do. Actually, I'm indebted to you for our conversation just now."

"You know."

"It just clicked then, while we were talking. The person I trusted the most has deceived me to a degree I cannot even fathom. I thought the lab raid was all nonsense, but you say there was actual equipment there?"

"Yes. We got video of it. And we saw your men loading meth into a truck."

"So what Chip told me was true. They were handling illegal drugs with my vans. Scooter Slovak. That deceitful son-of-a-bitch. He must be aiming to take over my company."

"Aiming to? I think it's pretty much a done deal. Reed and Hendricks? I'm guessing now that they were Scooter's dogs, not yours. Who knows who else he has on a lead at HardShell? And if you've allowed him to run whatever it is you've got going with the Iron Raiders, then they're not on your side either. All he has to do now is take you out. You'll be just another body buried up in Humboldt County."

"Not if I kill him first," said Rollins as he opened the car door.

I stepped forward and grabbed the door. Rollins glared at me.

"Best you step off, Madison," he said. "I'm going to sort this out right now."

"Rollins. Listen to me. If you think you can walk into your own company and take Scooter out, you're mistaken. He'll be ready for you and he'll have men to back him up. What have you got? An 'I'm The Boss' badge?"

Rollins pondered my words. "What do you suggest?"

"I've got an idea. If it works, you'll get to clean house for good, and get your company back into your hands. And I'll get what I need to free Chip."

Rollins cast his eyes out over to the beach and the windswept sea beyond. Then he shut the door, leaned his back against his car and nodded.

"Alright. I'm listening."

48

"Will this take long, Brad?" asked Scooter Slovak after Megan had shown him into my office. "I mean, you said an hour on the phone. Will it take that long? I've got a lot going on this morning."

I gestured for him to take a seat. "An hour at the most, I promise," I said. "Can Megan get you anything? Water? Coffee?"

"No, I'm good," said Slovak. "Let's get into it."

I went and sat behind my desk and leaned back and opened my palms as I surveyed the documents I had placed over my desk. "I just don't get it, Scooter. I'm just stunned by the verdict. I thought we had a good case. And I'm gutted for Chip. Aren't you?"

"Yeah, of course I am. Of course."

"But look, thanks for coming. I always do a thorough debrief after a trial. You know, go over everything with a fine-tooth comb to see if I missed anything."

"But you're going to appeal, aren't you? I thought that was your next step."

"Yeah, that's exactly right. So to do that I have to review all this shit." I picked up one pile of documents after another.

"Court transcripts, exhibits, briefs, you name it. Lucky me, I get to relive the whole thing, blow by blow."

Slovak had his fingers interlaced, and he was trying his best to appear relaxed, but it was clear his patience was at a low ebb. "I did wonder whether my testimony helped Chip's cause or made it worse."

I shook my head. "Don't be silly. You did great."

"But the prosecutor got it out of me that Chip saved my life and I know you didn't want the jury to hear that. I'm sorry I slipped up like that."

I leaned forward with my arms crossed on the desk. "Listen, Scooter. Don't beat yourself up about that. Believe me, Chip's not in jail because of anything you said on the stand. No, our real problem, the way I see it, was with the jury."

"How do you mean?"

"Well, I mean anyone who sat through the case knows that there was ample room for doubt about Chip's guilt. Yet they turn in a guilty verdict almost as quick as it takes to get a pizza delivered. No, something wasn't right there. That's my hunch. But none of these documents here are going to shed any light on what the jury was thinking. Court transcripts don't cover what went on in the deliberation room."

Slovak looked at his watch and lifted one side of his mouth. "I don't see how I can—"

"Sorry, Scooter. There's so much to go over. But the jury stuff, that's my problem. But I did want to review your testimony, if you don't mind."

"Sure."

"Something you said piqued my interest."

"What was that?"

"You said, now what were your words exactly?" I flipped through a wad of transcripts and after half a minute or so finally came to the page I was after. "Here it is. You said, 'He's not dumb enough to allow himself to be blamed for it either. I think someone wanted the money and thought this was a good way to get him blamed for it.'"

Slovak remained silent as he tried to gauge whether or not there was anything to read between the lines. "And?"

"And, well, I think you're exactly right. I think you described exactly what happened."

"Yes?"

"Well, who do you think would do that?"

"I said in court, I seem to recall, that I thought the guys from Bravo could pull that off."

"Yeah, I thought about that too. But then why would Chip be spared?"

"To frame him. Look Brad, is talking to me about this stuff necessary? Because it seems we're just raking over the coals. And, as much as I'd like to help, that's really not my job. It's yours."

"Right you are. I did think framing Chip might be the answer but then I thought of another possibility."

Slovak was no longer able to hide his frustration. "And what's that?" he asked flatly.

"Maybe the reason Chip was allowed to live was because he saved your life."

"What?"

"Yeah. Think about it."

"Madison, you're fucking insane," Slovak said, his eyes filled with scorn. "You go shooting your mouth off like that and—"

"Hey, relax, Scooter. I'm not saying you did it. I'm talking about Rollins. Shit, I thought that was obvious. I'm saying the fact that Chip saved your life might have earned him some grace."

Slovak checked himself. He said nothing. Then a cold resolve seemed to come over him. "You want to fuck with me, Madison? Is that what you brought me here for?"

"Easy, Scooter. Come on. We're on the same side here."

Slovak was leaned forward in his chair with a look to kill. "We're not on the same side, you fuck. I don't know what you're trying to pull here but you're walking on very fucking dangerous ground."

I found myself facing the man who everyone, including me, had underestimated. I understood the fear he could instill in some guy off the street who'd been roped into jury duty.

"Hey, Scooter. There's no need for that. Please, calm down. I'm sorry if I offended you."

Slovak jumped to his feet. "Shut your mouth, Madison." He put his hands on the desk and loomed over me. "You want to start throwing theories like that around then you'd better think about this. Think about that daughter of yours. Bella, right? I will shoot her in front of your fucking eyes, if you cross me. You got that?"

I held up my palms and backed myself hard into my chair, barely able to look at Slovak. "Scooter, I'm sorry. Please don't take this the wrong way. I'm not going to be telling anyone what I just said. I promise."

"You know how easy it was for me to drop Nate and Bo? I did it like that," he said, snapping his fingers.

Slovak pushed off the table and stood tall, the rageful power I'd provoked taking over his entire being. He looked at me with contempt.

"They were my friends. You think I'd have any hesitation to drop you and your little girl?"

I paused for a few moments, then unfurled myself from my near-fetal position. With my eye on Slovak, I leaned forward and pressed a button on my phone.

"Did you get all that, Ed?"

"Yes, we did. Loud and clear."

Slovak's face contorted into a maze of confusion. Then an instant later, when he realized what he'd just done, the flesh slackened in shock.

"Why don't you come join us, Ed and Quinn?"

At the sound of the door swinging open behind him, Slovak spun around. Quinn Rollins stepped forward and slammed his right fist hard into Slovak's cheek, dropping him to the floor. Ed Frierson shot his arm out to stop Rollins from moving in for the kill.

"Best let us take it from here, Quinn."

49

From my poolside table, the clear, jade water of Turtle Bay wrapped around the coastline and stretched out to the white lines of foam that marked the outer reef. With only the slightest of breezes and no swell, the shimmering surface was as smooth as brushed hide. The North Shore's famed surf breaks of Waimea, Banzai Pipeline, and Sunset were just a few minutes' drive away, but now, in mid-summer, even they were as flat and tame as a wading pool.

In the middle of the bay, I could see Bella on her paddleboard with two friends she'd made the very first day we arrived. I heard a gleeful cry and saw that they'd spotted a turtle and were paddling to get a closer look.

Bella and I had agreed to a partial digital detox. Our phones were to be left in the hotel room. So our time was mostly device free, and we filled it with just about every activity available under the Hawaiian sun. Bella loved surfing, and for the past few days, the trade winds had created a little swell that peeled around the point. Gentle and full, these ideal beginner waves would take us all the way to the beach. Playing in the warm sea water on cloudless days was a tonic for the soul.

Los Angeles felt a world away, as did Chip Bowman's case. He'd come to see me after his release from prison to express his gratitude. Rollins had asked him to return to HardShell to work as his trusted second-in-command, and Chip gladly accepted. The two of them were going through the entire personnel to weed out the bad eggs that had been corrupted by Slovak. It pleased me to hear that Cliff Loda was not just retained but promoted, even after Chip and Rollins discovered that his resume had been embellished.

Running the broom through HardShell was being aided by the fresh investigation launched by Frierson and his team. In building their case against Slovak, they'd been putting our drone footage to good use. A few of the men, when presented with video of them working at a meth lab, decided to turn on Slovak. Mercenaries to the end, they told Frierson's team everything they knew about Reed and Hendricks and the jobs they did for Slovak.

Piece by piece, Slovak's plan was unpacked. The men told Frierson that Slovak had a lot of them under his thumb, calling in favors against the sizeable sums of money he'd lent them. He had Reed and Hendricks by the balls more than most, as he possessed material from Iraq that could see them brought up on murder charges in a heartbeat. And fittingly, for this pair of rogue soldiers, it appeared he deployed them as hitmen. With his sights set on seizing control of HardShell, Scooter could not allow Henry Tuck to remove his money and cripple the business, so he had Reed and Hendricks do what they did in Iraq: commit murder and cover their tracks.

Frierson would have a tough job charging Slovak for Tuck's murder. In the case of Reed and Hendricks's murder, though, the prospects of a conviction were far more promising.

Rollins and I had spoken several times since Slovak's arrest. And as time progressed, the scale of his treachery had become apparent.

Rollins said the cops finally discovered what was left of the stolen money and drugs at a property Slovak leased under a false identity. When they went through the computer found at that location, they discovered he was selling the cannabis and the meth on the dark web.

Rollins believed Slovak planned the heist with two goals in mind. First, to get rid of Reed and Hendricks so they could never hold the murder of Henry Tuck over him. Second, Slovak wanted to build up a war chest to evict Rollins from HardShell, and then ramp up the company's illegal trade.

When Rollins ordered the HardShell vans to be pulled apart, secret compartments were discovered in the panels and floors of every vehicle.

"Chip was right all along," Rollins said. "But I trusted the guys who'd worked for me for years. I could never believe that Scooter, Nate, Bo—all three of them—were using my trucks to run illegal drugs."

After Slovak was arrested at my office, Frierson's men were delighted to find a lot of interesting material on his cell phone. A bank of WhatsApp messages saved onto the cloud treated the cops to a blow-by-blow account of how Slovak planned the heist.

They asked Cliff to swap shifts with Chip so that Chip would be on the job. When they got to the lot on Morrison Street, Nate's job was to knock Chip unconscious. Then Slovak arrived. He may have pretended to check Chip's vitals while he was lying on the ground, and used the opportunity to take his weapon. Slovak then stood up and shot his accomplices dead before using Nate's weapon to fire a bullet in Chip's leg to point the finger of blame at Chip. He could not afford to have Chip interfering in the illegal trade, yet he was reluctant to kill him. Making Chip the scapegoat was the perfect solution.

A waiter arrived with my second ice-cold beer. I felt lucky, and couldn't remember the last time I felt so relaxed.

A group of us were planning a farewell meal that night at the resort's bar and grill. I was initially disinclined to be social with other guests, but Bella's charm had spread throughout the resort and I found myself having to follow her lead. Her fans included not just the girls she was now out paddleboarding with but their parents too, whose remarks about my daughter made me immensely proud.

Bella was blossoming into a young woman whose future was something I'd feel privileged to witness.

I wasn't concerned with what she wanted to be, where she wanted to study, or when she might tell me she'd met the guy she wanted to marry. She was going to write her own story—a rich, original and, hopefully, happy one. I was humbled to be the father she loves. I'm sure Claire felt the same. When I thought of those two, I felt sad to know that they had grown a little further apart over the years. Nothing that couldn't be bridged, I thought.

"Dad!" I heard Bella cry out, the sound of her voice carrying clear across the water. Now that she had my attention, she flung her arms up in the air and did a backflip off her paddleboard into the water. When her head emerged next to the board, I could see she was beaming at me. I raised my beer in one hand and gave her the thumbs up with the other.

I intended to finish the beer and then grab a board and paddle out to join Bella and her friends. I'd noticed that the wind had picked up a little and there was a half-foot wave peeling around the point. This could be our last surf session before we checked out the next morning.

As I drained the bottle, the waiter approached my table carrying a tray. I could see him looking at me and I motioned to him that I'd had enough. He kept on coming, though.

"Sir? Mr. Madison?" he said.

"Thank you, but no more for now. I'm about to get back in the water."

"Sir, there's a call for you."

That's when I noticed the telephone resting on his tray.

"Oh, okay," I said. *Must be Megan*, I thought. *Couldn't she just leave a message on my cell?*

"Hello?" I said into the mouthpiece. "This is Brad."

"Brad, I'm so sorry to call," said a woman's voice that I didn't recognize immediately.

"Who—?"

"It's Nina, Brad. Nina Lindstrom." She sounded upset, her voice unsteady. Instinctively, I looked out over the water to Bella, who was now paddling her board toward me. She saw I was looking and pointed excitedly at the surf, knowing that there was some great fun to be had and wondering why I hadn't already noticed and come to join her.

"I'm sorry to call you like this. And I hate to be the one tell you."

"Tell me what?" My heartbeat dropped instantly. Nina was crying.

"It's Claire," she said tearfully. "There's been an accident."

"What kind of accident? She's okay, isn't she, Nina?"

I ran a hand over my head and looked out again at Bella, who was now paddling hard to catch a wave.

"No, Brad. No, she's not okay. You need to come home. Both of you."

"Is she in the hospital? What's happened?"

Nina coughed as she struggled for breath.

"Yes," she said, struggling to get her words out. "She was hit by a car."

I felt nauseous. I didn't know what to ask next. More to the point, I didn't want to leave myself open to hearing the worst. Nina was now sobbing, almost overwhelmed by grief.

"Nina," I said. "How bad is it?"

"You need to come back right away," she said, once she'd caught her breath. "We don't know how much longer she can hold on."

THE END

NOTE FROM J.J.

Thanks so much for reading *Blood and Justice*. I really hope you enjoyed the ride.

Could I ask you to do a couple of things to help the book's prospects? First, please write a review on Amazon. Second, please recommend the book to fellow readers. This support means a great deal to a small-fry writer like me.

All the best,

J.J.

Printed in Great Britain
by Amazon

12087769R00192